The
Four False
Weapons

John Dickson Carr Mysteries

The
Four False
Weapons

John Dickson Carr

PERENNIAL LIBRARY

Harper & Row, Publishers, New York
Grand Rapids, Philadelphia, St. Louis, San Francisco
London, Singapore, Sydney, Tokyo, Toronto

Originally published in 1937 by Harper & Brothers.

First PERENNIAL LIBRARY edition published 1989.

LIBRARY OF CONGRESS CATALOG CARD NUMBER: 89-45130

ISBN 0-06-081017-3

89 90 91 92 93 WB/OPM 10 9 8 7 6 5 4 3 2 1

Contents

1

The Summons

If anyone had told him, on the afternoon of May 15th, that only a day later he would be in Paris: that he would be involved in the rather sensational murder case which came to be known as the affair of the Four False Weapons, even as a spectator: he would have suspected someone of having surprised his dreams. And it would have embarrassed him beyond measure.

On the afternoon of May 15th he sat at his desk by the window, looking out dourly into Southampton Street, W.C.1. He was "Mr. Curtis, junior," or "our Mr. Richard," of the law-firm of Curtis, Hunt, D'Arcy, and Curtis. But at the moment he was reflecting that anyone who voluntarily becomes a solicitor must be a prize mug. It is true that he was lucky to be a junior partner, and lucky to look on even so non-hilarious a thoroughfare as Southampton Street, W.C.1. The offices of Curtis, Hunt, D'Arcy, and Curtis consist of a vast series of small cubicles or compartments run together like a maze round inner courts and air-wells. A visitor is under the impression that everybody must have to walk through everybody else's room in order to get anywhere. The premises are somewhat mouldy, and are not enlivened by spinster typists and pictures of dyspeptic-looking gentlemen with beards.

The truth of the matter was that Mr. Richard Curtis, Junior, was thoroughly bored with things in general.

A client (supposing one to have been sent in to him, which occurred seldom) would have been deceived by his appearance. A client would have seen a sturdy, solid, sedate-looking young man in blue serge, with an air of listening in courteous gravity to the client's troubles. This was due to the training of his father, the head of the firm, who had a beard like the men in the pictures. But the client would have been deceived. Under some papers, which he had arranged with a decent show of being busy, Richard Curtis had re-written the first lines of the *Lawyer's Ode to Spring:*

> "Whereas, on sundry leaves and boughs,
>   Now divers birds do sing;
> They mingle in aforesaid trees—
>   To wit: their carolling."

Which was one way of blowing off the steam of boredom, less obvious than shouting, "Yah!" and biting Miss Breedon, the senior typist. For it was

2

spring verging into summer through Southampton Street, to which his pulses responded.

Thus a client would have been surprised at the daydreams with which Richard Curtis peopled this office. While he looked his sternest, his imagination went another way. Into this office (say) would come a distinguished Personage in a black cloak with the collar turned up, and look round swiftly.

"Mr. Curtis," the Personage would say, "I have a mission for you to undertake. I must speak quickly, for we are watched. Here are three passports and an automatic pistol. You will proceed at once to Cairo, in whatever disguise you think fit; but take care that you are not followed by a man whose cufflinks take the form of a small black cross. Arrived in Cairo, you will proceed to the Street of the Seven Cobras, to a house which you will identify by—"

Some severely practical instinct at the back of Curtis's head told him that this was a lot of flapdoodle, and that even in dreams one ought to be right about the facts. But it was a fine dream; he rioted in it.

"—and there you will meet a Lady; need I say a beautiful lady?" the Personage would add, rather superfluously. "Here, then, are a thousand pounds for current expenses—"

At this point, in the actual world of the office, there was a knock at Curtis's door. It was not a Lady, a beautiful lady; it was Miss Breedon, the senior typist, and she said:

"If you please, sir, Mr. Hunt would like to see you in his office."

Curtis got up and went towards Hunt's office

without enthusiasm. Since his father had retired from active duty, Hunt was the senior acting partner. And young Curtis had been disappointed in Hunt. For a little time he had hoped for great things from the dry, lean, snuffy model of dignity which was Charles Grandison Hunt. There was a current rumor that there was More in Old Hunt than Met the Eye. It was even reported that he was fond of limericks. Curtis doubted this. To him the idea of old Hunt reciting a limerick was as fantastic as any Personage offering a thousand pounds for current expenses. All the same, he had sometimes imagined even Hunt saying, "Mr. Curtis, I have a mission for you to undertake—"

He tapped at Hunt's door, and was asked to enter in the familiar voice which always seemed to be preceded by a strong inhalation through the nose. Hunt sat at his desk, his pince-nez on his nose and his chin drawn in.

"Mr. Curtis," said Hunt, with an even stronger inhalation, "I have a mission for you to undertake. Could you be prepared to go to Paris by the evening plane?"

Curtis was not quite able to believe his ears.

"Could I!" he said.

Mr. Grandison Hunt deprecated this, eyeing him up and down. He sniffed again; he even dropped the formal style of address.

"No, no, Richard," he said. "This will not do. I perceive in you a certain unfortunate vein of—ah —pop and sizzle, which we must eliminate if we are to make you a credit to Curtis, Hunt, D'Arcy, and Curtis." He considered. "Now tell me frankly, Richard: do you consider our offices in the least a humdrum place?"

4

"Well, sir, what do you think?" inquired Curtis. "I've been sitting at that blasted desk—"

"Precisely," interposed Hunt, raising one finger as though he had proved a point. "Another question. You are aware, of course," he nodded towards the tiers of steel boxes behind him, "that our professional dealings are chiefly with the more conservative families of Great Britain, and certain English families abroad?"

"I've been allowed to know that much, anyhow. That's why—"

"Ah! That is why you consider it necessarily humdrum?" Over Hunt's face went a shadow which in anyone else's case might have been a smile. "At the moment, Richard, I have not the time to go into the matter fully. But a little mature reflection will convince you that dealing with such families is precisely the reverse of humdrum. In the nature of things it must be so. With such families there is leisure. There is money. There is a freedom from that stern respectability which makes England the most moral nation in the world. As a result, they produce more—more —ah—"

"Loonies?" suggested Curtis, with deplorable candor. "Here, I say! This is plain Socialism."

Hunt came as near a sputter as his nature would permit.

"Not at all," he said. "I believe it can be demonstrated that there is a higher level of intelligence and achievement in the House of Lords than in the House of Commons. You will say,"—he took his pince-nez off his nose, forestalling the objection,—"that this proves little. I agree. Nevertheless, I state the fact. What I wish to point out is

5

this: the more conservative the legal firm, the more dangerous will be the affairs it must handle. The most familiar legend of the great Doctor Samuel Johnson is that Boswell once asked him, "Sir, what would you do if you were locked up in a tower with a baby?" The great doctor appears to have been annoyed at this, and the whole world has united in terming it the outstanding example of an asinine question. I do not agree. Boswell was a lawyer, and knew exactly what he was about. It is precisely the sort of question which *we* must know how to answer, and precisely the sort of situation with which we must know how to deal.

"We will now return to business," Hunt concluded, setting his pince-nez back on his nose by way of emphasis.

"Well, sir?"

"I am sending you to Paris," pursued Hunt, "on behalf of a client of ours who lives there, a Mr. Ralph Douglas. You have heard of him?"

"If he's the one I think you mean," Curtis said, "I certainly have. Wine, women, and song, isn't it? His *Dame de Trefles* won the Grand Prix last year. Afterwards he had that party—"

"Yes, he has been rather a pink 'un," said Hunt with judicial gravity. He coughed, correcting himself. "However, that is not the point. What I wish to impress on you, Richard, is that Mr. Douglas is an irresponsible young man no longer. No longer! I am instructed to say that never has there been a more complete transformation. He sees the dawn up no longer. At the request of his future mother-in-law, he has even sold his racing-stable; though I fail to see," added Hunt, acidly, "that the sport of kings is not a sport for gentlemen. But his future mother-in-law, I believe, has stern views as to the morality of racing—"

"You mean Douglas has fallen in love and reformed?"

"Exactly," agreed Hunt, with a sort of pounce as though his companion had coined a refreshing new phrase. "He is to be married next month to Miss Magda Toller. His future mother-in-law is Mrs. Benedict Toller, widow, and now head of the travel-bureau called Toller's Tours. Do not form the wrong impression of Mrs. Toller, Richard: she is neither old nor dowdy. On the contrary, Mrs. Toller is a woman in the prime of life; extremely fashionable, extremely hard-headed; and you might call her handsome but for a very large, very thin nose, which tilts up slightly and is to me an abomination. Her moral views...but no matter. She has made strenuous opposition to her daughter's marriage to Mr. Douglas. Her own candidate, I believe, was Mr. Bryce Douglas, Ralph Douglas's brother, a go-ahead young gentleman in the Diplomatic Service. Her consent to the present marriage was gained with extreme difficulty."

Curtis still did not see where his own mission entered into this.

"Her consent?" he repeated. "Isn't the girl of age?"

"She has reached the age of discretion," said Hunt, "and therefore finds it more convenient to obey her mother. I should describe Miss Magda Toller as one of our—er, sensible beauties. Again, do not misunderstand. There seems no doubt that the young pair are altogether in love; but—there is a difficulty. That difficulty is a certain Mlle. Rose Klonec."

"An old flame of Douglas's?"

"Yes."

"Who wants to be bought off."

"No," said Hunt.

He opened the drawer of his desk and took out a closely written sheet of notepaper. After studying it again, with a sharper inhalation, he pushed it across to Curtis. It was headed, *35bis Avenue Foch, Friday night,* and ran:

Dear Hunt,

This is the fifth draft I've made tonight of a letter attempting to explain things, and still I can't get at it. It goes on and on, and gets much too complicated, so that I have to break off about the second or third page without anything really said. I have decided that the only way it can be done successfully is in person. It's like this: I am having a spot of bother, and I need advice. I should be damnably obliged if you could come over to Paris, if only for a few hours. I would come to London like a shot, only Magda and Mrs. Toller are here (at the Crillon) and I can't get away.

I suppose you know about my being mixed up, a couple of years ago, with a *poule-de-luxe* named Rose Klonec. I kept her for over a year, and ruddy expensive she was, too. Now, wait—my difficulty isn't what you're thinking, breach of promise or the like. La Klonec (she is Polish-English) is well known here, and had a string of backers before she met me. In fact, I seem to have been the only one who ever chucked her before she got everything he had. Probably because I met Magda and cooled off.

The trouble is this. When we first got together, I bought a villa on the edge of the Forest of Marly and installed her in it. It's one of those too-fancy places: red spotted marble like the Trianon, and windows going up to the roof, and all the trappings. When we broke up she moved out, and the place has been empty ever since. But there's something very, very fishy going on about that villa now, and La Klonec is concerned in it. That's all I'm going to tell you here, except that I think it's serious.

Could you possibly manage to come over here and have a talk?

As ever,
RALPH DOUGLAS.

Though Curtis's imagination was already at work, he read it through with a puzzled frown.

"But what's on his mind, sir? What's bothering him?"

"I have not the slightest idea," said Hunt with some austerity. "That is why you are going to Paris. You will take the evening plane, and put up at the Meurice. I will cable Mr. Douglas that you will call on him at his flat—make a note of the address—at ten o'clock tomorrow morning precisely. It is Sunday; but that should have a sobering effect on the conversation. I only ask you to remember Boswell and the baby. The matter may not be of the least importance. On the other hand, does anything strike you about the letter?"

"Yes. I was wondering whether the Tollers know anything about Rose Klonec."

Hunt frowned, an expression which gave to his face an acutely dyspeptic look. "That I cannot tell you. But I should imagine so."

"And do *we* know anything about her?"

"Not as yet. I knew, of course, that he was attached to some such—ah—*poule-de-luxe,* as many of our most distinguished clients are. His financial accounts alone showed that. The lady seems to have had a remarkable taste for jewellery. But, as to information about her, that was the next point I wished to bring up." Hunt considered him, drawing a deep breath, before he added: "Tell me, Richard: did you ever hear of a gentleman named Bencolin?"

Curtis had a feeling that his imagination had been not so far out after all.

"You don't mean," he said, "the greatest of all the French detectives? Or was, rather; he resigned during those political rows a couple of years ago. The man is so much of a legend that I've wondered whether he really existed."

"Henri Bencolin," said Hunt, eyeing the ceiling, "is a man after my own heart. I know him well. Do not be deceived by his grave airs and stately calm. I have never known a fellow with a finer taste in limericks. At alcoholic singing, particularly in quartets, he can carry the bass with remarkable effect. Yes, he has retired. I think you will find him far more mellow than the lean and hungry criminal-hunter you have been led to expect—"

"That's bad."

"I wonder," mused Hunt. "They tell me that in retirement he is a little—ah—gone to seed, sartorially. I have often thought that his famous white tie and Mephistophelian twirl were careful stage-trappings, which he found useful in his business. In his retirement he does not, thank heaven, grow roses. He spends most of his time fishing and shooting, for he must always catch something. But to business." He cleared his throat. "Bencolin has no longer any connection with the police, but he is in close touch with them. It may be very useful to us—you follow me, Richard?—to learn all we can about Mlle. Rose Klonec. I will give you a letter to deliver to Bencolin. His present address is unknown to me, but if you present your credentials to M. Brille, the present *chef de Sûreté*, at the Quai des Orfèvres, you will easily obtain it."

Hunt bobbed up behind his desk, a dry little figure with parted hair that looked suspiciously like a wig, and the wrinkles of his face suggesting that he meant to impart advice.

"That is all, Richard. I am depending on you to deal with this matter in a way that will reflect credit on Curtis, Hunt, D'Arcy, and Curtis. As soon as you have seen Mr. Douglas, you will, of course, report fully to me; by telephone, if necessary. Should I consider the position serious enough, it will be incumbent on me to join you. I do not anticipate such a contingency, but I shall hold myself in readiness...Ah, just one moment, Richard!"

"Yes, sir?" said Curtis, turning at the door.

"I wonder," said Hunt gravely, "whether you

11

have ever heard this one? 'There was a young girl from Hong-Kong—'"

He recited gravely, in the manner of one reading a lesson to a Sunday School. It was not until Curtis had gone on to his own office, controlling himself so as to avoid exploding in the face of Miss Breedon as she came in for dictation, that he realized he had really been admitted to the firm at last.

2

Rose Klonec's Last Bed

At just before ten o'clock on Sunday morning, Richard Curtis, slipping along the rue de Rivoli in one of those new, sleek, wine-colored taxis which have replaced the quacking cabs of old, breathed pure enjoyment. Over Paris floated a faint, warm haze of morning, through which the sun was breaking out across the Place de la Concorde. It caught a glitter from the forest of lamps, and from the green vista along the river, and flashed from the tops of tiny motor-cars crawling up the green hill of the Champs Elysées to where a great Arch showed misted in the sky. The occasional hoot or howl of a motor-horn emphasized Sunday morning. You heard them swish past, as you heard the swish of brooms when men in white aprons came out, lonely, to dust the pavement.

Here (Curtis thought) was a wider sky, and a redder skyline, and low-lying houses spread under a screen of trees. What sort of adventure couldn't happen here? He had not seen Paris for several years; he was not prepared for the way it took him. Even the smell of tobacco-smoke from a Yellow cigarette, which the taxi-driver was smoking—nobody in France ever does draw at a cigarette; it is simply allowed to waggle in one corner of the mouth until it burns itself out—even this smoke was associated with the town. As they crossed over into the Champs Elysées, he began to pick out landmarks. That slope of lawn where the white-covered tables were being set out, with skeins of lights above: that was *Le Doyen* on the left. On the right, behind those chestnut trees, was *Laurent;* and was the *Ambassadeurs* still there? All these new open café-fronts, frosted and painted inside like the stage of a theatre for musical comedy, were new but not alien; at night they would blaze. Mr. Curtis, junior, had to remind himself that he was here as a man of business. But there was no conceit in him, and he thought: what ruddy good is *my* advice on a morning like this?

He assumed a suitable gravity when he got out at number 53bis Avenue Foch. The Avenue Foch, under broadening sunlight, was shady and deserted. Possibly from its nearness to the Bois, you think of it less in terms of houses than of gardens. Few of the steel shutters were opened on the windows. But the concierge of number 53bis was astir, banging and beaming with a mop in the entrance hallway. *"Ah, Monsieur Dooglaz?"* she cried, as though at mention of the name she were hearing a great and surprising secret. *"J'espère qu'il va mieux,"* she added, with hearty sympathy. *"Quatrième étage, monsieur."*

Curtis, wondering what was wrong with him, went up in the lift. He had barely time to press the door-buzzer before the door was opened.

"Morning," said a genial if rather shaky voice. "You're from Hunt, aren't you? Good, good. Come in."

Even in the bearing of his host, as he was led into a back room where a breakfast-table was set by a window giving on a garden, Curtis felt a certain relief. Ralph Douglas almost bustled with relief.

"Surprised to find me up and dressed so early?" he inquired. Then he seemed to feel that this struck the wrong note, or required explanation, for he added, "Er—I had rather a bad night last night, unfortunately. But I'd got Hunt's cable, and I kept it in the back of my mind that I had to be on duty this morning. A Turkish bath put me right; I feel fine now. Coffee?"

"Thanks."

They appraised each other, and Curtis liked his host at once. Douglas was not at all the type he would have pictured as a playboy: he was not washed-out enough, not bored enough: he seemed too robust and interested. He was what the French might have called an Anglo-Saxon type, lean, fair-haired, blunt-nosed, with a broad mouth and an amiable blue eye. There was nothing at all distinguished about him except a certain sharp intelligence in that eye, or possibly a greater knowledge of the world than you might at first have guessed. Except for a slight puffiness of the eyelids, and a scrubbed look, he gave no sign of a night's drinking. He sat with his hands on his knees, his elbows poked out, studying Curtis; and his loose gray suit seemed to give him a great breadth of shoulder.

Then Ralph Douglas grinned.

"Well," he said abruptly, "I'm glad they didn't send somebody with a beard. I feel enough of a fool as it is."

"Don't let that worry you. Fire away or not, just as you like; I've got all the time in the world."

"You see," Douglas went on slowly, "what I want is not only legal advice. I want to talk to a countryman. The French are all right, but—" He stared out of the window. "I'm supposed to speak French very well; I've got a lot of friends here; I like Paris. And yet if I had to hear nothing but French spoken for six months, I think I should go crazy. Understand?"

"Yes," Curtis admitted, "I've felt the same thing."

"It's different, that's all I know. On the other hand, all the English or Americans I know here would only think my situation was funny. At least, I want a disinterested countryman, and no damned humorous—" He hesitated, his hand moving in the air, and then brought it down on his knee. "What's more, if we were at an office in London, I shouldn't be able to tell you what I'm going to. Not as honestly, anyhow. Values are different. I should stutter or dry up. There it is." Again he stopped. "Look here, what do you say to a drive? I can have my car round in half a tick. We could talk while we drive, and I could do with some fresh air. We might—drive as far as the Forest of Marly."

Five minutes later they were flying down towards the Etoile in Douglas's two-seater, Douglas lounging at the wheel and speaking as though to the wind-screen.

"Before I bring up my little riddle," he said, "I'd better emphasize whatever outline Hunt gave you. Magda, my *fiancée*, is the finest thing ever made. Mamma Toller is a bitch. B-i-t-c-h, bitch. In addition to her objections to me, she's got quite a crush on my brother Bryce, and wants him for a son-in-law. Bryce is a very decent sort; but he's one of these calm Foreign Office fellows who say the right, wise, and sensible thing on every occasion, like squeezing a toothpaste-tube; he can talk about everything and give you the impression he's really interested in nothing. Finally, when it comes to Rose Klonec—"

"Just a minute. Does Miss Toller know about Rose Klonec?"

"Yes. Everything, including the villa. Good Lord," said Douglas, turning his head with a violence of surprise, *"she* doesn't mind in the least, provided it's all over. I told her all about it. And I think she's even rather pleased about having ditched a notorious charmer like Rose. She's interested: she asks was Rose this, was Rose that, and so on; but she doesn't mind."

"What about Mrs. Toller?"

"No, Mamma Toller doesn't know anything. That's part of the trouble."

"I'm not going to give any advice until I hear about it," Curtis told him meditatively. "But one thing jumps up here. As man to man, now: if you love this girl, and she loves you, why don't you tell Mamma Toller to go pickle her head in brine, and marry the girl?"

Douglas seemed to be aiming viciously at a pedestrian as they swung into the Avenue de la Grande Armée.

"That's easy enough, in theory," he said, letting off steam, "but you don't understand the family situation, or the stranglehold that old vixen has on Magda. It isn't an ordinary question of wanting to obey mamma, or not wanting to obey her: it's blackmail, in a way. By God, that's what it is: it's blackmail! It's—well, I'll tell you about it when I get the rest of the story straightened out.

"Now, about Rose Klonec. I was tied up with her for over a year. I was never in love with her. Oddly enough, it's Magda who's the really beautiful one and Rose who's the more or less plain one. But Rose has something: oh, definitely. Red hair. All that. And something that isn't in the least what we call sex-appeal; a stimulation, a sort of mental twistiness, that's made saner men than I go broke. Mind you, she'll break you if she can. She isn't consciously cynical; it's as natural as breathing, not greed at all; and it's this naturalness that Philistines like myself can't understand.

"Rose is—I can't help if it's an old term—Rose is a lady. I've never heard her use a crude word, or an obscene word, as long as I've known her. She has really good manners, and a real delicacy. You'll say it's only my Philistinism towards foreigners which could be surprised at that. But again, there it is. On the other hand, I once asked her, 'Are you capable of really falling in love?' She said, 'Yes, I am sure of it.' I said, 'Supposing that, would you go with anyone for love alone, without

18

a question of money?' She said rather sharply, 'No, of course not. There is no relation between the two. Of course, when I am old and do not attract men any longer, I shall have to pay them to make love to me.'

"That, my boy, is what makes my mind freeze up. It's practicality gone mad. At least it's simple. But I have a simple mind too, and I don't follow it. Now I'm inflicting all this on you...and it's a relief to get it off my chest...for just one reason. Rose and I parted the best of friends, rather like a film-divorce. She went over to a chap named De Lautrec, who's been after her for some time. I think Rose is genuinely fond of me, as I am of her. But if she saw the opportunity of picking up a few thousand extra francs by getting in the way of my marriage, and ruining things, Rose would do it. There would be no animus. It would merely be *pratique*."

Douglas had been speaking with great animation, his voice deepening, his foot unconsciously pressing harder on the accelerator so that they whipped out through the dingy-looking suburbs round the Porte Maillot. He turned round and added:

"Well?"

"The question is," Curtis said, "what you have to be afraid of. Not breach of promise, as you said yourself. It doesn't matter whether you've written any letters or made any promises"—he thought he saw Ralph Douglas flush—"in her case. Are you worried about whether she might give the show away to Mrs. Toller?"

"No, not in the least. I shouldn't mind telling the old girl myself."

"What is it, then?"

"There are three queer incidents; that's my puzzle. The first of 'em, you may say, isn't much. I've had an offer to buy the villa—it's called the Villa Marbre—with its furniture, all in a lump. A jolly good offer, too. But the offer comes from that fellow De Lautrec, who took over Rose. You'll say Rose was attached to the place, and wanted him to buy it for her. You'll say De Lautrec, being practical himself, thought it would be cheaper to get a bower ready-made-and-furnished rather than fit out a new one for her. But—to me it had a wrong sound. The offer came too late; Rose has been with him eight to ten months.

"That may not be important; but the next part of it is. De Lautrec rang me up on Thursday. I said I had been wanting to sell the place anyway, especially since I was getting married, and wouldn't he come round and talk the matter over? De Lautrec said he was going out of town for a few days; but when he returned he would get in touch with me.

"Right! So far so good. On Friday morning I thought I'd drive out to the villa—where we're going now—to have a look round, and make sure tramps or burglars hadn't been fooling about. As I wrote to Hunt, it's empty ever since; and the furniture and general fittings are rather fine stuff. It isn't big enough for a caretaker, being merely a setting for a fancy lady. But I paid the nearest *agent de police* to keep an eye on it when he went his rounds, and a gardener to look after the grounds occasionally.

"Well, it was all locked up; shutters on the windows, covers on the furniture, dusty, and just as

20

gloomy and undisturbed as when I'd left it. Just as I went in, automatically, I touched the light-switch in the hall. When my finger was on it I realized that the light wouldn't go on, because I had ordered the light and water cut off; the trouble was that, lo and behold, the light did go on.

"I thought that was funny, because I distinctly remembered 'phoning the company about it. But I began to wander through the place. Nobody had been there in my absence, that was certain. Then I went upstairs, to what had been Rose's room—elaborate place, with a bed like Du Barry's at the Little Trianon—and had a look round. When Rose went away, with her severely practical soul, she took all the table-linen and bed-linen; she said she had a use for it. Yet I looked at that confounded bed, and there were pillows and bed-linen on it."

Douglas was so engrossed in his story, turning round to look at his companion, and hitting the flat of his hand on the steering-wheel, that he had almost ceased to notice where he was going. But Curtis did not call his attention to the road. Ralph Douglas's very face was becoming more human with the relief of pouring this out.

"Mind you," he went on jerkily, "it wasn't as though anybody had been living there, or using the place. The linen was absolutely untouched and new. It was just—there. I tell you, I stood in that stuffy place, with the very faint light coming through the slits in the shutters, and I began to get a creepy feeling.

"I went downstairs again, to the kitchen, and tried the water-taps over the sink. The water was on. Then I heard the electric refrigerator humming, and I opened that. The refrigerator was fully stocked with stuff for a late supper: truffles, *foie gras*, things like that. And in one corner were six half-bottles of Roederer Champagne. By the way, Rose Klonec always drinks half a bottle of Roederer before going to bed at night. But there was one more reason why I knew I *had* ordered the light and water shut off, and someone had later countermanded the order to the company in my name. That reason was the electric clock."

"Electric clock?"

"Yes. There's an electric clock that stands on top of the refrigerator, and is connected with the same base-plug that runs the refrigerator. The clock was going, but it was pointing to some crazy hour. Now, that clock's an excellent timekeeper; I found that out. But you see what had happened? When the current was shut off by the company, the clock stopped. When the power was turned on again— at someone else's order—the clock simply picked up action again where it had left off before.

"Well, I was feeling a bit queer. I went out and got hold of the policeman, a chap named Hercule Renard, I had paid to keep an eye on the house. And it seems somebody *had* been hanging about: round the walls of the villa, at least. Hercule had seen a very queer customer on Wednesday night, and again on Thursday, who always disappeared. Hercule said he was 'like a scarecrow,' and wore a corduroy coat.

"I don't know what I'm suggesting. All I know is that there's something damned funny going on. The trouble is that I don't dare see Rose to find out, or even ring her up. The Tollers are in Paris, and I'm in constant attendance on them. If something should slip...This is where we turn."

Paris lay well behind them now. They were in a rolling country of whitewashed villages straggling into each other, which fell away now at the crest of a hill where the Forest of Marly showed almost colorless under noonday sun. A good road branched off at the edge of the forest, and they drove for some quarter of a mile along it.

"There it is," said Ralph Douglas curtly.

What impressed his companion, as the car stopped, was this wood's absolute quietness, even secretiveness, under that blaze of sun. When the noise of the motor was shut off, it was as though stillness slipped in physically and took its place. Curtis heard each beat of the motor as it died. When he stepped out, he heard his foot swish loudly in the grass at the road-side. They were in the shadow of a high stone wall, fronting on a sanded pathway inside the grass-bank, and pierced by two gates. With the same air of secrecy, beyond the wall rose up a square of tall poplars, grayish-green, set close together, with a sort of dry shimmer under the heat.

"The gate's open," said Douglas, his voice sounding very loud. "Here! I had it padlocked."

The iron gate creaked as they went inside. At the end of a sanded path they saw the Villa Marbre as though framed in trees. It was built of reddish mottled marble, long and low, with two short wings towards them. Its arched square-paned windows, stretching to the terrace like doors, had their frames and joinings painted white. Though it was two storeys high, the top-most one resembled an attic, with its windows as miniatures of the white arches below. All these windows were closed with steel shutters, having blank lines of slits. And there was something wrong with the villa. Through slightly wavering shadows of branches, sunlight reflected the polish of its red marble; and its terrace was banked in color, the yellow of iris against the blue of delphiniums; yet there was a dry, oppressive look about it. It seemed drained, or on the edge of decay.

Then one of the shutters moved, and began to fold back.

They were within half a dozen paces of that ground-floor window. Ralph Douglas cursed once, and ran up the two shallow steps that led to the terrace, as the leaves of the windows were pushed open. Out on the terrace jumped a little, middle-aged woman in black, with a white apron.

"Ah, my God!" said the woman dramatically. "Truly, you have made my heart jump."

She stared at Ralph, blinking and wrinkling her already-wrinkled eyes as though to get closer into his face. She was a sturdy body, with a face grown coarse from too-intensive use of powder to lighten her complexion, and a square sagging jowl. On the bridge of her nose there was a deep red mark, as of glasses. Then suddenly she seemed to recognize Douglas. The drama dropped from her, as her hand dropped from her bust; even the tone and pitch of her voice altered. She ceased to peer. Her voice grew cheerful, even respectfully jocose and wheedling.

"It is you, Monsieur Dooglaz!" she said heartily. "Good morning, Monsieur Dooglaz! I am stupid. You slept well, I trust?"

"I—" said Douglas, and stopped.

She became respectfully confidential. "But I did not hear you go out, monsieur. You were not in your own room; and of course—considering—I did not wish to wake madame, you understand."

"I do not understand," replied Ralph, in husky French.

"The chocolate is prepared, which monsieur may wish to take up himself." She became deprecating. "And now perhaps monsieur may wish to give me my little gift, and permit me to return to Paris? Monsieur may be good enough to add the bus-fare. And"—reaching into the pocket of her apron, she took out a folded handkerchief and carefully spread it out to reveal a pair of eye-glasses with one lens gone and the other split—"without doubt monsieur would wish to replace the poor glasses, on which monsieur stepped last night?"

"Who," said Ralph, "who the devil are you?"

"Monsieur?"

"I said, who the devil are you? What are you doing here? What is this about glasses? And—" Again he stopped, putting his hand to his collar.

"But I am Hortense, of course. Madame's maid. That is to say, I left her service two years ago; but, as I told monsieur last night, I was happy to be invited to serve her again, if for one evening only—"

"Madame who?"

"Madame Klonec, who spent last night here, as monsieur did himself."

"Would it interest you to know," said the other, "that I did not spend last night here; that I have not seen madame for nearly a year; that I think this is a—"

A new and sharper expression had come into Hortense's wriggling eyes; but she drew back, and became heavily reproachful. "Monsieur, you are mocking me. Ah, no; this is too much; it is not *gentil!* It is certain that you were here. You gave me my instructions yourself. You said—"

"Where is Madame Klonec now?"

"Upstairs, in her room, asleep. You said—"

Douglas pushed her gently to one side, and took one step through the window; but on the threshold he turned round to Curtis. His naturally high color had come back, and his expression was one of heavy earnestness.

"Look here," he insisted. "The first thing you're going to think of is that I'm putting up some sort of game on you, dragging you out here, and...oh, anything you like to think. I swear to you I wasn't here. I swear I don't know what this woman is talking about. All I know is that some sort of game is being put up on me. Come on."

The room inside, a very long drawing-room which occupied most of the wing, was almost dark. Hurrying through this room, Ralph Douglas went out into a large central hall, and up a fine staircase at the rear. The door towards which he went was of the rearmost room in the left wing. He banged on it sharply. They heard Hortense's squeaking shoes come up the stairs.

"Rose!"

He banged the door again, rattled the handle, and found that it was open. Without more ceremony he went inside.

Curtis, following him, found that it was as dark as the rest of the villa. Though the shutters were not closed on the high windows facing them from across the room, heavy tasseled curtains had been drawn across the windows, so that there were only chinks and glimmers of light. It was sufficient for them to make out that the biggest article of furniture in the secrecy of this room was the bed against the right-hand wall. There was a feeling of humankind here, an atmosphere as of powder and dishevellment, which they felt even before they saw the outline of a person under the coverlet. The woman lay very peacefully on her back, the coverlet drawn up almost to her neck. Though Curtis did not like to approach closely, he could see that the waxy eyelids were closed, that the large plump face was composed; and her long bobbed hair, of a deep auburn color, was spread out on the pillow. She wore what looked like a peach-colored night-gown, and one heavy bare arm was crooked across her breast outside the coverlet.

Ralph Douglas took her none too gently by the shoulder, and then he stepped back.

"Rose!"

Again he touched her shoulder, tentatively; this time he drew back with even more quickness, and remained moving his own shoulders a little.

"I say, Curtis. Come over here and touch. She's stone cold. I think—"

3

The Stiletto in the Bath

Curtis went round to the other side of the bed.
The arm and shoulder had more than a marble
chill and smoothness; they were stiff. The two
watchers remained staring down, not even looking at each other. From the doorway Hortense's
high voice, eager to take alarm, sang out at them.

"Elle est malade?"

"Elle est morte," said Ralph, almost absently.

They were not prepared for Hortense's screams,
which were as quick as though someone had
turned on a tap; or for the incredible quickness
with which Hortense flung out of the room, still
screaming.

"Grab her," said Curtis, "quick! Grab her and
shut her up, or—"

"Right." Ralph seemed in complete control of

himself; but, when he turned round after taking a few steps towards the door, his face was almost as waxy as the dead woman's. "So help me God, *I* had nothing to do—"

"After her!"

Alone by the bed, Richard Curtis first thought of what a mess this was; and his strong suspicion was that Ralph, in spite of all this buoyant earnestness, had arranged it and put them both into it deliberately. At the back of his mind he was certain, even then, that this was no natural death. Yet at first glance there was nothing in Rose Klonec's appearance to suggest otherwise. He found himself wondering wherein her attractiveness had lain in life. But the stimulation, the vivacity, whatever it might be, had all been drained out of this clay; so that there remained only a short sturdy woman, age about thirty-five, with a good figure but a rather plain face. There was even a shrunken look about her. Afterwards he tried to remember what had first put the idea of murder into his mind. Probably it was the fact that on the padded coverlet, near the exposed right forearm of the dead woman, there was a small dried smear of what might have been blood.

In any case, they must have light...

The semi-darkness of the place had a greenish tinge from the trees which closed in the villa; its thick air, of waxed floors and old curtains, had become stifling. Curtis pulled back the heavy drape on one of the windows, nearly stumbling over a large round table which had been placed near it. Outside the window ran a small balcony. Then he turned back to the room, wondering.

It was a room of no great size or height, papered

in that very dark-red satin peculiar to France, which in certain lights seems to have black in it, and picked out with wooden framings of dingy gilt. A small crystal chandelier had been fitted with electric candles. In the wall opposite the windows was the door to the hall, and also a very fine black and gilt marble mantelpiece, surmounted by a marble clock that would not run and a great gold-leaf mirror that would not reflect. In the wall to Curtis's left was the half-tester bed, just beside a half-open door to a bathroom. Finally, in the wall to the right was another half-open door to a boudoir or dressing-room.

But what chiefly gave the place its cluttered appearance was the large round table, together with two chairs and a small serving-table on wheels, which had been pushed near the window. And now Richard Curtis began to encounter queer things. The serving-table was all right, being loaded with food and drink for an intimate supper: especially drink for there was one opened bottle of champagne in a cooler, and two sealed ones beside it. Although dregs in two glasses showed that the first had been touched, nothing to eat had been set out on the round table. Plates, cutlery, and linen were neatly arranged on the lower shelf of the serving-table.

Then Curtis looked at the big round table. Its polished top bore just three things, and highly incongruous things. These were: (1) a china ashtray on whose edge ten half-burnt-out cigarettes were neatly ranged round at intervals like the spikes in a wheel; (2) a large straight-bladed razor, closed, with an ebony handle; (3) a small pair of carpenter's pliers.

"Here!" Curtis said aloud, as Ralph Douglas might have done.

Ralph entered the room at that moment. It was something of a relief to see his 'typical' Anglo-Saxon countenance, dubious of him as Curtis had become.

"I've got Hortense locked in the lavatory downstairs," he reported. "It's the only place she can't break out of. She's raising the devil. She says— well, not to put too fine a point on it, she says Rose was killed. You know: murdered." With an effort he looked Curtis steadily in the eye. "Either by me, or for her jewellery. There's nothing in it, is there? That is, she *looks* all right."

"I don't know. Was there anything she might have died of? Heart trouble, or the like?"

"Not that I ever heard of." He stared at the bed; then, glancing back, he caught sight of the razor on the round table. "What's that thing doing here? Yes, and look behind you. There!—down on the carpet by the window."

Curtis turned round. Brushed by the tasseled curtain, an edge of bright metal was shining. It was the blunt barrel of a .22 calibre automatic pistol, of silvered steel except for the black grip.

"Razors and guns," said Ralph. "Yes, we've got to have a look at her."

He went back to the bed. After a hesitation he disengaged the coverlet from under the crooked right arm, and pulled the coverlet down. So far as they could tell, there was not a mark on the body in its peach-colored nightdress, either back or front, and no trace of blood. Curtis had to replace the coverlet: his companion's eyelids had suddenly begun to twitch with dangerous tensity, and his hands shook.

"Poor old—" said Ralph, expelling his breath. "You know, it's just beginning to soak through my mind what this thing means. I don't want to think about it. At least she wasn't killed with—" He nodded towards the razor, and then towards the pistol. "The trouble is, she's dead. I was wondering. She used to take sleeping-draughts pretty regularly: chloral hydrate, or some such stuff. Do you think she might have got an overdose?"

His eyes wandered to the half-open door of the bathroom. He reached inside and switched on the light by the door. The bathroom, which was a very modern addition to the villa, had no outer window; it was tiled in black, and had a shallow sunken bath. On a shelf over the washstand Curtis saw a small round cardboard box, standing beside a tooth-glass. *Strickland, English chemist, 18 rue Auber,* said the printed label, without further directions. Using his handkerchief, Curtis opened the box and found it nearly full of small white tablets.

"Did she ever take stuff like this?" he asked.

"Yes," said Ralph. "That is, I remember the name of that chemist. And the pills looked like that; though I don't know what's in 'em."

"There seem to be very few gone out of this box, anyhow. Was it a very strong drug? Dangerous?"

"I can't tell you that. She used to take two of them at a time."

"This place," grunted Curtis, staring round, "is an arsenal. So far there are three things you could kill with: a pistol, a razor, and a drug that would be poisonous. If—"

He looked down into the bath. And this time, with the shock of death wearing off, he found his heart turning sick inside him: for he saw the fourth weapon. At the same time he remembered a small spot of what might have been dried blood on the coverlet, near the woman's right forearm. At the bottom of the bath, near the drain-opening, lay a dagger of the stiletto pattern, thin and long, its triangular blade being surmounted by a hilt of wrought silver. It looked as though water had been splashed over it; but the water had only diluted and made gritty certain bloodstains before it dried. It was spotted with such pale stains. The bath, black tiles gleaming, itself looked blurred and damp.

"I know how she was killed now," Curtis said abruptly.

"But, damn it, she wasn't stabbed!" insisted Ralph. "We'd have seen the mark, and there wasn't a mark on her—"

"No, she wasn't stabbed."

He went back to the body. After getting the better of his reluctance about touching it, he slid his fingers gingerly under the crooked right arm. They found a long unpleasant gaping, like a mouth; it moved at his touch, and had certain dried edges which made him yank out his hand. But it was what he had expected to find. The large artery in the underside of the forearm, concealed until now, had been severed by a long slash.

"She bled to death," Curtis said, rubbing his hands together. "Don't you see it? The way the Romans used to do in committing suicide, except that they opened a vein and the blood flowed more slowly. She was in that bathroom, or someone took her in there. Someone cut the artery with that dagger; someone either put her in that sunken bath, or put her on the floor with her arm hanging over the edge of it, and let the blood run. She's—drained dry. Then someone neatly put her to bed."

There was a silence. They looked at the large, plain, sunken face, entirely without cosmetics.

"Then it's murder after all?" Ralph demanded.

"Yes. Now pull yourself together and listen. I'm supposed to be here to advise you, and I'll try to until I can send for Hunt. You can tell me the truth. Did you do it?"

"My God, *no!* Why should I kill her? And, even if I had, do you think I'd have chosen this place to do it? The whole mess is bound to come out now. Every time I look at this—this place, I feel disgusted. I wish I'd burned it down."

"Steady. That woman downstairs, Hortense, swears you were here last night. It ought to be easy to prove. If you weren't here, where were you?"

"Ah, that's better." Ralph was evidently beginning to reflect. He took a few lumbering strides back and forth, smoothing his fair hair. "Well, I had dinner with Magda, at Fouquet's. Afterwards we went for a drive in the Bois, in my car. Then I delivered her back to her old lady, at the hotel—"

"What time was that?"

"Quite early. About ten-thirty, I think. Am I proving an alibi?"

Curtis grinned. Ralph Douglas was bobbing up again like a cork, and they both felt better. "We can't tell yet. What did you do afterwards?"

"I was supposed to go and see my brother Bryce, on business. But I didn't feel like it. I had almost persuaded Magda to tell the old lady, as you put it, to go soak her head in brine; so I was feeling on top of the world. Besides, I knew you were arriving here this morning, so I intended to turn in early. I thought I should just drive round for a while, at random, and then go home...No, wait! Don't groan: I read detective stories too. I drove 'at random,' but I know quite well where I was. I dropped in at a little café at Passy, just on impulse, to have a drink before I went home. It was one of those dingy places I like, full of cab-drivers and so on. I got to talking to them, and standing the drinks all round. I wasn't particularly under the weather, mind you!—"

"Do you remember the name of the café?"

"No, but I know the name of the street, the rue Beethoven; and I could find the place again...Well, the result was that I didn't get home until nearly half-past three, feeling guilty and with a rotten headache. I had to play a tune on the buzzer and shout to wake up the concierge, which is unusual; she put her head out of the pen and told me it wasn't *gentil*."

"Did the concierge see you?"

"She must have."

"That," Curtis said reflectively, "is all to the good. If you didn't get back to your flat until half-past three, why does this woman, Hortense, swear that you were here—?"

It was just such a situation as he might have imagined in his office in Southampton Street, yet it did not fascinate him; it only worried him badly.

It was alien, and twopence-colored, and it had even a different air from Southampton Street. Yet it was as real as the dark-red wallpaper which shut them in, or the brutality with which Rose Klonec had been murdered. A woman lay dead in a room where there were four possible weapons, a revolver, a razor, a box of drug-tablets, and a dagger-stiletto. Yet the only one of these weapons which had been used was the one which should not have been used; for who would dig to sever an artery with a sharp point only, like a stiletto, when your obvious choice was a touch of the razor? Materials had been prepared for a supper. Yet the only objects on the round supper-table were a china ashtray, with cigarettes ranged in a mathematical circle on the edge, and a pair of small pliers.

It was nothing but "yets." Curtis became dogged.

"How long was it," he went on, "between the time you left your *fiancée* at her hotel and the time you dropped in at the café?"

"Not more than twenty minutes or so, I'm pretty sure."

"Do you think you can prove what time you left the café?"

"Yes, I should think so," answered Ralph. "It's an all-night place for cab-drivers, as I told you, and there's a big clock on the wall in case anybody should have to notice the time. Several of us left together. I couldn't give you the time exactly, but it was well after three. So if Hortense—"

"If Hortense what, monsieur?" interposed a cold voice in French. The door to the hall opened, and Hortense walked in. She was in a shivering kind of rage; yet she was full of dignity.

Behind her stood a policeman, peering.

"Monsieur forgets," Hortense stated formally, "that a woman may at least break a window and scream for help. And now, papa, judge whether I tell lies."

To Curtis it seemed curious that the agent hesitated, hunching his shoulders under his short cape, before he pushed past her. He was an oldish, burly man with a gray moustache but a jaunty twitch to his cap. Not only did he seem short of breath, but there was an odd discomfort, almost furtiveness, about his choleric face. After one sharp glance at the bed, he stood teetering, reaching behind him with one foot to tap on the carpet with the toe of his boot, after the fashion of agents.

"Good morning, M. Hercule," said Ralph dryly.

"Good morning, M. Dooglaz," replied Hercule gruffly, from deep down in his throat. He jerked his thumb over his shoulder. "The old woman," he said, returning the insult, "has accused you of having murdered Madame Klonec."

"She's mad."

"That is evident," agreed Hercule, going to the bed. "For she accuses you of having cut madame's throat with a razor. Well, her throat is not cut! But madame is dead. A heart-attack, perhaps?"

"No, she was murdered." At this point Hercule's expression, which had been verging on relief, altered again. But Douglas stood his ground. "The artery in her arm was cut, and she bled to death in that bathroom there. But I did not do it."

"Oh, the devil," said Hercule under his breath.

"Also, I should like to ask Hortense why she is

so sure Madame Klonec was killed with a razor."

Hortense herself had seemed a little taken aback at Douglas's statement; but it was a small room, and ever since she entered her weak brown eyes had been fixed on the round table. She had now moved forward until she was scrutinizing it with the expression of one peering through a microscope.

"To begin with, because the razor is there," she answered, pointing calmly. "And also because I saw monsieur sharpening it last night, putting a fine edge on it. And also, as I remember now, because monsieur promised me a hundred francs extra to keep out of the way."

4

The Pink Spot

Ralph Douglas's expression changed a little, a broadening of the broad mouth in something like horror, as Curtis had little doubt his own did as well.

"Then it was you—" Hercule began in a rush; but he checked himself abruptly, and regarded the woman with an even more congested eye. He seemed unable to make up his mind about something. "This is not true, Monsieur Dooglaz?"

"No," said Curtis, feeling that it was time to interfere. He addressed Hercule with formal politeness. "May I introduce myself? I am an English advocate, a friend of M. Douglas. Here is my card." Hercule regarded it without much enlightenment. "I had better tell you that this lady seems to be under some extraordinary delusion. She

41

seems to think that M. Douglas spent last night here, at the Villa Marbre. Now, we know that is not true. We can offer proof that he was not here at any time."

"Well, truly," cried Hortense; "no, now, that goes beyond all—"

Hercule's face cleared. "Be quiet, grandmama," he growled. "A delusion, you say?"

"Or something we don't understand. Mightn't it be as well to question her?"

"Good. I will do it," said Hercule. From under one opened button of his tunic he produced a notebook, and from somewhere in the lining of his cap a pencil. These he studied carefully, while the woman looked on with an air of extreme intensity. "Your name and address?"

"Hortense Frey. 41 rue des Halles, seventh."

"Your occupation?"

"I am a lady's maid."

"Madame Klonec's maid, then?"

"No, not at present. I left madame's service a little over two years ago, before monsieur there became acquainted with her. No, it was not that, grandpapa," said Hortense quickly, and folded her arms. "I was not dismissed for any reason *you* would understand. My references are there for all the world to see. It was because of my eyesight."

"One moment," interrupted Ralph hesitantly. "That's true, Hercule. I have heard Madame Klonec speak of it. When Madame Klonec was in a temper, and you couldn't find what she wanted, she always said you had 'eyes like Hortense'; it was a sort of proverb. That's how I came to hear of it. She said Hortense was always mislaying her glasses, and getting herself into a temper about mislaying them—"

"*Bien aimable, monsieur,*" said Hortense, folding her arms tighter and wagging her head. "So you have heard of me? I have heard of you, too, and recently." From the pocket of her apron she took out a soiled letter, which she unfolded with care. "Be so good as to read this, grandpapa. It is in English. Do you read English? No. Then I will translate it."

She did so, with sing-song rapidity and remarkable perfection.

Dear Mlle. Frey:

I have heard you spoken of by Mme. Klonec, whom I believe you used to serve, as a person of tact and delicacy; and I should like to entrust to you a mission of some delicacy now. I was at one time an intimate friend of Mme. Klonec, although we have been separated for some time, and during our acquaintanceship she resided at the Villa Marbre, near Boissy, Forest of Marly—

"I had heard of it," Hortense interrupted herself curtly.

I have now reason to hope, I am glad to say, that our differences may be made up. Madame has granted me a rendezvous for the evening of Saturday, May 15th, at the Villa Marbre. She will, of course, require the services of a maid for that night; and there are reasons why I think it unwise for her to be attended by the maid she employs at present. If you will accept this commission for one evening, I can promise you good wages; and, even about the future, who knows?

Go to the Villa Marbre on Saturday afternoon. (I enclose keys to the gate and the villa; the route is by bus or tram from the Porte Maillot to Boissy, where you can get directions.) The villa will need be set in order a little but you need do no more than make it presentable. Prepare the suite of apartments, bedroom, dressing-room, sitting-room, for madame in the left wing; and my own rooms in the right wing. You yourself will occupy a room on the ground floor by the kitchen, which I trust you will find comfortable. You will find the kitchen fully stocked, and any household materials you may need in your own room. I expect to arrive in the evening early to give you any further instructions, though I do not expect madame until late.

As good faith, mademoiselle, I enclose a hundred-franc note; and you may be sure that there will be four more of them in your purse on Sunday if you obey me faithfully.

Yours,
RALPH DOUGLAS.

"Ah, that is all very well," Hortense burst out, on the edge of hysterics or blubbering. "You and your promises, faith! 'Even about the future, who knows?' That is a nice thing. I am not rich. I have not had work for months. When I receive that letter of yours on Saturday morning, I am so overjoyed and so full of hope that I—"

"Hortense," said Douglas, "I swear you shall have ten hundred-franc notes, here and now, if you will only tell the truth."

You would not have imagined that such a squat woman had Hortense's agility. When he tried to look at the letter, she bounded back; one hand was at her nose, as though holding an invisible handkerchief while she sobbed, and the other clutched the letter. In the revulsion of feeling after her welcome of this morning, her screwed-up face wore a look of horror.

"It is too late for that now," she said darkly. "I *am* telling the truth. You shall not touch me. You are a murderer, and I will have nothing to do with you. Murderer! That is you. Mur—"

An uneasy solicitor thought it time to intervene. Ralph Douglas, genuinely touched, had taken out his wallet and was beginning to wave banknotes at her. The excitement seemed to be contagious: Curtis wondered how this scene would have looked in the offices of Curtis, Hunt, D'Arcy, and Curtis.

"Hortense," he suggested, "we must see the letter, at least. Give it to Hercule, and let him hold it up. You trust the police?"

"Good. That is practical," growled Hercule, taking it out of her hand without more ado. It was a typewritten note; he dangled it in the air.

"Well?" Curtis asked in English.

"This is getting to be a little too much. That's my signature; I'd swear to it," said Ralph. "I know that's my signature. It even looks like the type-writer—Look here, what's the game? I didn't write it."

Hortense, who had dried her eyes with her hand, now seemed to have reached the bottom of misery, though she was beginning to look at Douglas curiously. Curtis addressed her.

"Did you understand what we were saying just now, mademoiselle? You speak English?"

"A little. I am sick of you!"

"You must understand it very well. There are some hard words in that letter: I only wish I knew as much French. It struck me, from the way you read it, that you may have shown it to someone and got a translation—"

"Is it of consequence, monsieur," she inquired with cold dignity, "if I did? Do you take me for a professor at the Sorbonne?"

"To whom did you show it? A friend?"

"To a place where it is their business to know such things. To a travel-bureau. To MM. Toller's Tours, in the Boulevard des Italiens. And to a friend, yes. I have the honor to be acquainted with M. Stanfield, the chief of the whole bureau at Paris, who knew madame well, and used to arrange her bookings when she travelled."

"That was very discreet," said Ralph in a hollow voice.

"It was necessary. Also, it was confidential."

Moodily Ralph began to pace about her, his hands in his pockets; and he spoke to Curtis out of the side of his mouth: "George Stanfield—as she says, the head of the whole blooming show here in Paris, and a great pal of Maw Toller. I say, this is even worse than I'd thought." But Hercule, now puzzled and impatient, intervened.

"Well, well, let us return to business," Hercule growled. "All this is nothing. You do not acknowledge this letter, then, M. Dooglaz?" He flourished it. "Good. I write it down. We progress. Now, grandmama, continue your story, and take care what you say, for my pencil awaits you. You received this letter on Saturday morning, you learned what it meant; and what then?"

"I came here, naturally," retorted Hortense. "There was much work to be done, and you can see for yourself I did it well. But it was not necessary to hurry, since M. Dooglaz did not arrive until night—"

"Ah! M. Dooglaz arrived here, then? At what time was that?"

"At just nine o'clock."

"You hear, M. Dooglaz?"

"I hear," answered Ralph, "and I could not wish for anything better. Now listen to me, Hercule: at nine o'clock last night I was having dinner at the Restaurant Fouquet. My *fiancée* can swear to that, the maître-d'hôtel can swear to it, the waiters can swear to it; there is nothing easier to prove."

"And you hear, woman?" demanded Hercule, expelling his breath upwards so slowly that his big moustache was agitated. "Eh? Tell us what happened."

"I am telling you the truth! At nine o'clock someone rang at the door. I opened it. It was monsieur there. He wore a raincoat and a black hat. He spoke to me in English. He said—"

"I cannot understand this," said Hercule in perplexity. "If you are not lying, it must have been some person pretending to be M. Dooglaz. Look there, grandmama! Can you identify that gentleman? We have heard your eyesight spoken of—"

"*Justement.* But my eyeglasses were not broken

47

then," Hortense snapped, fishing the remains of them out of her pocket. "As for identification, it is the English type: red face, blue eyes, blond hair. You cannot mistake it, never in your life. Besides, he spoke to me in English and presented himself as M. Dooglaz. But I was speaking of my glasses. I took his hat, and I was taking off his coat for him when he stumbled on the parquet. His back was to me, and his shoulder struck me—like that!" She brought her hand across the bridge of her nose, with a highly realistic gesture. "It was a painful blow; it brought the water to my eyes; and the glasses were knocked off. Even while he was apologizing, he said he was afraid he had stepped on them and broken them."

There was a pause, broken by Hercule's asthmatic throat-clearing.

"I think we understand," Hercule said. "It would be easy, eh? First you had a look at him... there was a light?"

"Yes, a good light. It is the light in the hall downstairs."

"And then the glasses are broken. Good. But what about his voice?"

"Oh, it is the same voice; and in any case all voices are alike when they speak English."

Richard Curtis was pulled up short on several new realizations. He supposed this must be akin to his own countrymen's belief, not only that all Chinese looked exactly alike, but that most French or Italians were distinguishable only as types. It had not occurred to him that this might work the other way. It occurred to him how little attention he himself had paid to the identification of voices, when they were voices speaking another language; the distinction was only one of high or low pitch; and that beyond this there was no quality of utterance by which he could tell Jacques from Jules among a hundred speakers, after meeting them only once before. Curtis began to think concretely of the murderer. This was a murderer of quality. He did not hide. He walked boldly under the light of all the lamps, protected by the screen of Hortense's weak eyes and the sound of another language.

All of them seemed to realize this; but it was Hercule who was the most flustered.

"It is evident—" he said, and stopped. "Tell me, M. Dooglaz: is there anyone who wishes to do you an injury, and who resembles you enough to pass himself off as you?"

"Look here...no, there is nobody I know of."

"A relation? A brother, perhaps?"

"There is nobody. I have a brother, yes; but he could never be mistaken for me under any circumstances. He is shorter, he has a moustache, and," said Ralph, summing it up in one gesture of inadequacy, "you do not know him. Even if it were a question of disguise—go on, Hortense. What happened then?"

"He—you—oh, I do not know! He was very nice. He took me into the drawing-room and talked to me. He explained why he had sent for me instead of madame's own maid. He explained that madame was then the little friend of a certain M. De Lautrec, who was furiously jealous and violent. Something terrible! It was thought that madame's maid had been put with her by M. De Lautrec, as a spy. But M. De Lautrec was leaving Paris for the week-end: that was how madame could find time to see M. Dooglaz.

"Well, I asked him if he would like to take something to drink, and make himself comfortable. He said no, not at the moment: that he was obliged to return to Paris—"

"To return to Paris?"

Hortense nodded. "I have said so. To return to Paris for a short time, on business which concerned madame, but that he would return to the villa the same night. He said he might be a little delayed."

At an acquiescent nod from Hercule, Curtis took over the questioning.

"At what time did he leave?"

"I think it was about twenty minutes past nine."

"Did he come and go by automobile?"

"*Tiens*, I don't know!" said Hortense, startled. "I did not hear one."

"While he was speaking to you, had you an opportunity to study his face?"

"I could not, monsieur, without my glasses. It was a sort of pink spot."

"He spoke to you in English the whole time? Yes. And then?"

"And then, monsieur," pursued Hortense, a little thawed by Curtis's courteous manner, "nothing of importance happened until madame herself arrived, at past eleven o'clock. I heard her drive in —her auto is in the garage here now—and I went to meet her. She was alone; she carried two valises; she was astonished to see me. I said, 'Ah, madame had expected to be her own maid over the week-end, eh, since the poor M. De Lautrec is so jealous and madame cannot trust her own maid?' And to my surprise, imagine, her expression became as black as a pit. She said, 'Yes, he is jealous enough, curse him; you don't know what this week-end has cost me. It is droll.'"

"What did she mean by that, exactly?"

"I don't know, monsieur. She refused to talk about it, except to say that she hoped M. De Lautrec enjoyed *his* week-end."

"But how did she act? Did she seem eager to see M. Douglas, for example?"

"Ah! She did indeed. Very, very much so. She was in formidable high spirits, like"—crooking her elbows at her sides, Hortense imitated the swaggering step of a soldier—"like that! When madame was in good spirits, she was magnificent. Like a savage. At the same time, I thought something was worrying her or on her mind. I could not see every line of her face, you understand, but I know all her moods. For instance, I know she was annoyed that M. Dooglaz was not there to meet her, or did not arrive soon afterwards; though she tried to conceal this."

"Did she say how M. Douglas had communicated with her, to ask her to come out here?"

"I understood he had telephoned to her."

At this point, Ralph, who had been shifting from one foot to the other, interposed gruffly. "Why was she so anxious to see me?"

"Does monsieur not know?" inquired Hortense. "I understood monsieur was the only one who ever threw her over before she was ready. Well, I showed her this suite of apartments. I unpacked her valises in the dressing-room there," she pointed, "while she made herself comfortable in the sitting room beyond. I put away her clothes and her jewel—God in heaven!" cried Hortense, slapping her forehead. "I had forgotten the jewellery!" Before they could move she had darted into the dressing-room; but she was back quickly, panting with relief. "No, it is all right. They have not taken her jewellery, as I thought; it is in the little box in the drawer of the dressing-table. But some wretch has put down a sticky bottle on that beautiful rosewood dressing-table, and left a mark...Shall I continue about last night? Yes. I helped madame to bathe, and afterwards assisted her into an evening gown: she would not *receive* monsieur in negligée. By this time it was past midnight, and still monsieur had not come. She told me that she would not need me any more, and that I could go to bed. You would like to see?"

With her brisk steps she again crossed to the half-opened door of the dressing-room. Here the shutters were closed, but there was enough light for them to make out a rich shell of a room, modern except for a bare black-and-white marble floor. There was a profusion of scattered toilet articles on the dressing-table; Curtis could even see the ugly ring where the bottom of a bottle or glass had eaten away the polish of the rosewood. But no clothing of any kind was to be seen, except a pair of yellow satin mules under the dressing-table. After a glance round, Hortense went on to the sitting-room.

Fresh, cool air brushed through side windows that were neither draped nor shuttered. They stood open on a marble balcony, a series of arches like a grotto, shaded by leaves through which the sunlight was falling, and with an outer marble staircase. The room was panelled in gray and gold, furnished in blue with the romantic luxury of the First Empire. Its crystal chandelier tingled slightly to their steps on the bare parquetry. On the mantelpiece was another clock that did not run. But there was a grand piano, and a shelf or two of books. Round the windows opening on the balcony, a cleared space seemed to have been made—with chairs opposite each other, and two silver candelabra thrown together on a side table as though awaiting some purpose. On the center table (incongruously) stood another wine-cooler. But there was no bottle in the wine-cooler, and no glass.

"I left her here," Hortense explained simply. "Those windows were open then as they are now; and, faith, it was a beautiful night."

"You went to bed then?"

"Not immediately, monsieur. That reminds me." She pointed. "Madame asked me to bring her up a half-bottle of Roederer. You know perhaps that every night she drank half a bottle of it no matter what else she drank; and sometimes she used to drink much. She told me that she expected to drink much more, after monsieur arrived. But she said she would begin now with the half-bottle. For she was annoyed—she was furious; yes, I could tell, in spite of all her smiles—that monsieur had not arrived. I walked softly. I did not wish her to flare out, on such a beautiful night."

Mention of the Roederer champagne seemed to interest Hercule, who had the eye of a toper. He stumped forward.

"So? Then where is the half-bottle now, grandmama? I do not see it. There are bottles in the bedroom, for the little supper they intended to have; but they are all large bottles ..."

She was ironical. "Now here is something! How should I know? Do you think the truth of poor madame's death depends on the absence of a half-bottle of champagne?"

"All the same, I note it down. *Mem:* 1 demi-bout., which is missing."

It was not, Curtis thought, a bad principle in this affair; and he was to endorse this view before many days. At the moment he went after Hortense again.

"You brought the half-bottle, then. And after that?"

"That was all. Madame had also instructed me to prepare a little supper against the return of monsieur—that little supper grandpapa speaks of —but I was not to carry it upstairs. I was to put it on the serving-table, and she said monsieur would bring it up when it was necessary. Well, I prepared it. When I had finished I closed up the house and went to bed in my little room by the kitchen. It was then ten minutes to one o'clock, and monsieur had not come in. I remained awake, because I wondered whether I should have to let him in. At ten minutes past one he came in by the back door. I know this because I turned on my light and looked at the clock in my little room. You understand, I was terribly frightened when I heard the back door opening, and I called out, 'Monsieur Dooglaz, Monsieur Dooglaz, Monsieur Dooglaz,' until he answered. Then I opened my door and looked out into the kitchen. At least I could still make out the brown raincoat, and the black hat, and the pinkish-white spot of a face.

"I told him about the supper, which was prepared on the serving-table. He said yes, he knew that. He told me that, as he was coming round the side of the house, madame had called to him from the balcony of the sitting-room. He said," abruptly Hortense spoke in English, to imitate a sing-song, "he said, *'Now go to sleep like a good girl, and don't disturb us tonight, and you shall have another hundred francs.'*

"Naturally I was pleased at that, you understand. I shut the door and lay down again. But he did not go upstairs immediately, as I had expected. I heard him walking about the kitchen. I though, *Tiens,* what kind of an amant is this? But of course you can never tell about the English. Then I heard a sound I did not understand; it was a sound continued for a while, though it was not loud; and I thought it must be the sound of something being sharpened on a whetstone.

"I thought, What is he doing, when madame expects him upstairs? I got up out of bed very softly, and I opened the door a little of a crack"—Hortense held up her pinched thumb and forefinger, to show how small a crack—"and I looked out. Monsieur was standing with his back partly to me. He had in his hand something oblong, grayish, with a shine on it like oil. I knew this for the little whetstone block. He was passing up and down the block something which also shone.

"But naturally I did not think anything of it then, though I was impatient. I thought he must be sharpening a knife to cut the roast chicken. But it did not go up to a point, as a knife does. The last I heard of him was when he went past my door on his way upstairs. He was wheeling the serving-table, for I heard the wheels creak, and the dishes rattle, as he pushed it along."

"And the time was then?"

"A quarter past one," said Hortense, who had become pasty-white.

The silence was broken by a snort from Hercule. "No, now, this goes too far," he said, running towards the balcony. "There is someone watching these windows from over there in the trees."

5

The Arrival of the Scarecrow

What Hercule had seen, or thought he had seen, they could not tell. After one gruff roar, Hercule stood at the windows waving his thick arms and saying, "*S-ss-t!*" as though he were trying to drive a dog away. When they reached his side there was nothing to be seen.

"He is gone," Hercule said unnecessarily. "But he was there in those trees, I swear it."

Curtis thought of asking, "Is that how you try to catch him?" It seemed to him that there was something to be questioned even about the solid Hercule's behavior today. But they were already on the good side of the gendarmerie, and it was best not to annoy him.

"Who was there?"

"The tall man in the old coat. I have seen him before."

"The one you called the 'scarecrow'?" demanded Douglas. "The man you saw twice in the grounds before this?"

"You drink too much, grandpapa," said Hortense, who was looking very sick but standing her ground. "No doubt you are in the habit of seeing scarecrows walking."

He turned round. "Holà, little one! Just as you are in the habit of seeing men wearing raincoats on fine nights, eh? That's a very pretty story you have told us, but there are reasons why we don't believe it, these gentlemen and I. As for my scarecrow, I call him that because he was wearing an old hat such as they put on scarecrows; but he was smoking a pipe. Now, about your story. You say the man was sharpening a razor—on a whetstone block! It is plain you do not know how razors are sharpened..."

"I saw what I saw."

"Also, you have heard these gentlemen say that madame was not killed with a razor."

"So they say. With what, then? Have you looked? I should like to know whether you have done anything at all, except to talk about the importance of missing half-bottles of champagne? Have you made a report to your Commissaire about this, as it is your duty to do?"

With an evil look at her, Hercule brushed past her shoulder and lumbered through the dressing-room towards the bedroom, while she followed like a nagging wife. Ralph touched Curtis's arm, and they stayed behind for a moment.

"I can't stand much more of this emotionalism,"

Ralph said. "It sets *me* going. But in a way the old girl is right. What ails Hercule, do you think? I'm certain he's honest enough, and he's well known in the district. Here: what are we going to do now?"

Curtis was making notes on the back of an envelope. "You heard those time-schedules Hortense gave?"

"You mean about the times the mysterious stranger was sneaking about?"

"Yes. He got here last night at nine o'clock. He left, 9.20. He arrived back, 1.10, he went upstairs, 1.15. You can prove you were at Fouquet's until after nine; right? What about the neighborhood of one o'clock? Can you prove you were at that café in Passy then?"

"I'm pretty sure of it."

"Then we're all right," said Curtis, feeling that he could do with a long, powerful drink. "You don't need to be afraid of the police, and we may be able to stifle some of the publicity. If they're convinced somebody was masquerading as you—honestly, haven't you got any idea who might have done it? You see how it stands. It isn't any question of an elaborate disguise out of a detective story, where somebody dresses up as somebody else and fools his own wife. This would be easy. Hortense is as blind as a bat without her glasses. The murderer gives her one good look, to fix the appearance in her mind—the disguise can be as superficial as you please—and then he breaks the glasses. Without that alibi, you would have been in the soup. The general design of the business seems straightforward enough: but what about the trimmings? Why is that arsenal of weapons laid out..."

They were interrupted by a hail from the next room, and by the noise of an altercation. Beside the round table in the bedroom, Hercule—wearing gloves—was examining the razor. Its blade was now open; he turned it round in the sunlight.

"Hortense," he decided, "has at least told the truth about one thing. See now! Some fool has undoubtedly whetted this on oiled stone. He has blunted a part of it by drawing it the wrong way; there are the scratches. Also, there is a good deal of oil on it. But *this* was not used to cut the artery in madame's arm. There's no blood on it at all; and the assassin could not have washed off blood without washing off the oil." In a fume he closed the razor and put it down again. Curtis's respect for his intelligence was increasing. "So why must he sharpen it, if Hortense is to be believed?"

"Should you touch that," asked Curtis, "before the Commissaire—?"

"I attend to my business," said the other with dignity. "Now, that pistol on the floor by the window. Did you see that in the assassin's hands, grandmama?"

"No. I never saw it."

With an asthmatic grunt, Hercule picked it up. "An automatic of English manufacture. Good, that is important. Fully loaded, and no one has fired it. Good. But where is the weapon with which madame was killed?"

Curtis directed him to the bathroom. All four of them gathered round the edge of the black-tiled bath, looking down into it. The thin triangular blade, with its silver haft and its mottling of pale stains, made Hortense draw back.

"But I know that!" she declared. "That thing in the bath. It belongs to madame herself. It comes from Corsica. M. Stanfield, the gentleman I spoke of at Toller's Tours, gave it to her as a little present three or four years ago. She liked it, and always kept it by her."

Hercule peered suspiciously. "An extraordinary toy, grandmama. However, I note it down. Did madame bring it with her last night?"

"Assuredly. I put it away in the drawer of the dressing-table."

"There are many things here I do not understand," said Hercule explosively, after a long pause while he stared at the stiletto. "Madame bleeds to death: good. That weapon is used to cut her arm, since there is blood on it: good." With great effort he bent down and gingerly touched the bottom of the bath, still damp in places, with the tip of his gloved finger. He held it up stained with a slight brownish sediment. "*That* is blood, eh? Yes. We must agree that the assassin held her over here, or put her into the bath, while she bled. But how did the assassin persuade her? Madame was a strong woman. She must be attacked: she would shout, she would scratch, she would fight. And there is not a sign of a fight. It is possible she may have been struck on the head and stunned."

"Look at that cardboard box over the wash-basin," said Curtis. "My friend thinks they are sleeping-tablets."

Hercule picked up the box and sniffed at it.

"Well, grandmama?" he said.

"They are sleeping-tablets," agreed Hortense.

"But what of that? You could not force madame to take sleeping-tablets, any more than you could force her to bleed: faith, no, not without a fight!"

"Imagine, then, that madame has taken them of her own accord?"

Hortense regarded him with such pale skepticism that it was like a light. "It is easy to see that you are old, grandpapa! Madame doses herself with sleeping-tablets on the same night that she burns with impatience to meet her lover? Whiskers to you! You make me laugh."

"Nevertheless, why is the box there, then?—and a glass beside it?"

"Why, why, why! You ask me that. Why are there revolvers and razors all about, and why is poor madame dead? Why does anything happen? Don't ask me. Ask these dirty English, who brought it all on us. Oh, my God!" cried Hortense. Her nerves suddenly collapsed altogether, and she burst into a spasm of weeping.

"Listen," urged Hercule, raising his hand. "Ssst! Grandmama, be quiet and listen."

They had all caught the sound. All the doors were open through to the front of the villa, and to the open windows of the drawing-room. In the silence they heard the noise of a motor-car pulling into the drive which curved round the left wing of the villa.

Ralph walked swiftly to the nearer bedroom window. Untwisting its catch, he pushed it open and stepped out on the balcony; but he came back with equal quickness.

"That's torn it," he said calmly. "It's Magda."

"What does he say?" asked Hercule.

"I shall have to see this through," Ralph went

on, not heeding him. "Why in blazes do you suppose she's here? If Ma Toller—it's going to take plenty. Come along, old son, and lend me moral support. I need it." He turned to the others. "It is my *fiancée*. You understand the difficulty I am in. For God's sake do not come downstairs until I have had time to explain."

With Curtis following, he hurried out into the hall, and down a flight of back stairs to the kitchen. The back door was unlocked. A few steps led down into a shady garden planted with box hedges. Through rows of tall blue delphiniums the sanded path ran out to a small round building of marble, a sort of temple, with pillars and circular seats. But they were not looking in that direction now. A girl was walking rapidly round the side of the villa, flashing into strong sunlight as she turned the corner.

Somewhere—possibly from a hint dropped by Hunt about "one of our sensible beauties"—Curtis had got an impression that Magda Toller would be tall, stately, and bloodless: a blonde. She was the reverse of all these. Magda Toller was small, with black hair bobbed something after the fashion of Rose Klonec; and, despite a certain subdued air, she was very far from languid. At first glance, after the broad charms of Rose, you might have thought Magda slight. This would be at first glance: after which your glance would return, and return again, until you realized her attractiveness was not merely beauty of complexion, or of hazel eyes and high-arched eyebrows that gave her an air of detachment. Two dimples marked the corners of her mouth when she smiled. But she was not smiling now. As she came swinging round the corner of the villa, her hands were dug into the pockets of a light tweed coat; a fillet of ribbon bound down the hair to keep it from blowing in an open car. Despite a calm manner she was plainly under an intense nervous strain.

She stopped dead, blinking.

"Ralph!" she said. "Is that you? But—"

"Yes. What are you doing here?"

"I didn't think—that is, they said there was trouble...Are you in trouble?"

"No. Who told you that?"

"I don't know. Some person on the telephone. I got here as soon as I could; but I had to go to church with mother before I could slip away, and then I had to change, and then it took me hours to find the beastly place."

They stood looking at each other. By this time Curtis was getting his second or third glance, with results which strangely depressed him. He had begun to realize why Douglas might have thrown over several Rose Klonecs for this unassuming young lady.

"So this is the place," she said, eyeing it speculatively. One thought was evidently in her mind as she considered it; she suddenly became aware that this must be apparent in her face, and went pink.

"I forgot," said Ralph in some haste. "Some introductions are in order. Mr. Curtis, Miss Toller. Curtis is my solicitor, Magda. He's just come over from London."

Her pinkness increased as she saw a stranger, and she froze under an aloof air. Curtis was so anxious to make a good impression that he himself was rather stiff in manner.

"How'djoudo?" said Miss Toller.

"How'djoudo?" said Curtis.

"Look here, Magda: I've got to tell you, so we'd better get this over with quickly. There *is* trouble, in a way, it's about Rose Klonec—"

"I see," said Magda. "And hence the solicitor, and we may all speak frankly and get you out of the mess. Oh, Ralph, you idiot, have you been carrying on with that trollop again?"

"No, I have not. It's worse than that. She's dead, Magda. Somebody murdered her—up there. We don't know who it was. Curtis and I found the body this morning, and if it weren't for certain fortunate happenings I might be on my way to the police station in handcuffs this minute. Don't faint, now."

"It's your tactful way of breaking the news," she told him after a pause. "I'm not going to faint. But can we find a place to sit down?"

They went down the sanded path to the little marble building, where they sat and looked at each other.

"I'm going to put in my case before anybody else gets a chance at you, my girl," Ralph went on grimly. "Now tell the court under oath: where was I round about nine o'clock to nine-twenty last night?"

"I don't kn—stop a bit, of course I do. We were having dinner. I say, was that when they did it?"

"Tell her about it; that's your job," said Ralph. He lit a cigarette moodily while Curtis took up the story from the beginning. Speaking slowly and giving as few as possible of the lurid details, he pointed out each fact in favor of innocence. She sat with her hazel eyes fixed on him, the lashes hardly winking; and at the end of it she almost smiled.

"I'm sorry I was rude to you a minute ago," she said. "I think you could keep him out of trouble if anyone could. Ralph, you idiot—!"

"Damn it all, why am *I* an idiot?" shouted the other, stung. "What have *I* done? How could I prevent it? I didn't kill her—"

"Ralph, please control your language. I don't care whether you killed her...that is, I suppose I do, rather, because I'm going to marry you myself and I shouldn't want any precedents set. But I mean that isn't the main point."

"I know the principle. When in doubt or difficulty of any kind, call me a fathead and then everything seems to appear in brighter colors."

"Darling, you have plenty of intelligence, or I shouldn't like you. The only trouble is that the kind of intelligence you have is no good in a case like this." She hesitated. "You see, things are jumbled up at a very bad time. I shouldn't be surprised to see mother out here this morning..."

Ralph looked up.

"Then the party *would* be complete," he said. "Why should she come here?"

"Because there was a row after you took me home last night. Nothing in particular started it: it simply grew. It ended with my making the decision you've been wanting me to make. I said 'down with gratitude,' and that I was ready to marry you any time you'd have me. It was beastly of me; but moral lectures in Paris seemed so completely out of keeping that it was the last straw." She turned to Curtis. "You'd better know about this, as—er—legal adviser. You see, my father was a convicted murderer."

Curtis did not pretend to misunderstand.

"Mrs. Toller is not your real mother, you mean?"

"That's it. My father was hanged at Pentonville in 1908, a few days before I was born. My mother died in childbed; I suppose that's odd, for she was a street-walker. I was the sensation-baby of the day. Mrs. Toller, who was then even more pious, adopted me out of the ditch. My full name is Mary Magdalene Toller—repentant sin, you know. I was the full-blown product of crime and sin; and I've been told a great deal about them since."

She spoke without any affectation, or even concealed bravado. She was merely stating facts. Once Ralph opened his mouth as though to protest, but he stopped. At the end of it she smiled suddenly, so that the dimples deepened at the corners of her mouth; and gave a slight shake of her black bobbed hair.

"I can tell you, Mr. Curtis, I've probably had more impulses towards crime and sin than most anyone I know. But, Although Doctor Freud Is Distinctly Annoyed, I still haven't done anything yet. Still, that's the trouble. When this mess comes out—well, I don't mean that I shall be accused of being mixed up in the murder. At least nobody could ever mistake me for a tall fair man who looks like Ralph. But those antecedents will be dug up by somebody...and with mother raving..."

Ralph stirred. "Here! I hadn't thought of that—"

"*I* had," she told him succinctly. "That's why I felt so sick. Where's your brother?"

"Bryce? What's Bryce got to do with this?"

"Where is he? He's supposed to have a lot of influence with the police, or with the government, or both. Of course, the murder can't be hushed up; but if you and I could be prevented from dancing hand in hand through the newspapers—Still, why not?" She grinned. "Maybe it would be rather a lark."

"But Bryce!" Ralph was puzzled. "Influence with the police! This is all news to me." His expression conveyed that Bryce Douglas was the last person he could conceive of as having influence with anybody. "I can't believe it. He's too—pale. He's only something in the Foreign Office, as far as I know. I told you about him, Curtis; he's the fellow who says and does exactly the right thing on all occasions."

"Well, that may be a recommendation, even in the Foreign Office," said Curtis. "And we certainly need something like it now. What kind of position has he got?"

Magda looked thoughtful.

"Of course, it may be all rot. But he's dropped various dark hints to mother and me—"

"He's in love with you."

"Well, I can't be expected to resent that, darling. Anyhow, it's certainly true that he spends half his time between London and Paris; and he always stalks about with a briefcase, and whatnot, and looks terribly important. Still, I don't suppose it's much good. It's a question of whether he'd use his influence even if he had any: unless I asked him nicely. Oh, damn. Whatever you say, Ralph, we're in the middle of a most dreadful mess; and the question is, what are we going to *do*?"

"Perhaps," said a new voice, *"I might be able to suggest something."*

It was a deep, rather slow, faintly genial voice, speaking in English. In the little temple where they were sitting, broken reflections of sunlight gleamed from the under-side of foliage, and moved a little on the white marble floor; the shadows of the pillars lay across it. Another shadow had now fallen among them, a very long shadow. Curtis first noticed the smoke of the rankest and worst tobacco he had ever smelled; then the sleeves of the corduroy coat, worn at the elbows, of the man in the doorway. He was a tall, lean, stringy man, in the middle fifties, and his appearance was not improved by his hat. He was smoking a pipe. A genial eye was turned on them from under a wrinkled eyelid, and he needed a shave. Yet nothing could have exceeded the gravity with which he removed the pipe from his mouth and lifted his dilapidated hat.

"It is possible, Miss Toller, that I may be of service to you," pursued the tall man. "I am a land-owner of this district. My name is Bencolin."

6

Through the Shutters

No other name in France could have surprised Curtis quite so much. He was even, in the depths of his soul, a little shocked. He wondered what Grandison Hunt would have said if this apparition, once noted for its sartorial nicety, had strolled into 45 Southampton Street. On the other hand, it was possible that Hunt would have greeted him with a limerick. If this were Henri Bencolin—and every intonation of the voice, every gesture told him that it was—certain things were missing, like the Mephistophelian eye. Or were they? He was not quite sure.

For the apparition, receiving a gesture of assent from Magda, gravely fitted on its hat again and sat down on the marble bench, stretching out its long legs affably. Despite the fact that he needed a shave, his moustache and black beard were now trimmed so closely that they were like a graying stubble. An eye twinkled under the hat, out of a spreading of wrinkles. He spoke in good American, fluent to overpowering, if somewhat pedantic: as though he had first thought out an elaborate sentence in French, and then turned it carefully into English.

"Good Lord," said Douglas, "you're not *the*—?"

"I am," said Bencolin. "I may add that for the first time in my life I am thoroughly comfortable. Miss Toller, I beg your pardon: I am afraid this pipe annoys you. I will put it out." He did so, with a snap of his powerful wrist, and odoriferous results. "It is not the best Virginia; but I find that it is good for the wasps."

"That's quite all right," beamed Magda, coughing with a good deal of moisture in her eyes. "But if you *wouldn't* mind a cigarette—? What on earth are you doing here?"

Curtis was beginning to understand that this was the Bencolin of whom he had heard, in whatever way he chose to present himself. Such was the enormous vitality of the man, the sense of certitude he conveyed, that it was as though they had been waked up: they almost forgot the matter in hand. Bencolin chuckled.

"I am a landowner," he said. "At least, the term has a noble sound, and I can show you the land down the road. My ample leisure, out of the shooting season, I spend in reading those classics, both French and English, which one thing or another has hitherto prevented me from devouring. I am at present in the midst of an epic poem which is devoted chiefly to repeating every line three times. It appears to concern a Red Indian family living near a place incredibly called Git-chee-Gumee." He looked doubtful. "You see me, then, eating my dinner at peace in my garden, with an improving book propped up before me, and the damned wasps circling round my wine-glass. Holà! Who could wish for better?"

"You *have* retired, then?" asked Ralph in a curious tone.

"In a manner of speaking."

"Because I was wondering if you weren't Hercule Renard's 'scarecrow.'"

Bencolin straightened up. "You would like to get down to business at once, then?" he asked politely.

There was something in the way he said it that caused a silence.

"I heartily apologize, but I have been watching you," he went on. "I have been listening. Still, I think I may be of service. At the moment Rapet, the Commissaire of the district, is on his way here; and a car from the Sûreté should arrive presently; I thought it was best to summon them. Yes, I know all about Rose Klonec." He looked at Curtis. "You are Mr. Douglas's lawyer?"

"Yes. And," said Curtis, "I have a letter for you."

From his inside pocket he took the envelope addressed in Hunt's small, neat handwriting. Bencolin's eyes narrowed as he opened the letter; but he had not read far before his expression became one of amusement, not to say relief.

"This," he said, "puts an entirely different complexion on the matter. Come, this is excellent!" He got up. "Mr. Curtis, may I have a word with you in private? You will excuse us for a moment?"

Curtis walked slowly down the sanded path beside him, Bencolin at a long and rather shambling stride; he had begun to fill his deadly pipe again. One faint remark floated up to them from the temple, "So that's the old geezer," as they turned the corner of the villa.

"I am the old geezer," said Bencolin. "I feel flattered that Mr. Douglas did not apply a stronger term. Shake hands, my friend. Any associate of that old reprobate Hunt, who next to Jeff Marle is the greatest friend I have in England, is both welcome and trusted. Now read this."

He held out the letter, which said:

Dear Henri:

The bearer of this, my partner Mr. Richard Curtis, will explain to you as much as is necessary of the affairs of a client of ours, Mr. Ralph Douglas, who has become mixed up with a woman called Rose Klonec. As a favor I should like to ask you to find out what you can about this woman, along your own ways: it may be useful to us. I am unable to verify what I am writing here, and so I will not risk inaccuracy by instructing Mr. Curtis on the point; but it occurs to me that a woman of that name was employed—about five or six years ago—by Masset on your secret police. You remember that business of the Deputy from Provence? If it is the same woman, what's up?

Show Dick a good time; he is a good fellow, and he is now about to prove whether he is made of stern enough stuff to support the excitements of an English solicitor's life.

Remember the Albanian countess?

Kindly burn this letter. It is *not* an official communication.

Curtis looked up, to find Bencolin smoking placidly.

"Secret police—?" Curtis repeated.

"Well, that is only a side-line, of course. Masset occasionally employed her. And now, my friend, you must not immediately have visions of sinister spy-plots to blow up the Quai d'Orsay or start another war. When I say the secret police, I mean something much more domestic and much more practical, if a trifle less romantic. Let me put the situation like this. There is to be a meeting of the Cabinet, or even a meeting of a committee of the Cabinet. The subject under discussion is whether the franc shall be inflated or devalued; of the six new cruisers that are to be built, at what shipyards they shall be built, and by whom; even whether the International Exposition shall be held in 1937 or 1938: but all matters in which the Stock Exchange is interested. The decision of the Cabinet is not known until from twelve to twenty-four hours after the decision. If, during that time, one or even half a dozen persons knew the decision in advance; if (in short) there were an informer to give the tip—"

"There would be fortunes made."

"And a beautiful explosion afterwards, when the leak became known," said Bencolin. "We have suffered too much from that sort of thing. Our Parisian sees treason, and immediately wants the heads of everybody in sight. Over goes the government; and the parade of colored shirts then resembles a revue at the Folies Bergères. It must stop."

In the driveway past the side of the house there was an open blue sports car, presumably Madga's. Bencolin sat down on the running-board and frowned.

"I will not trouble you with politics," he went on. "It is to be hoped that politics will not enter too much into this case; for it promises to be a fine puzzle, a stimulating puzzle, a noble challenge to the wits. Forr-rard the Buffs!" beamed the former *juge d'instruction,* drawing out his *r's* with a long rumble from the throat, and rubbing his hands exultantly. "To be frank, I am a little tired of Gitchee-Gumee. However, this I must tell you. The leak in the Cabinet, which I confess has a sinister sound, is believed to be the confidential secretary of a minister we need not name. But the secretary's name is Louis De Lautrec."

Curtis whistled.

"You mean the fellow Rose Klonec has been living with? I see. Then the secret police shoved her on to De Lautrec to find out?"

"In this case, no. A woman who took nearly a year to find out something from her lover would be useless to the secret police or anyone else. No; she has been in Masset's pay for only a week or two. I understand the government does not set such traps in England, my friend?"

"It is doubtful."

"It is practical," said Bencolin simply. "I myself came into the affair by accident. As Mr. Douglas shrewdly guessed, I am Hercule Renard's 'scarecrow.' Hercule knows me, though not in such clothes as this; and I did not dare take him into my confidence. He talks too much at the local wine-shop...Now see what happened! A fortnight ago M. Masset, the head of the bureau of secret police, came to me as I sat at ease in my garden, reading an improving book about Don Quixote; and M. Masset's moustaches drooped exactly like Don Quixote's. He did not want advice. He merely wished to drink a glass of wine in congenial company, and utter prolonged squawks concerning his woes. Among them was the De Lautrec affair. I was interested, since I knew that Mme. Klonec had formerly lived at this villa here.

"And then—well, I was drawn into it in spite of myself. Have you wondered why Hercule Renard was allowed to see me quite so obviously? I was compelled to draw his attention to me. Otherwise he might have seen someone who was there as well as myself: someone who was also interested in the house. Twice I noticed an intruder here. Once...let me be certain of these dates...once was on the evening of Wednesday, May 12th: four days ago. Once was in the early evening of Friday, May 14th: the night before last."

Curtis arranged dates in his mind. He also remembered what Ralph Douglas had told him that morning. On Friday, May 14th, Ralph had come out here to look over the villa and see that it was in good condition, after De Lautrec had offered to buy the villa from him. (Why, come to think of it, had De Lautrec made that mysterious offer?) On that same Friday Ralph had discovered that the lights and water were in working order, that the bed had been made in Rose Klonec's room, and that there were six unaccountable half-bottles of Roederer champagne in the refrigerator.

Curtis felt Bencolin's eye fixed on him.

"You were thinking?" Bencolin prompted softly.

"Nothing much. I don't know about Wednesday, but the man you saw on Friday may not have been an 'intruder' at all. Mr. Douglas himself came out here on Friday."

"So? At what time?"

"In the morning."

Bencolin shook his head. "No, this was in the evening. Also, for a reason I will indicate, I am certain it was not Mr. Ralph Douglas.

"Now let us get our days in order. Wednesday, to begin with. I saw my intruder when I was driving back from Boissy, with provisions for my simple country cottage; and I noticed him because he was climbing up over the wall. I saw him on top of the wall, in some very passable moonlight. He was carrying a large covered basket over his arm. He wore a brown raincoat and a black hat."

"The same costume as the murderer wore last night, according to Hortense?"

"The same."

"You didn't see his face?"

"It may be a long time," said Bencolin in a curious tone, "before we see his face. Well, I drove my horse and trap—yes, my friend, it is a horse and trap, and without lights—a little way along the road, after which I returned to investigate. Unfortunately, at that moment Hercule came rolling home from the wine-shop, with his paunch wabbling above his bicycle, and damnably inquisitive with his bull's-eye lantern. I was obliged to go home and read an improving book.

"However, I was intrigued. The intruder had not looked like a burglar; and he was carrying a filled basket. For two successive nights I kept an eye on that villa from the hedge opposite, meditating on the beauty of the country and keeping the wasps off with my pipe. On Friday evening there was another visitor—but not the same one. This fellow was shorter and had a different air from the man in the raincoat. He opened the padlock of the gate with a key. At the same time, I did not think it was the owner, Ralph Douglas; I had seen Douglas several times from a distance, when Rose Klonec was living at the villa.

"Here, then, was the situation. The villa is empty: Madame Rose, now a police spy, has gone to live with De Lautrec. On Wednesday night, a man in a raincoat and a black hat climbs the wall with a filled basket over his arm; on Friday night another man opens the gate and goes in. All these things might have no connection whatever. They probably did not. But they interested me so I followed the man through the open gate.

"He went round the left hand side of the villa —walking softly—and down the drive where we are standing now, towards the back. The villa was shuttered, but I could now see that there was a light in the kitchen. So there was still another person here tonight? As soon as he saw the light, the man I was following drew back. Then he began to approach the back windows of the kitchen with some caution; and tried to look through the slits in the shutters. To get a really good view through such shutters (my police experience could have told him) is almost impossible. But he saw something, and the expression of his back told me that he either did not like or did not understand it. At this point the light in the kitchen was switched off. My man jumped back from the window. For about two minutes we both stood quite still.

"Ah, well. You can understand by this time the pitch of my curiosity. After several years' inaction, I was myself again. I had smelled powder. I had seen a red herring. I felt better, thank you. Therefore I came up to him from behind and put my hand on his shoulder. I do not like the fellow, but give him his due: even at that unexpected touch he never moulted a hair. This can be ascribed to his Foreign Office training. He was Mr. Bryce Douglas."

"Bryce Douglas?"

Sitting on the running-board, Bencolin leaned back against the side of the blue car, which pushed his dilapidated hat a little back. Curtis could see the many wrinkles spreading out round his pouched black eyes when he smiled, and the cords in his neck when he chuckled. But there was now a restlessness about the big figure. He drew in his chin for grave speech.

"Bryce Douglas, yes. You don't need to look so suspicious, my friend. I knew the man and I knew his errand: he has been cooperating with Masset in the De Lautrec affair—"

"Then he does have influence with the police after all?"

Bencolin shrugged his shoulders.

"With the government, if you prefer. There is a difference, as any old brigadier of the Sûreté will inform you with some profanity. Our friend Bryce has been acting as a sort of liaison-officer, on the quiet, between the Quai d'Orsay and Whitehall. There seems some reason to believe that a part of the money used to bribe De Lautrec comes from England.

"In any case, there he was—remarkably well-tailored, flower in his buttonhole, even a brief-case. I know that brief-case. It is a symbol. He had intended to meet Rose Klonec there, and to get a report on De Lautrec. So much he admitted; and Madame Rose had chosen the Villa Marbre. Why? Why? Why does madame have such an affection for the Villa Marbre; and how does it fit in with certain other activities?"

He hesitated, his eyes narrowing.

"Still, what did he see when he looked through the window?" asked Curtis. "Rose Klonec?"

"No," said Bencolin. "He saw a man in a brown raincoat and a black hat."

This figure was becoming something of an obsession.

"Doing what?"

"Nothing that could be called significant, on the face of it. The man appeared to be handling what Bryce described as great numbers of bottles of champagne. It was impossible to see with any clearness, including the man's face. The bottles, which he seemed to be putting in or taking out of a refrigerator, were identifiable by their shape and color. Then the light was turned out in the kitchen. Unfortunately, that made our Foreign Office gentleman turn tail. The situation was—hum—domestic. He believed it must be his brother Ralph, stocking the larder for an evening party. He had no desire to go into the villa under those circumstances. So he left the grounds. It does not seem to have occurred to him to wonder what Ralph Douglas might have been doing alone, in a dark and shuttered house in the Forest of Marly, playing with champagne-bottles. Nor, I admit, does the explanation occur offhanded to *me*."

"Just a minute, sir," Curtis said sharply. That 'sir' slipped out inadvertently. He regretted it: but he was too used to giving respect in the offices of Curtis, Hunt, d'Arcy, and Curtis, and there was something about Bencolin which compelled it. "You know why I'm here?"

"To protect the interests of your client, naturally."

"Yes, that's it. Why should Bryce Douglas think it was his brother he saw in the kitchen? What made him think so?"

"What made Hortense think so, the night afterwards?"

"Hortense is nearly blind."

"Try to look through one of those shutters, my friend; you will be nearly blind as well. Do not misunderstand me," continued Bencolin quietly. "I am not trying to make out a case against Ralph Douglas. Listen to me! I have heard the very clear account of the whole affair you gave to Miss Toller out there in the temple. And I tell you this much: if his alibi holds good, as I presume it will—for he would not be such a jackass as to call a café full of taxi-drivers for witnesses unless it did—then he has not *that* chance of being suspected." He snapped his fingers. "Are you satisfied?"

The suavity of his explanation was marred by the fact that at the end of it Bencolin scratched his beard with the stem of his pipe, and turned a quizzical eye on his companion. Curtis had a feeling that he was being weighed or measured. Consequently, he was not certain whether he trusted or distrusted, liked or disliked.

"For God's sake, Jeff—" the other pursued; "I beg your pardon. You remind me of a stubborn but dependable friend of mine. For God's sake, Mr. Curtis, let me in my declining years be free of the popular belief that I never do or say anything without some subtle reason behind it. My friend Baron von Arnheim, during a little encounter of ours on the Rhine, once said to me, 'I wish you would play a joke, for no reason except that it was a joke. I wish you would go to the theatre, for no reason except that you wanted to see the play.' Petrone Galant sang a similar tune. Well, I am tired of playing bogeyman to scare the under-world of Paris. I am a provincial, *voyons*. I only wish to see the play...Are you with me?"

"Yes, hang it all, I am!"

"Good. And now let us consider the play."

He was silent for a moment, staring at the tops of the poplar trees.

"This enigmatic man with the brown coat and black hat is seen on three occasions. On Wednesday night I saw him—carrying a filled basket. On Friday night Bryce Douglas saw him—doing something with champagne-bottles. On Saturday night, the night of the murder, Hortense Frey saw him—sharpening a razor. Is there any connection in those things?"

"I certainly can't see any," Curtis said gloomily. "Any more than why the room should be strewn with so many weapons. The champagne business crops up again, too. Hortense said that she served Rose Klonec with a half-bottle of Roederer last night: but the bottle now seems to be missing. None of it seems to make any sense."

"Come, surely it is not as bad as all that. Surely it is clear that the——"

From the roadway in front of the villa came a sound of several motor-cars with brakes screeching as they swung sharply through the now open gates. Bencolin got up with an eagerness he could hardly conceal.

"That will be Durrand and his crew from the Sûreté. I telephoned them from my own house. I should not be at all surprised if I were invited to direct matters for the present; in which case, my friend Richard, you will have the opportunity to see exactly how we work. Go and join your friends in the little temple. I will be with you in a moment."

7

The Missing Champagne-Bottle

In the temple Curtis found Ralph and Magda smoking cigarettes with the same air of concentration.

"You were a devil of a long time," the former complained. "What are the omens?"

"They seem pretty good. Bencolin himself is going to take charge, I gather. The police are here. So keep your chin up; they'll be here in a minute—"

"Oh, my hat!" said Magda suddenly; "and look who's with 'em."

The open space round the back of the house was now swarming with men. In the midst of them was Bencolin, shaking hands with a burly man who wore a sinister-looking slouch hat. But another figure had detached itself from the group, and was walking hesitantly down the path towards the temple. He was a middle-aged man of the sort called well preserved, displaying a certain well-tailored leanness; and he wore full morning costume. His bearing was unobtrusive, but he held his head a little back as though he were always looking someone in the eye. He had one of those large, grayish, grizzled faces which suggest intentness, and a slight stoop. A slight gray moustache, hardly more than the outline of one, lent an odd touch of dandyism in an obvious office-man and family man.

"It's George Stanfield," said Magda, tossing her cigarette away. "The manager of mother's Paris office. He was at church with us this morning."

She checked herself, for Stanfield was within earshot. He hesitated; then he took off his silk hat, revealing the fact that he was as bald as a turnip. On the step of the temple he hesitated again, struggling; and what he managed to get out was:

"By heaven, I hardly know what to say."

"I'm glad somebody feels like that," said Ralph. "Shall we keep it at that?"

Stanfield looked straight through him, coldly, in a way that made Ralph Douglas's jaw come forward. Then Stanfield sat down with a quiet air.

"You realize, Magda, that you have deeply offended your mother?"

"Have I? There's something more important than that."

"The murder? Yes, I know. I rode out in one of the police cars." Despite his quiet air, he seemed fussed by a thousand cares. He brushed this aside. "You're facing a serious scandal, Magda. My experience has been that anyone in France

86

can be bribed; but I'm afraid this has gone too far. I had no idea...in church this morning...that you and your mother—that there had been trouble last night—" Again he stopped. "Magda, your mother is seriously ill."

"I know that game," said Magda, leaning back against the bench and closing her eyes. "So you were sent after me, were you?"

"Not exactly. I felt it was Bryce's business to come; but your mother insisted that he stay and—and see to her. And then there was another unwise business." Something like a smile, as much a ghost as the moustache, showed on his face, at the same time that his restless, pale-blue eyes were roving and studying. "After you had gone this morning, Bryce and I were both summoned. It was just as well. Your mother had been foolish enough to ring up the police and send out a general alarm for you. That would have cost us something in the way of scandal, I can tell you! I had to quash it. Naturally, at our office, we have a good many dealings with the police. I went to the Prefecture and saw Bourdeau. He told me that the report had just come in about—" Stanfield nodded towards the villa. "Who is this gentleman?"

Curtis was introduced.

"Yes, that was wise," Stanfield said grimly. He looked at Ralph. "Well, young man, you got yourself into this mess, and the least you can do in decency is to keep Magda out of it. It's none of my affair; I'm not going to preach; I've seen too much of the world to preach; but why did you have to kill her?"

Curtis interposed. "We needn't discuss that now. Mr. Douglas did not kill her. We will talk all about that at a more proper time."

Stanfield folded his hands in his lap.

"Just as you like," he agreed dryly. "I only thought it would be better to put all the cards on the table, so that we can see what we're up against. For I suppose we shall have to support him; at least, to see that he avoids the guillotine. He may have a great deal to explain, like that row a year ago last March."

"What," said Magda, "was the row a year ago last March? Don't let him talk to you like a Dutch uncle, Ralph; he's only mother's mouthpiece. Speak up and answer him."

"I am sorry," said Stanfield, after a pause. "In a way, I suppose that's true." A certain vein of kindliness was evident in his worries. He remained looking at the floor. "Lord knows, everybody seems to have been against you, Douglas. But there are reasons, if you can understand them. I've been in this town for twenty-three years, earning my bread and raising a family as I should in Surbiton. When we see you young blades come over here only to spend your money and raise the devil, and regard it as a kind of extra-mundane haze where no values count, we don't like it. Things which seem fine and wild at your age only look foolish at mine."

"All the same," said Magda quietly, "what was the row? You didn't tell me, Ralph."

"I didn't think I needed to. It was no secret: it was in the papers at the time."

"Yes?"

Ralph lifted his shoulders. "All right. It was at one of those night-clubs where they have music-hall turns on the cabaret floor. One of them was a knife-throwing act: the management announced that if the knife-thrower missed his board the people at the tables would get it in the eye. For some reason that made it popular." He brooded. "Rose and I were there with a party. The table with the fellow's knives on it was pushed almost against our table. Rose reached out and took one of the knives to look at it. She was quite sober: only excited. I grabbed her arm and tried to make her put it back—and I got a cut along the side of the jaw. It wasn't deep, and it didn't leave a scar; it was an accident. But it was a mess."

Magda Toller looked at him curiously.

"But that's not all?"

"That's absolutely everything," declared Ralph. "Ask anybody. Ask De Lautrec, for instance: he was there. I mean, those are the *facts*. The version that went round was quite different. It turned the thing into a brawl. It also said I grabbed Rose and said that, if she ever did anything like that again, I'd spoil her looks with a knife and see how she liked it. Now, that's not only untrue; it's plain damned idiotic. If I were a sufficient swine I might hit her, though I doubt that. But it would never occur to me, or anybody I know, to think of using steel. It's not natural. You don't think of it. If you get into trouble, you use your fists. And that's all I—"

"*Ss-s-t!*" Magda warned.

Bencolin and the burly man with the slouch hat were coming down the path, the latter talking animatedly. He stepped up to the door of the temple, removed his hat formally, and spoke through his moustache.

"*Messieurs et mesdames!* Do not derange yourselves, if you please. I am Inspector Durrand, associate of the chief of the Sûreté. This is M. Bencolin, in charge of the investigation. M. Bencolin asks that M. Richard Curtis, who discovered the body, will accompany us to the villa."

"Why can't we all go?" asked Magda Toller.

Even Inspector Durrand looked surprised. Ralph and Stanfield turned towards her. It would have been difficult, Curtis thought, to describe her expression then: there was no cruelty in it, and no morbidity, but rather a half-guilty fascination.

"By all means, Miss Toller," said Bencolin heartily. "I shall be very pleased. Now, then, Durrand, lively!"

"But this is impossible," the inspector growled.

"Completely impossible," agreed Stanfield. He had begun to talk in fluent, rapid, colorless French, as though he were dictating. "Mademoiselle does not know what she is saying. No. I forbid it."

"Now 'forbid,'" said Bencolin critically, "is a word I definitely do not like. You are Mr. Stanfield, Durrand tells me? Will you walk here ahead of me? I have something to ask you."

Magda walked defiantly, between Ralph and Curtis, as the little group began to straggle. "I wanted to see the body," she said in an undertone, replying to Ralph's muttered question. "Was it very wicked of me, darling?"

"You realize that chap only wants to get us all under a microscope to study us?"

"Well, *I* didn't kill her, and you didn't; so what should we worry about? Now that I've thrown my bonnet over the windmill, I want to do and see everything I can. I've said I won't be Mrs. Benedict Toller's pride and joy any longer, and that gratitude is a washout. So I want to take advantage of it. Darling, you'd be surprised what a low mind I have."

Nevertheless, she flinched in spite of herself when they came into the bedroom where Rose Klonec lay. All the curtains had now been drawn back fully, so that the room was dazzling. Yet the dark-red walls had blacker lights, the black marble mantelpiece looked tawdry, and beyond the bed were spread out conspicuously the stale supper-materials beside the round table. The room was now full of intruders at work, including a fat man in a top-hat, who was examining the body. Bencolin spoke exactly in the style of a lecturer.

"These are some of my associates. Dr. Benet, the medical examiner. Dr. Mabusse, the director of the laboratory of technical police. M. Grangier, his assistant. The work of the other two you can understand. You have heard a great deal about fingerprints; but have you ever seen any developed? You see those reddish marks on the light surfaces?—on the two champagne-glasses, for instance, beside the wine-cooler on the serving-table? The powder they use is red lead. For dark surfaces, like the handle of that razor on the round table, the powder is lead carbonate, which brings up the print in white. In England I believe it is customary to use 'gray powder,' a mixture of mercury and chalk, and powdered graphite. Then the prints are photographed with Leica cameras; no flashlights, you see, are necessary. The work of the medical examiner is sometimes less pleasant.

I should suggest, Dr. Benet, that you pull up the bedclothes."

The doctor grunted.

"Is there any report, Dr. Benet?"

The doctor in the silk hat took out his watch and examined it with an air of concentration. "Ah, that. She died not more than twelve hours ago and not less than ten. But allow a space. It is now past one o'clock. Say that she died between one and three o'clock this morning."

"And the weapon?"

"It was that stiletto in the bathtub, without doubt. The wound is jagged, done by dragging the point of the stiletto across the forearm, and there is a piece of the point broken off in it. It is a terrible wound, very deep. Still, there are other things here I don't like: not natural . . ."

Bencolin nodded to his four companions. "Come with me. We will take these rooms in order, beginning with the sitting-room."

Magda, Ralph, Stanfield, and Curtis followed him through the dressing-room, with Inspector Durrand stumping in the rear. In the sitting-room they found Hortense and Hercule, the former with her arms folded and the latter looking glum. Somewhat deflated as he recognized Bencolin, Hercule began some explanations; but Durrand cut him off.

For a long time Bencolin stood motionless, looking round the room. It was very quiet in the gray-panelled room with the crystal chandelier, except for a rustle of leaves outside the balcony. Bencolin looked at the door communicating with the hallway. He looked at the empty wine-cooler on the table in the middle of the room. He looked at the cleared space round the line of open windows, where furniture seemed to have been pushed back. Finally he began to walk round the table, his steps sounding loud on the bare parquetry, and glanced out of the windows as he did so. From there he went to the door communicating with the hallway. It was locked, with its key on the inside.

"Mademoiselle Frey!"

"Monsieur?"

"Repeat your story, everything you have already told these gentlemen," said Bencolin, turning round. Though still defiant, Hortense was for the first time a little scared. Again she gave the account, which was the same as before; he did not interrupt her, but his sharp black eyes remained fixed steadily on her face as he towered over her. "Good, that is clear enough. Now, that letter you received on Saturday morning, presumably from Mr. Douglas, telling you to come out here... give it to me, please. Come, hand it over! Thank you. I will take good care of it. I understand that you took this letter to Mr. Stanfield there"—at this point Hortense shot an uneasy glance at Stanfield, who was impassive—"in order to have it properly translated. But we will return to that. We will commence with the arrival at this villa of the strange visitor—who introduced himself as Mr. Douglas—at just nine last night. You have told us that he was wearing a brown raincoat and a soft black hat. What else was he wearing?"

"I don't know, monsieur."

"Consider a moment. When he stumbled, and his shoulder struck your nose, you were helping him off with his coat. What did he wear under it?"

"I tell monsieur, I do not know! That was when my glasses were knocked off; and, besides, he did not take off the raincoat after all. But if he only pretended to stumble," said Hortense, evidently in a cold blaze over her lost glasses, "I tell you it was very, very realistic. Ah, wait! I remember his trousers. He had what they used to call 'Ossford bags,' from England. That was another reason—"

"Another reason you knew he was English? We were coming to that. You say that he always spoke to you in English. Are you certain it was his own language; or might he have been a Frenchman speaking English? Are you familiar enough with the language to be certain?"

Hortense blinked, and looked doubtful. "Perhaps not, monsieur. But I certainly thought so. Besides, he spoke my name many times, and he did not pronounce 'Hortense' as a Frenchman would."

"You say that, if he only pretended to stumble, it was very, very realistic. What makes you say that?"

"Because I heard his heel slip on the polished floor, and I almost had to catch him."

"Very well. We will leave him for the present, and go on to the arrival of Mme. Klonec. You tell us that she arrived at a little past eleven; that you brought her up to these rooms, with her valises; that you unpacked for her; and that afterwards you helped her to bathe and dress. When she had her bath, how many bath-towels were used?"

("What the blazes—!" muttered Ralph under his breath.)

"Bath-towels, monsieur?" repeated Hortense, as though she had never heard the word before.

"Why, two. One to dry madame, and one for her to stand on."

"What did you do with them afterwards?"

"I threw them into the hamper in the bedroom. Monsieur, why—?"

Bencolin snapped his fingers towards Inspector Durrand, who nodded and went out. He returned within a minute.

"There are three bath-towels in the basket now," Durrand reported. "Two of them are still a little damp. The third is dry, but it is stained with blood."

"To continue, Hortense." Bencolin spoke absently, with a frown under his dilapidated hat. "When she dressed afterwards, what did she wear?"

"An evening-gown of black and silver, with black stockings and shoes."

"Where is the gown now?"

"It is hanging up in the wardrobe there in the dressing-room. I noticed it when we passed through the dressing-room this morning."

With the same absent and frowning expression, Bencolin strode into the dressing-room. He opened the door of the wardrobe, to find a number of dresses on neat hangers, with a black and silver gown as the outermost. A negligée of peach-colored lace was hanging opposite. On the floor were several pairs of shoes, with stockings folded in compartments just above.

"The devil!" he said.

From there he went to the dressing-table. Curtis, standing in the doorway, could see his reflection in the glass. He glanced at an open jar of cold cream, with its lid on the table beside it. He pulled away the little chair in front of the dressing-table, to look under and beyond it. Finally, he examined the door of the dressing-room giving on the hallway, which was also locked on the inside. He returned, shaking his head.

"Tell me, Hortense. Was madame a neat person, neat and tidy?"

"Extremely so, monsieur."

"H'm. I am now going to ask you a question which I want you to consider carefully; but we must have the proper answer if we are to eliminate the fantastic from this case. You were madame's maid for a long time. Can you tell me from any signs you see here whether it is certain—beyond any doubt, remember—that madame must have undressed herself, and might not have been undressed by the murderer after she was dead?"

Hortense let out a crow of mirth. "We think of all sorts of things, do we not? I beg your pardon, monsieur! And I will tell you. It is certain that madame undressed herself. One cannot be madame's maid for some years, as you say, without knowing the little tricks, the little (what do I wish to say?) mannerisms. Look! There are the stockings she wore last night. She had an unusual way of folding a stocking afterwards, that I have not seen in anyone else—so. There is the gown she wore. On the hanger she always placed the weight of it one little inch to the left—so—because one of madame's shoulders was a very little bit higher than the other. She had other habits, which I know. No, monsieur: whatever you have in mind, it is certain that madame undressed herself."

"You would swear to that in court?"

"I would swear to it anywhere, monsieur."

Whatever he had in mind, Bencolin looked relieved.

"In that case, let's go back to the time you left her in this room last night, dressed in her black and silver gown... She told you to bring her up here a half-bottle of Roederer champagne. After you had done that, she told you to prepare in the kitchen a little supper which Mr. Douglas would bring up when he arrived; and then she said you were to go to bed? Good. Is the villa well stocked with champagne?"

Hortense seemed doubtful.

"I do not know what monsieur calls well stocked. There were a number of bottles standing in the ice-box—and not lying down in the cellar, as they ought to be." Her tone implied a certain liveliness in the habits of bottles. "There were three large bottles of Pommery, sweet; and I think two or three bottles of Mumm, dry; but only one half-bottle of the Roederer that madame liked. I know. I brought it."

"The half bottle that is now missing?"

"So they say. At least, I do not see it here now. I brought it up in the wine-cooler which stands on the table there now."

Ralph, looking troubled, cleared his throat to attract attention.

"Wait a moment!" he interrupted. "I don't know whether it's of any importance, but there has been a change in that refrigerator during the last forty-eight hours, if Hortense is telling the truth. I was here on Friday morning. There were then six half-bottles of Roederer... you remember my telling you, Curtis?... and nothing else."

"*Bien aimable, monsieur,*" said Hortense viciously. "Of course, I am lying again."

Bencolin waved her to silence. "I assure you, little one, that if we didn't believe you we should have no case to work on at all. Now! You brought the bottle up here, after which you were instructed to prepare supper, and then go to bed. In what room did madame intend that they should have their supper?"

"Monsieur?"

"I said, in what room did she intend that they should have their supper?"

"Is it of importance?"

"It is of the greatest importance. I ask you: isn't it true that they were not to have it in the bedroom at all, but that the table was to have been brought in here? Here is the natural place, by these open windows on to the balcony. Someone has cleared a space in front of the windows where the table was to have been set. Those two candelabra, placed together on that little table by the window, where they don't belong, are candelabra for a dinner-table... Listen to me, Hortense. You are keeping back information for the sheer joy of keeping back information. You like to have facts drawn like teeth. I warn you to be a good girl, or I will forget my politeness and kick your behind from here to the Palais de Justice. Were they to have supper in this room: *yes or no?*"

"Yes, yes, yes, yes!" shrieked Hortense. "At least, that was what madame said. Ah, I wish I had a brother! I meant no harm. I was only—"

"At what time did you leave madame here last night?"

"At a quarter past midnight."

"By which door did you leave this room? Through the dressing-room, or through the door to the hallway?"

"Through the door to the hallway, there." She pointed, using the fingers of her other hand to wipe her eyes surreptitiously.

"Did she lock it after you?" Bencolin persisted.

"No."

"But you notice that it's locked now? Also, the dressing-room door giving on the hallway is also locked?"

"As monsieur says. I did not notice."

Bencolin drew a deep breath. For a time he remained staring out of the windows at the marble balcony and the little balcony staircase at the end of it. He was even more a scarecrow figure as he reached under the ancient hat to scratch his head; but, when he produced his pipe and turned round again, his eyes looked pleased.

"Inspector Durrand... my friend," he said, with a long rumbling throat-clearing as though he were going to begin an address. "We have here a fine example of facts which cannot possibly mean what they seem to mean. Every mirror gives back the wrong reflection. Every natural action has the wrong ending. I like it. But I think that before long we had better try to reconstruct what happened here last night, or we shall never have a notion of where to look for the murderer. It would appear, however, that the truth may depend on what one person considered so foolish—a missing half-bottle of champagne.

"On Friday morning there were six half-bottles of Roederer in the icebox. On Friday evening the man in the brown coat and black hat comes to the villa, and is seen through the kitchen window indulging in some mysterious jugglery with champagne-bottles. (Ah, you open your eyes, Mr. Douglas; you hadn't heard of that, had you?) Well, on Saturday night there are three large bottles of Pommery, and two or three of Mumm; but only *one* of the sort Rose Klonec invariably drank. Curious eh? It looks as though someone were trying to make her drink that particular bottle: as though someone were forcing it on her as a conjuror forces a card..."

He was snapping his fingers absently, as though talking to himself; but in reality, Curtis realized, talking to them. It was Magda Toller who accepted the challenge, despite Stanfield's "Shh!"

"Why should that be?" Magda asked with composure. "She was not poisoned, was she? What else could have been in the bottle?"

"What about a sleeping-draught?" said Bencolin.

There was a silence.

"You yourselves have noticed," he went on, "the impossibility of holding a person in or over a bathtub until she bleeds to death—all without an outcry, a struggle, a disturbance of some kind— unless that person is either stunned or drugged. Now, consider the murderer's position. He dares not, he cannot, come face to face with Rose Klonec: she is expecting Ralph Douglas, but the murderer is not Mr. Douglas. He can deceive a half-blind woman like Hortense, who has never seen him before; but assuredly he cannot deceive Rose Klonec. Therefore he must make certain she is drugged before he arrives. That is why he is so late in getting here. I myself have noticed that through the line of open windows here"—he pointed to the windows—"a watcher in those trees opposite can get a good view of what goes on in this room. She was sitting here with her bottle. He saw her drink it. He waited until he knew he was safe, and then he came in by the back door."

Again there was a pause. Ralph and Curtis looked at each other, and the former struck his fist into his palm.

"I believe you've got it!" the former said excitedly. "I never thought of that: of course he wouldn't have dared to meet her face to face. And he didn't; that's why he kept out of the way all evening. The champagne had knockout-drops or something in it—"

Bencolin looked at him.

"You believe that?" he said doubtfully. "For myself, I find it almost incredible."

"But you said—"

"Well, I confess I enjoy hearing myself talk. At the moment I see a number of strong objections to the theory. First, to introduce a drug into a sealed bottle of champagne, and to do so undetectably, would be almost impossible. Second, why should the murderer afterwards *steal* both bottle and cork? Even in the unlikely event that he wished to hide the fact of her having swallowed a drug, why not simply rinse out the bottle and leave it: what is the purpose of removing such a dangerous souvenir? That bottle begins to assume even more enigmatic qualities. Third, there is no drug powerful enough to strike without any warning, especially in a drink that is taken slowly like

101

champagne. She would have felt what was happening to her: she would have rung the bell for Hortense, and made some fight against it. But you have noticed the careful, leisurely way in which she undressed.

"Fourth, there is the behavior of the murderer himself. If he expects to find her in a coma when he arrives, why does he take the trouble to carry upstairs a weighted serving-table with supper for two? What about the opened wine-bottle in the other room, with the two glasses which have both been used? What about all the other appliances he brought up with him? We know only this. We want the man in the brown coat, and we want him badly. There is much to be done; and we cannot speculate until we hear the result of the post-mortem examination. At the moment I am nicely balanced between two beliefs. On the one hand I cannot quite believe in the theory of a drug in the champagne bottle; on the other hand it seems possible that at some time, for some reason, a drug was given to Rose Klonec..."

"Monsieur," said Hortense.

"There is something in your expression, little one, which—"

The woman's eyes shifted a little. "It is possible that a while ago I may have spoken ill-advisedly. Since you make so much of a drug, it is possible that madame may have herself taken some of the sleeping tablets, from the little box in the bathroom."

8

Concerning an Electric Clock

The bedroom had now been cleared, and the body taken away in a wicker basket. Only Dr. Mabusse, head of the laboratory of technical police, remained: he stood by the mantelpiece, on which was a large black leather box or case, and he was checking over a sheaf of notes. Mabusse, a saturnine man with a broad mouth and long sideburns, chuckled when Bencolin came in.

"Ah, I've been waiting for you," he said. From the mantelpiece he took the little cardboard box that had been in the bathroom, and the glass that had stood beside it. "I suppose you want these? Benet told you a while ago he didn't like certain things about that body; nor did I. The little congestion of the retina, to begin with."

"The cynic," said Bencolin. He frowned and

103

rattled the box. "What are these things?"

"I could make a guess. I can give you a practical test now, if you prefer, though I'd rather wait until I got to the laboratory."

"Now.—Well, well, Hercule?"

Swelling with wrath, Hercule was stammering behind him. "*M. le juge,* let me call these gentlemen as my witnesses. They will tell you that I have not done so badly! Listen! I myself deduced what you have done about those tablets: that madame herself must have taken some tablets. But grandmama there," and he looked heavily at Hortense, "grandmama there at that time chose to swear that Mme. Klonec did not take any tablets and would not have taken any. She said, 'Madame does herself with sleeping-tablets on the same night that she burns with impatience to meet her lover?'—and she flounced herself and was damned high and mighty. Ask these gentlemen! Now it suits her to swear something very different."

"Why not?" said Hortense, coolly. "Why not, grandpapa? I did not know then what I know now. I had not then looked inside the box, as I have done since—when your old back was turned, grandpapa."

"Well?" said Bencolin.

"Well, there are three tablets gone from the box. I still don't know why madame should have taken them; madame must have been crazy. But she must have done it, because they were there last night. I tell you I know! I unpacked the valises. I found that little box and put it in the right-hand drawer of the dressing-table. You warned me not to hold anything back, so there! And I counted the

tablets because I wondered whether I might—
you know—borrow one. But there were twelve,
and I knew madame would notice it if I did. Now
there are nine." She folded her arms.

"Were three tablets her usual dose?"

"No, she used to take only two. But I have
known her to take three."

"That's all," said Bencolin with restraint. He
motioned to two plainclothesmen in the hall outside the bedroom door, and they hustled out a still
protesting Hortense. Then Bencolin chuckled:
the news seemed to raise his spirits greatly.

From the great leather box Mabusse took out a
spirit-lamp, a small test-tube, and a wire tongs.
He dissolved a tablet in alcohol in the test-tube,
and added ten drops from a small bottle which
gave out a strong smell of ammonia. Then he held
it over the lamp, whose flame moved witchlike in
yellow and blue as though there were a wind in
the room. Curtis was surprised to see the brilliance of the flame above the mantelpiece: until
he realized that it must be late in the afternoon,
and that there were shadows in the room.

"Now we have it," Mabusse was rattling on.
"Ammonia isn't the best alkali, but it will do. You
see those clear white drops on the side of the
tube. Smell it. That's chloroform. The basis of the
tablet is chloral hydrate; I should think about
twenty grains to each tablet. Are you satisfied? If
so, I'll shut up shop. The lady chose a strong sedative."

Bencolin was whistling between his teeth.

"Yes, I know that. So she swallowed sixty
grains, if Hortense is to be believed. Still, it was
not—?"

"Oh, no; it wouldn't kill her, if that's what you mean. On the other hand, it wouldn't leave her in A-1 condition for a night of love, I can tell you. Sorry, mademoiselle!" said Mabusse to Magda, with a cheerful lack of apology in his voice. He tipped a hand to his saturnine forehead. "But it is best to know these things, eh? Ha-ha-ha! I agree with Hortense; I don't see why she did it. Now, I know a poule at Neuilly—"

Magda smiled back at him, the dimples deepening in her cheeks; and at that moment a tension, which had been on them all ever since they came into these rooms, suddenly broke.

"Damn your impudence," Ralph said in English.

"Easy, my lad," Stanfield told him, coming into the conversation with equal promptitude. He spoke in an easy tone, as though from behind a desk; even as though from inside his collar, like a man giving advice; and he went on in English: "M. Bencolin, we all thank you. We've been obliged to you for an amazing afternoon, seeing you at work. It's been most instructive. But you'll admit that the circumstances could have been happier. Now, I am acquainted with many people in or associated with your department... Bourdeau, the prefect... Célestin, the procurer-general... all good friends; and I know they wouldn't be pleased if this informal third-degree were carried too far. We understand each other, I think. Consequently, if you don't mind, we'll just—" He stopped dead. "May I ask where you got those things?"

Stanfield's voice remained level, but his mouth seemed to acquire a broader, flabbier curve as he stared. From wandering about the room, Bencolin had now sat down on the foot of the bed facing him. For the first time Stanfield noticed that Bencolin had in one hand the .22 calibre automatic, and in the other hand the silver-hafted stiletto. He juggled them. Curtis had a feeling that something was closing in around their group, something alien and sinister. He thought that he was probably wrong; but he could not rid himself of the idea. It was as though the stolid Inspector Durrand had moved closer, the saturnine Mabusse had moved closer, even Bencolin had taken on a foreignness which could not be associated with Grandison Hunt.

Bencolin spun the stiletto into the air and caught it with a flat smack against his palm.

"My good friend," he said, "there is no thought of any third-degree. A car is at your service, and you are welcome to return to Paris whenever you like. Would you like to go now?"

"I was only wondering—"

"You recognize one of these weapons, I think? Or both of them?"

Stanfield laughed slightly. Over his face had come the expression, not quite so deep as contempt, nor quite so light as indulgence, which is many years older than Waterloo.

"I certainly thought I had seen that knife before. I gave one of them to Mme. Klonec many years ago. It's a souvenir of a Corsican trip. I used to keep it on my desk at the office, to open letters with; and she admired it, so I—"

"Did you know her well?"

"Professionally, yes."

"I wish to put this with great delicacy, my

friend. Her profession or yours?"

"Mine," said Stanfield dryly. He smoothed at his ghost of a gray moustache, his face wearing the same expression of dry good-humor. "I don't object to these insinuations, because I know it's always customary to look for the woman. But I'm a home-loving man, Mr. Bencolin, with four noisy children to support; and I leave such foolery to younger men. No: Mrs. Klonec was merely a good client. She travelled a good deal, she did all her bookings through us, and I always attended to her wants personally. The gift of the stiletto was a trifle—"

"I see. You say that you gave it to her 'some years ago,' as though you were speaking of an episode of your lost, airy youth. When did you give it to her, precisely?"

"Oh, three or four years ago. I don't remember."

"But she valued it highly enough to take it with her even when she came out to this villa for a week-end?"

Stanfield looked thoughtful. "No, that won't do. I happen to know that she always took it with her wherever she went. She carried it as a sort of—well, protection, as some women might travel with a small pistol such as the one you've got there. Incidentally, she couldn't stand the sight of firearms. She said she would not be able to fire one to save her life. But she was fond of steel; she was fascinated by steel, for some reason. You may have heard of the incident in the night-club, when she interrupted a knife-thrower's act to look at one of his knives, and stirred up a row with Douglas here. No: the presence of the knife here doesn't even mean she was expecting any kind of trouble. It was simply a protection against non-existent burglars, as much a part of her travelling-kit as brushes or combs."

Bencolin sat motionless, an apparition with humped shoulders. Twice he spun the stiletto into the air before he spoke. "Were there any fingerprints on this thing?" he asked Mabusse.

"Yes. The dead woman's on the haft; not blurred, either; nobody else's."

"The haft; now that's very interesting. But no fingerprints anywhere else?"

"No. The only thing—" He hesitated. "Tell you later: same thing is on the back of the pistol. Another point: the murderer didn't wear gloves, but handled the stiletto with a towel. There's towel-lint, with a little blood, dusted all around the blade. I've preserved it as usual."

"Mysteries?" inquired Stanfield, pleasantly, after a pause. "So the dead woman's own fingerprints were on it, and nobody else's! There's a solution that would satisfy everybody. Do you think she may have cut her own artery and killed herself?"

"And put herself to bed afterwards. No, that's doubtful," Bencolin said. "However, I call your attention to the fact that, when Hortense unpacked madame's belongings last night, Hortense *says* she put the stiletto in the drawer of the dressing-table. Let's go on with our questioning, Mr. Stanfield, about Hortense. Yesterday morning —Saturday—Hortense Frey brought a letter to you to be translated. This letter."

From his pocket he took out the typewritten note signed "Ralph Douglas."

"Yes."

"Do you still insist that you weren't intimately acquainted with Rose Klonec, except in business hours at Toller's Tours?"

"I most certainly do."

"Then didn't it strike you as odd that her maid —her personal maid of previous days, not now connected with her—should come to you with a letter which concerned a most delicate private matter? Hortense knows enough English to know what the letter was about. She would be careful to use extreme discretion, since she was hoping to get her old job back. She must have any number of friends, particularly women in the same line of business as herself, with a thorough knowledge of English. Why should she come to you?"

"You had better ask Hortense about that. *I* can't tell you. Still, you would be surprised at the troubles people bring to a travel agency."

"The contents of the letter distressed you?"

"Well, I was annoyed about it, naturally," replied Stanfield with asperity. "From the long story Hortense was telling you in the other room, and the general comments that seem to have been made on it, I gather that this 'man in the brown raincoat' wasn't Douglas at all, and that the letter was a forgery. For Miss Toller's sake, and even for his, I'm glad; though it will cause enough trouble, whatever happens. But at the time I had no reason to believe the letter wasn't genuine, and when I heard that Douglas seemed to be picking up this affair again, after his engagement to Miss Toller, I—"

"Then," said Bencolin quietly, "it was natural that you should mention the matter to your friend and patroness Mrs. Benedict Toller, eh?"

There was a pause. Curtis had a feeling that Stanfield had put one foot into a trap, from which he had not quite time enough to draw back before it closed. Stanfield stiffened.

"I did nothing of the kind," he replied briefly. "That's all I have to say."

"Just as you like. The reason I asked was because of something I overheard when I was ill-mannered enough to eavesdrop on the conversation between Miss Toller, Mr. Douglas, and Mr. Curtis in the little temple. Yesterday morning Hortense brought the letter to you for translation. Yesterday evening Miss Toller broke away from her home, and announced her intention of marrying Mr. Douglas out of hand, because of a grand riot she had with her mother. Grand domestic riots always have a cause: even if it is a hidden cause. I can't think of a better cause than *this* news." He waved the letter, and then tossed it on the bed. "Perhaps you would care to tell us, Miss Toller. Did your mother know about this? If so, did she mention it to you?"

Bencolin's amiability was not assumed. In himself and in this girl there was the same spark of devilment, which made them obscurely kin, and which had been evident from the first in the way they treated each other. But Magda Toller was not easy now. Her hazel eyes had a hard luminousness, as though from strain. They did not move from Bencolin's face. When she reached up a hand to smooth back the black bobbed hair, with its prim parting and its fillet of ribbon, the gesture had almost a quality of stealth. But she managed to smile; and to control her hands.

"No," she said. "Though my mother mentioned

many things, she didn't mention that."

"So. Did Mr. Stanfield tell you?"

"No."

"Suppose someone had told you, Miss Toller: what would you have done?"

"Had it out with Ralph," she answered promptly. Then she considered. "Or no, stop a bit! If I'd had reason to think anything like that, I'd have stuck as close to him as a limpet, all night if necessary, and made jolly certain he wasn't sneaking out with anyone else. But I went out to dinner with him last night, and I didn't have any reason to think so. If someone had told me, that's what I'd have done at first. Afterwards I'd have..." She stopped. "What you really want to ask me is whether I might have killed her."

Bencolin spread out his hands in a magnanimous gesture.

"Well," she continued, "I honestly didn't. I'm not the man in the brown raincoat, even if I walked on stilts and had a baritone voice like Ralph"—she gave a gobbling imitation from deep in her throat—"but that's not the point. I don't think I should have killed her in any case. I don't know how your Frenchwomen are supposed to act from jealousy, though I suspect they're not nearly as wild-eyed as we like to think, either at this or that. But as for killing her..."

"Why not?" asked Bencolin.

She suddenly caught his broad grin, which altered the whole expression on his face, and she relaxed.

"Oh, *damn* you! All right: not worth the trouble. I've seen this Rose Klonec; and, to be quite vulgar about it, I don't think she had so much."

"Miss Toller is very young," Stanfield explained.

"She is very natural," said Bencolin harshly. "With your permission, Mr. Stanfield, I like it."

"You have my permission, M. Bencolin."

The two bowed to each other with some gravity; then a smile appeared again between Bencolin's cropped moustache and beard, and he got briskly to his feet.

"The third-degree, as you put it, is over," he announced. "I think that's all I need trouble you at the moment. I must examine all the exhibits in this room, with the technical assistance of Dr. Mabusse, and I will not bore you with it now. You had better return to Paris: Miss Toller and Mr. Stanfield, that is." He snapped his fingers towards the plainclothesman in the doorway, and then made a curious flat opening-and-shutting gesture of his palm. "There is still trouble in store for you, Mr. Douglas. You will be, as you know, under technical detention for a few hours. You must go before the Commissaire of the district; then to Paris before the *juge d'instruction* and registrar of the district-court. You are in for a stiff questioning—"

He glanced at Ralph, who merely nodded.

"—but if your alibi can be verified there will be no difficulty. Mr. Curtis may, of course, go with you as your counsel; and the *juge d'instruction* will advise you if a point of French law should arise. Now let me take you downstairs."

("Polite old beggar, ain't 'e?" whispered Magda under her breath.)

"I am," said Bencolin. "Also, it is growing late. It—" He looked at the useless marble clock on the mantelpiece, and paused. "It must be easy to forget the flight of time here. Another clock that does not run. There is one in the sitting-room of this suite, and I noticed still another downstairs." He pursued the point as they descended. "It must sometimes be a trifle awkward. Tell me, Mr. Douglas, is there no clock in the house that works?"

"These must be the tactics you're famous for," Ralph said gloomily, but with a quick look at him. "Blame the antique-dealers, not me. They're all museum-pieces. But there's an electric clock in the kitchen."

"Whereabouts in the kitchen?"

"On top of the refrigerator. You plug it into the same socket as the refrigerator—there."

Bencolin had pushed open the door of the white-tiled kitchen, where a weeping Hortense was being comforted by a stout man with a bowler hat. In the rear wall, between the window and the back door, was a high refrigerator; and on the refrigerator stood a glass-encased clock with a busy look, its hands now pointing to twenty minutes past three. Bencolin inquired the time of the man in the bowler, who drew himself up proudly to say that he was M. Rapet the Commissaire, and that the time by his watch was also twenty minutes past three. Curtis suddenly noticed that from studying the clock Bencolin had turned his attention to something else. About a foot to the right of the refrigerator, over the light-switch by the back door, showed a very small round bulge. A white-headed drawing-pin had been driven deep into the plaster wall above the white tiling.

"Hortense," Bencolin went on, "this is the clock

by which all the times of your testimony are given?"

"Eh? That one? Yes, monsieur."

"But I think you said the clock you used was in your little bedroom off the kitchen?"

"It is still true, monsieur," replied Hortense. "When I went to bed, I took the clock, and carried it into the bedroom, and connected it to the socket in the wall there. You need not think there was anything wrong with the clock, no! I set it by the church-clock when I arrived; and I swear to you I must have looked at it every fifteen minutes of the day or night afterwards; for, do you see, every minute I was expecting somebody."

"In that case, we need not trouble about it at the moment. M. le Commissaire, Inspector Durrand!—Hortense and these two gentlemen will accompany you. I wish you good day, and good luck, and good champagne."

In turning round, he had detached from the back of the refrigerator a piece of black thread or cord some ten inches long; and had the end of it now looped round his finger. He was twirling it round amiably. Though he shook hands with both Curtis and Douglas, Curtis saw a certain twist to his leathery jaw, a certain expression of the eye. And what Curtis felt, in a sunlit kitchen among prosaic things, was a twinge of uneasiness that might have been fear.

9

The Second Alibi

At nine o'clock in the evening, two men sat at a table on the terrace of a café at the top of the Champs Elysées, taking an after-dinner brandy. They were Richard Curtis and the now not-so-impeccable Bryce Douglas.

Curtis was tired. He was not so tired as Ralph Douglas, who had gone off for a quiet dinner with Magda after having been released, "with honor," as the examining magistrate said. Curtis's consolation was that he himself had not done so badly on his first case: possibly not acquitting himself with honor, but at least, as he put it to himself, bloody well. As the result of a telephone-call to London, Hunt had told him to handle the entire business himself. Hunt could not get away; and D'Arcy, their expert on French law, was then in America. But it was not too difficult. The procedure was different, and prejudicial to the accused. What you chiefly had to do was forget the law but keep your head.

With the swift nets of the Sûreté raking in each witness almost as soon as a witness was mentioned, Curtis had been stirred to admiration. The parade passed. Two waiters from Fouquet's testified to the presence of Ralph Douglas and Magda Toller, whom they knew, in the restaurant from 8.30 to 9.15. Six assorted habitués of the wineshop, "The Man Who Was Blind," rue Beethoven, Passy, (including the proprietor) testified that this young gentleman had been drinking there from about 10.55 to 3.15. And Hortense could not be shaken as to her positiveness about the times.

At Curtis's insistence—to forestall any manoeuvre as to possible jugglery in time—the electric clock from the Villa Marbre was brought from Boissy to Paris. It was examined by a jeweller from the police laboratory in the presence of the *juge d'instruction,* with Curtis pressing questions.

Was the clock accurate. *Yes.* Was it defective in any way, or was there any sign whatever that it had been tampered with mechanically? *No.* They believed Mlle. Frey to be a truthful witness, didn't they; or else Mr. Douglas would not be here at all? *Yes.* They had heard Mlle. Frey say she had been watching the clock all day and night—and that was likely, wasn't it, considering that she was looking forward eagerly to a remunerative job in the future? *General agreement.* It was therefore certain that she must have noticed any alteration in the clock. *Probable, yes.* What Curtis wanted to do was to get all this into the official records, of which he asked for and got a copy. When it was all over he crossed the street to a café opposite the Palais de Justice, joined Ralph and Bryce Douglas, drank three bock-beers in rapid succession, and felt better.

Bryce Douglas had also been of assistance with the police. From what he had heard of Bryce, Curtis had been expecting to feel some antagonism towards him. He did not feel it. The person who had been described to him; "the person who can talk about everything and yet give you the impression he's really interested in nothing"; in short, that air of complete detachment that all honest people dislike—all this was for the most part a defense. It fell off in time of difficulty. It concealed uncertainty: fear of looking a fool, fear of making a mistake, fear of the boot. It also concealed, Curtis rightly guessed, a fondness for the ways of the thriller as great as that of Curtis himself.

He remembered Bryce in the café across from the Palais de Justice, a gloomy cavern of a place with a zinc bar and sawdust on the floor. Bryce stood with his bowler hat pushed on the back of his head, trying to keep from spilling beer on his trousers. He was as immaculate as a tailor's dummy never is; he had a stiff back, a long nose, a small but bushy brown moustache, and an eye grown friendly from the necessity to defend someone. That Bryce was really attached to his brother, except in the way of duty, Curtis doubted. What he liked was being the Unseen Power behind the throne or the stock-market, or whatever term you like out of thrilling literature: except that he was not a power, and there was no throne.

Curtis had touched the truth that afternoon, when they were hanging over the zinc bar.

"Meet me," Bryce had said, "nine o'clock to-night, at the Café Mogador, near the Etoile." He added in a more gloomy and more natural tone: "A lot of things have gone bust."

At nine o'clock Curtis, who wished that Bryce's fondness for curt and military effect had made him give more explicit directions so that there would not be so much difficulty in finding the damned place, sat down at one of the red-topped tables. Bryce sat opposite with a brief-case in his lap and an expression of satisfaction on his face.

"I have something to ask you, and something to tell you," Bryce said slowly. He offered cigarettes. "But the circle isn't complete yet. There's another guest to come. Until then—what do *you* think of the case?"

Curtis shook his head. "I don't know. But if you want opinions, you have plenty to choose from. Have you seen the evening papers? Every amateur criminological-writer in Paris has spread himself on an analysis of it, and without mincing plain words, either. 'Our expert' is all over the place."

Bryce's face showed more of a sense of humor than the long nose would seem to warrant.

"Ah, yes. Yes, rather. I notice that you are described as 'the brilliant young advocate whose fiery eloquence was so instrumental in persuading the *juge d'instruction*.' Wait till old Hunt sees that. He'll have your hide."

"I suppose so."

"Still," Bryce said thoughtfully, "maybe you had an incentive to be at the top of your form. Miss Toller was in the hall outside, getting most of it. May I ask you a question without offense? It struck me that you were very much attracted to her."

There was no offense in his tone. He sat looking with great solemnity at the traffic in the street, a serious-minded little figure with a bristling sandy moustache and a straight back.

"Wait a minute," he added vaguely. "You were going to say, 'I met her for the first time this afternoon,' weren't you?"

Curtis laughed. "What makes you think that?"

"I'm in the *cliché* business," said Bryce. "I hear nothing else. I'm like a guide who conducts people day after day and year after year round the same museum-exhibits; I know everything people will say in commenting. But you haven't answered my question. Of course, if you feel it incumbent on you to say nothing—" In spite of himself, an aloof kind of expression began to freeze over his face: a thing that he could not help, and that had made him all his enemies.

"I feel it incumbent on me to say that Miss Toller is engaged to your brother, and that it's hardly our business."

There was a silence.

"Really," said Bryce at length.

Another silence.

"There are no circumstances," continued Bryce, "in which I should acknowledge myself in the wrong. It's bad policy. 'Never complain, never explain,' is an excellent motto—though I see by your face that you don't like it. But it's possible that I may have approached the question from the wrong position. The trouble is that I like Magda very much, and when I see her...see her..." His fist began to pound slowly on the table. "Oh, hell!" said Bryce Douglas. "Here, have another drink. Waiter! Two more brandies. What do the experts in the papers say about the case?"

Curtis was relieved to have this way out, very much relieved.

"Thanks, I don't mind if I do. Well, a fellow called 'The Thinker' in *Paris Minuit* says that your brother is probably a master criminal who has devised a perfect alibi." He drew out a sheaf of papers, while Bryce looked at the street. "On the other hand, somebody who has the nerve to write under the name of 'Herlock Sholmes' practically accuses De Lautrec of killing her—"

"Ah, that affair at the Villa Marbre!" interposed the waiter, whisking their glasses across the table. "That's a good one, eh?"

"Have you a theory, *mon gars?*" inquired Curtis.

The waiter reflected. "To me it is simple enough. The woman was M. De Lautrec's mistress: she went to another man's house for *zizipompom:* M. De Lautrec killed her. There you are."

"But what about the man in the brown raincoat?"

"I suppose it was M. De Lautrec himself who impersonated this Englishman; eh, monsieur? He suspected that his mistress was deceiving him with the Englishman: he arranged this little trap to test her: she fell into it: and he killed her."

"That doesn't take much account of the details."

"We who read the newspapers, monsieur," said the waiter profoundly, "have not time to bother with the details; but we always think we know the assassin, and we are usually right. Besides, if M. De Lautrec did not kill her, who did?"

Curtis saw Bryce, who paid no attention to the opinions of the pavement, nod with satisfaction towards the opening in the hedge of the terrace.

Bencolin came in. He was not the scarecrow of that afternoon; he was fresh from the barber's; but there was so much unobtrusiveness about his soft black hat and soft black topcoat that Curtis felt he had meant what he said about retirement. He sat down at their table and ordered brandy.

"Now there's the question," Bencolin commented, "that all Paris is asking tonight. 'If De Lautrec didn't do it, who did?' De Lautrec has got his head into a beehive. Open your ears—attention—and you will hear it buzz. I got your message, Mr. Douglas, and here I am. You said you had something to tell me. Good evening, my friend Richard. You see that what I promised you has happened; your client has been released with a good character."

It was Bryce who answered. These two preserved towards each other a sort of amused civility: the attitude usually existing between the official police and the Foreign Office agent. Bryce was staring him in the eye.

"Thanks very much," he said. "But since all three of us here know the facts, we can speak frankly. The trouble is that we don't know whether you figure in this as a friend or an enemy. What's all this about clocks? Are you still suspicious of my brother, or not?—Stop! You were going to say, 'I am suspicious of everybody—'"

"I was going to say—"

"'—and at this moment I must not tell you what I think.' Right?"

"Well, my friend," observed Bencolin, getting out his black pipe and whacking it on the edge of the table, "I can't possibly be indiscreet if you ask all the questions and then answer them for me. Go on. Continue my interesting conversation with you."

"Look here, shall we drop this fencing?"

"Very well," said Bencolin quietly. He put down the pipe on the table. "Now listen to me— both of you—and I will tell you God's truth, at least so far as it extends to me. In a way I am suspicious of everybody. If I were not absolutely certain that neither of you is the man in the brown coat, I should be suspicious of you, friend Bryce; and even of Richard Curtis. The odd part of it consists of this: I know who the murderer is. I can even prove who the murderer is. And therefore I am at an absolute dead-wall and dead-end."

Curtis wondered whether he had been hearing aright.

"Hold on!" he protested. "You say you know who the murderer is, and can prove it, and *therefore* you're stumped? Is this some kind of play on words?"

"No. It is the plain and painful truth. And, unfortunately, it is no credit to me that I know the murderer. There were one or two little indications which led me to think so, yes: I looked for the proof: and there it was. If you think I'm talking wildly, let me state a similar case. Suppose you are reading a detective story with an intriguing situation. A corpse (let us say) is found strangled, sitting in a chair by a window, and wearing a domino mask; and all the clocks in the house are found with their faces turned to the wall. You are carefully warned that the blazing clue to the truth is the fact that there is a teaspoon in the victim's side pocket, and that, without all these things being just as they were, the crime could never have taken place.

—You follow me? No clue was left merely to confuse; or because it was a reminder of the victim's past misdeeds (that saddest device of all); or because the murderer thought it artistic. Each indication was a necessary part of the pattern."

"What's the explanation?" demanded Bryce, his face lighting up with interest.

Bencolin looked at him. "I suggest you think of one," he said politely. "Or apply yourself to a study of Rose Klonec's murder. But to finish this mask-clock-teaspoon puzzle. Now, suppose at the denouement the identity of the murderer was revealed—for the simple reason that his fingerprints matched those on the collar of the strangled man. Would you feel cheated? That's exactly what might happen in life; but would you feel cheated? You know damned well you would. There is no doubt as to the identity of the murderer. He admits the crime. Then he shoots himself. Consequently, you never know the significance of the mask or the reversed clocks, or what deduction you should have drawn from the teaspoon. Page 315, 'The End.' What would you do? You would strangle the author, lynch the publisher, and shoot the bookseller. Yet why do you complain? You know the identity of the murderer, don't you?"

He had been speaking in English, with deep and measured eloquence, and a face as solemn as an owl's. Now he broke off to address the waiter:

"It is not much; but I feel better. My boy, another brandy."

"Monsieur is ill?"

"It is only that I have spent my leisure in reading improving books," said Bencolin. He turned to the others. "I'll do better than that: I'll even

125

give you murderer *and* motive. But you see my situation."

"You don't mean to say that the murderer left his fingerprints on the stiletto or the body or something?" demanded Bryce. Curtis saw that he was a little shocked.

Bencolin was sardonic.

"No, there were no fingerprints, or footprints, or convenient buttons torn off a coat. But there was something that our police laboratory can identify just as well. Which leaves me stranded, gnawing my nails. Through little effort of my own I have reached the end of the case; and I still know almost nothing about it. I have got to the middle of the maze, but for the life of me I can't get out of it. There are as many theories as there are material objects scattered about that suite of rooms at the Villa Marbre. I don't know why a harmless half-bottle of champagne should have been stolen. Some of the weapons I can explain, but others leave me in a state of hideous perplexity. Even if I could guess what a pair of pliers has to do with ten cigarettes ranged round on an ashtray, their presence is still to be explained. I don't know why—but you understand. Of this much, however, I am certain. Of all the clues in those rooms, not one is either unimportant or misleading, if they are properly interpreted. Consequently, I can't even clap the murderer into the cage, and blaze away with questions, because I haven't enough evidence. I should not even know what to ask. I should not know how to approach. 'You killed her.' 'No.' 'We know you killed her.' 'No.' And there I stop. No, I am going to give the murderer some rope: at least, until I get the post-mortem report. The post-mortem report may

126

solve a few of my difficulties."

Bryce Douglas drew a deep breath.

"As usual, you've managed to take the wind out of my sails," he complained. "I got you here to give you some information that you don't know and that you probably would not have found out. Your department is pleased to think ours consists of a group of gentlemen-amateurs who couldn't even keep tabs on a film star.—I came here to tell who didn't commit the murder."

"Well, who didn't commit the murder?"

"De Lautrec didn't. But if you know who did commit it, I don't suppose that'll interest you much."

For a moment Bencolin sat staring at him, his wrinkled eyelids moving under the brim of the soft black hat. Bryce got his sensation: he savored it with composure, smoothing his moustache. Then Bencolin took hold of the table as though he were going to push it forward.

"Are you certain of that?"

"Quite certain. As you pointed out, everybody in Paris is saying De Lautrec must be guilty. If they knew the other thing—that De Lautrec has been suspected of selling government information, and that Rose Klonec had been spying on him—they'd be certain. But we happen to know he's innocent, and you can strike him off the list of suspects. Look here." He took a letter out of his brief-case. "No, I am not shouting secrets at a public café. Masset issued the statement this afternoon, and it'll be all over the place tomorrow. In the first place, we were after the wrong man; De Lautrec hasn't been selling information. The real leak has been found out. It was a typist in the

Ministry of State: one of our men took her off the plane to London last night."

"That proves nothing about the murder."

"Wait! You know Mercier, in the same service? Yes. Well, last night—when all the dirty work was done—Mercier and I went out on what looked like a good tip. The tip said that De Lautrec was supposed to be going out of town for the weekend; but that this was wrong. The tip said that if we would follow him when he left his flat at ten-thirty that night, we should see where he went to get his pay and his instructions. If we nabbed him when he left the house to which he was going, we should find our evidence. At the time, of course, we still believed De Lautrec was our man; and it looked like the trap we'd been praying for."

Bencolin scowled. "Then the tip itself was a hoax? A—what do you call it?—a wrong steer? Ah, I see. You got it from Rose Klonec?"

"Yes: that's the beauty of the thing. She rang me up in the afternoon. Apparently she knew quite well that De Lautrec wasn't guilty. She simply wanted us to nab him so as to make certain he didn't interrupt her projected meeting with Ralph. Before you say we were led by the nose, let me ask you what *you* would have done under the circumstances?"

"Go on."

"Mercier and I were on hand before ten-thirty. De Lautrec lives in a new block of flats in the Boulevard des Invalides—"

"Did Rose Klonec keep a separate establishment, or did she live there with him?"

"She lived there. De Lautrec didn't actually leave the flats until a quarter to eleven, so I suppose that's why she didn't get out to the Villa Marbre until well past eleven. Anyhow, De Lautrec drove off in his own car, and Mercier and I followed in a taxi. With all the several million taxis in this town, and the fact that most of them look exactly alike, it never excites any suspicion to be followed by one. Whenever you look out the back window of your car, you'll almost always see a taxi behind you in any case; and who's to know it's always the same one? A little device of my own," said Bryce, "which the official police might copy with profit.

"Well, De Lautrec led us by way of the Avenue de la Bourdonnais, over the river at the Pont d'Ilena, up through Passy, through the Bois, and out on a dismal-looking waste of a place between the Bois and Longchamps. There was a house among some trees on a hill, with a stone wall round it, and not a light showing anywhere. De Lautrec parked his car a little distance away from the house, and we followed him up on foot. He made some sort of rattling noise at the gate; and a concierge came out of a lodge just inside, still without showing a light, and let him in. I began to be certain we'd got on to something good. We reconnoitered a bit; but we had to be careful, because it was bright moonlight, and several other people came up to the house in the same quiet way, to be let in.

"Damme!—you understand? I was now convinced we'd got hold of a really big thing. There were only two gates, front and back, and Mercier and I could make certain he didn't leave without our knowing it. I wondered whether we ought to get help, or whether I ought to climb the wall and investigate. But we couldn't leave our posts in case he came out; and we couldn't spare the chauffeur and the taxi in case we needed the cab when De Lautrec came out. So we watched for over three mortal hours; and once, when I got too close to the wall, the concierge came out and looked round. At just twenty minutes past two De Lautrec left the house. He is a surly looking young fellow, on the tall side; he was at Harrow, and he speaks almost perfect English. We waited until the concierge had let him out, and then I gave the signal that we were to—ah—close in—"

"You whistled like a night-bird," said Bencolin gravely.

Bryce drew back. He had been engrossed in his recital, with a shining and crafty eye, and a whole-heartedness that was reminiscent of Ralph. Curtis could image him before the gates, with his bowler hat and his brief-case. But now he drew back, and his manner assumed its usual acidity.

"As a matter of fact, I hooted like an owl," he corrected, with a sort of grandeur. "It is rather an accomplishment of mine, though it is seldom of any great value socially. We closed in on De Lautrec when he was about twenty yards from the house. We asked him to come with us to the Quai d'Orsay. He refused, and said we were mad. Then he tried to cut up a row—"

"What did you do?"

"I laid him out flat," said Bryce, surprisingly and calmly. "Small people like myself must have some knowledge of the principles of wrestling. Mercier searched him. At first I was sure we had struck oil. In his wallet, though we found no papers, there was one packet of twenty thousand-franc notes and one packet of fifty hundred-franc notes. Also, he had on him several valuable

130

pieces of women's jewellery..."

Bencolin sat up.

"I need not dwell on the unpleasantness afterwards," Bryce said gloomily. "Of course he thought we were thieves. When he became convinced of our good faith, he raved. He demanded to be taken back to the house to show where he'd got the money. We suspected a trap, but we went." Bryce settled back in his seat with an air of cynicism. "Do you know what the place was? It was nothing but a very small, very select private gambling establishment, run by the Marquise de la Toursèche, with her lady friends as a side-line. There were only six people there last night, at baccarat. As I knew two of them socially, the position was—er—embarrassing. I did not honestly feel that I owed De Lautrec an apology, since we had only been doing our duty. In any case, he had won the money at cards. I've learned only today that De Lautrec is in very bad financial straits. He's been visiting the marquise's place frequently to regain his losses. As for the jewellery, he finally consented to explain that, though with a very bad grace..."

"What were the pieces of jewellery?" demanded Bencolin sharply.

Bryce looked at him. "Jewellery? Oh, yes. I didn't make a note of them, after he had explained; but there was a five-jewel emerald pendant, and a blue diamond bracelet, and something else I can't remember. You see, when her guests are short of ready cash the marquise is in the habit of advancing sums on jewels. De Lautrec had borrowed the stuff from Rose Klonec that afternoon. As a matter of fact, he didn't need to pledge it, and hadn't taken it out of his pocket that night,

131

because he was winning. He arrived with two thousand francs in cash and ran it up with phenomenal luck to twenty-five thousand at the tables. But that's the point, don't you see?

"De Lautrec went into that house at 11.00. He came out at 2.20. During that time both Mercier and I can swear he never left the house. What's more, all the people in the house can swear he never left it—I've got their names here—because they were at the table watching the run of his luck. When he left the house, we caught him and brought him back. It was easily 3.15 before we straightened out the mess. Consequently, he *couldn't* have been the murderer in the brown coat and black hat. Your prize witness, Hortense, says that the murderer arrived at the villa at ten minutes past one. We've also heard that the medical expert swears Rose Klonec was murdered between one and three o'clock. And there you are." With an air of dour finality Bryce shut up his briefcase. "Send the dogs out again. Let's have another go at it. De Lautrec has not only got an alibi: he's got an alibi of such rounded and beautiful construction that it's almost as good as Ralph's."

10

Confidences in a Rifle-Gallery

The rifle-shots, fired rapidly, had a waspish quality about their noise. In the open they would have been little louder than cracks of a whip, but in this basement they made strong echoes, and at the end of each was the clang of a bell. The sharp-shooter, who seldom missed, leaned almost negligently over a counter built waist-high. His elbow was on the counter, supporting the barrel of the .22, his nose was down along the sights, and his left hand jerked regularly to eject the cartridge-cases. At the end of the long shooting-gallery facing him, built of corrugated iron painted black, ran slow-moving figures painted white: a line of policemen, a line of priests, and two wheels of diving rabbits, with targets at intervals and a bell in the center. Electric bulbs in wire cages showed several other doors in this underground place, to a gymnasium, to a swimming bath, to a lift.

This yellow light showed that the marksman was a wiry young man, something over middle height, wearing a white silk shirt and with the sleeves of a white sweater knotted round his neck. His heavy black hair, with a high polish, was clipped so closely at the sides that this part of his jaw was white. He had one of those faces which can only be called typical in France—a certain prominence and staring sharpness about the dark eyes, a lengthening of line in the face despite a square jaw—yet at the same time there was a suggestion of the English about him.

The uniformed attendant touched his arm. "There are some gentlemen from the police here to see you, M. De Lautrec," the attendant said.

Bencolin and Curtis arrived at the block of flats, number 81 Boulevard des Invalides, at ten o'clock. Bencolin's suggestion that Curtis and Bryce Douglas should accompany him was accepted quickly by the former, though Bryce had to go to the Crillon to "comfort" Mrs. Benedict Toller. They had left the Café Mogador in Bencolin's car before Curtis picked up the attack he meant to make.

"Am I allowed," he said, "to ask the court a question?"

Bencolin grunted.

"Then what about that damned clock? There's the point that sticks me. The champagne bottles and the four weapons can wait; but what about that clock? You've said, whether with or without the intent to deceive,"—he saw amusement in Bencolin's face as Bencolin swung the car down the Avenue Marceau,—"that you believe Ralph is innocent. Then why did you get such a funny look when you saw the clock, and what hocus-pocus could there have been about it?"

"Was it a funny look?" inquired Bencolin. "Well, possibly old habits are asserting themselves, and I show my teeth merely for the salutary moral effect on suspects. My friend, you are seeing subtleties where there are no subtleties. And you are missing the whole point about that clock."

"But what's wrong with the clock?"

"Nothing, so far as I know."

"Right. I've been thinking about all sorts of wild possibilities. For instance, can someone who isn't there tamper with the clock by means of the electric current that runs it? Swing the hands forwards or backwards at will? It would be a brilliant scheme if you could work it; but I can't see any way. Aside from that, where's the loophole? Hortense is completely positive about her times; and all last night that clock was in her sight—"

"At last you come to the point. All last night that clock was, apparently, in her sight. And just how good is her sight?"

There was a pause.

"Here is a woman," argued Bencolin, "whom you describe as blind as a bat. She can't even distinguish the features of a man in the same room as herself. Then how is she so certain as to the time as shown on a small clock, the only wor!:able clock in the house? You and I, with good eyesight, are sometimes deceived at first glance, especially when the hands are in that dubious position round twelve or one o'clock. Yet the most vital testimony in the case depends on her statement that the man in the brown raincoat arrived at the Villa Marbre at ten minutes past one.

"Also, note the position of the clock. It stands pushed well back on top of a very high refrigerator, which I wished to see. Add to this the fact that over the clock is a thick glass case not free from dust after having stood for so long in an empty house. After nine o'clock that night—when the brown-coated man first arrived and her glasses were broken—Hortense's evidence would not be worth *that* in a court of law." He snapped his fingers. "It is true that she says she went to bed at ten minutes to one, and that at this time she transferred the clock to her own bedroom. At this time she may have flattened her nose against the glass round it in an attempt to tell the time (a thing she would probably not have done every fifteen minutes all evening); but even then it is inconclusive. Still more inconclusive is her statement that the brown-coated man arrived at ten minutes past one, when she 'turned on her light and looked at the little clock,' without getting out of bed. No, no, no. Hawkeye the Scout, out of another improving book, would hardly be so vehement. Put Hawkeye Hortense up before a tribunal, and I will guarantee to prove that the murder was committed at any time that suits my taste."

Curtis uttered an inner groan.

"Then those alibis—"

"No, it is not as bad as all that," Bencolin told him cheerfully. "Remember, we have Dr. Benet's word that the murder was committed between one and three o'clock. Of course, I might point out that nothing is more uncertain than medical evi-

136

dence as to time of death. But one thing is sure: if either Ralph Douglas or Louis de Lautrec committed the crime, either must have done so at well after three o'clock and nearer to four. You see the position. The tipplers at the café, 'The Man who was Blind,' give your friend Ralph an alibi between 10.55 and 3.15. To drive from Paris to the Villa Marbre is a matter of close on half an hour. Similarly, in De Lautrec's case we have another horde of people, this time at the home of the Marquise de la Toursèche, to swear to his presence between 11.00 and past 3.15. If either arrived at the villa afterwards, this brings up the time of this arrival to nearly a quarter to four... Consequently, it does not seem likely that the medical examiner, who is the soundest man in Paris, can have been so *entirely* off the track as to fix the time between one and three. Yes, I am disposed to accept the innocence of both Douglas and De Lautrec. All I wish to do is to warn you, as a friend, not to swallow incautiously everything that is vehemently stated by Hortense Frey."

Curtis looked at the windscreen, and found theories uncertain.

"Then I've been making a fool of myself all afternoon?" he asked with some bitterness. "Lord, I could kick myself all over the place for not thinking about that point of the eyesight—"

"Not at all," said Bencolin. "Between Hortense's positiveness and your fluency, you have convinced all Paris that your client is innocent. What more could you have done? Only, don't link your fate with Hortense's too far."

"Here! Do you mean Hortense is the murderer?"

"I will now make mysteries," said Bencolin, with sardonic and full-blown hatred. "All my life I have been accused of making mysteries; and now, when I have no wish to do so, I can't help myself. I told you I knew who the murderer is; I know who it must be, I can prove it; and yet at the same time I don't believe it. Actually, that is what is bothering me. That is behind the rush of words with which I afflicted you at the Café Mogador. I do not believe plain evidence. If only I could discredit the fact that a certain person must be guilty, I might be able to fit into place a few of those cursed inconsistencies. Therefore I will violate all precedents. If you will drop in to see me at the Quai des Orfèvres tomorrow morning, I will tell you who must be the murderer before we are halfway through the investigation. In the meantime, let us see what M. De Lautrec has to say."

The block of flats at 81 Boulevard des Invalides was a new acre of innovations in white stone. At the Caisse they were informed that De Lautrec was hiding from newspapermen, of whom there were a good many in attendance. An attendant took them down into the cellar, where a negligent marksman was firing round after round at a ringing target as though to relieve his feelings.

The uniformed attendant touched his arm. "There are some gentlemen from the police to see you, M. De Lautrec," he said.

Twice more the bell clanged before De Lautrec, with steady hands, put down the rifle and turned round. The wiry young man in the white shirt faced them with a courteous stiffness, a buttoned-up air as though at a mildly unpleasant interview which had to be endured. At the same time, there was a look of strain about his eyes.

"I have been expecting you all day," he said. "You are M. Bencolin? I know you by sight, and I am glad that it is you." He made a slight, sharp gesture with his left hand. "But what can I say or do? It is a horrible affair, truly horrible. I was never—really close to her, you understand, in spite of her being what she was. And yet—"

"We understand your feelings, M. De Lautrec," Bencolin informed him. Bencolin hesitated. "I have an unusual request to make. Would you mind conducting our conversation in English? This is Mr. Curtis, of London, Mr. Ralph Douglas's lawyer, and he speaks only a few words of French."

"With pleasure," answered De Lautrec, abruptly and heartily.

Curtis was conscious of a shock of incongruity. De Lautrec had one of those accents which are not associated with any institution of learning except the British Broadcasting Corporation. Anyone who has heard a Frenchman flash out the words, 'Look here, old chap,' will have experienced a similar shock. It seems wrong for the speech to come tumbling out in that way, especially since it is fluent and almost perfect in pronunciation. Oddly enough, the use of another language seemed to put De Lautrec at his ease. He relaxed. He even smiled. Hauling himself up with his hands behind him, he sat down on the counter.

"How do you do?" he went on in the same abrupt way. "I'm very glad to give you any assistance. What would you like to know, gentlemen?"

"I'll begin," said Bencolin, "by saying it is fortunate for you that you have a complete alibi as regards last night—"

De Lautrec expelled his breath. "So you know that. Yes, thank God," he brought his fist down on the counter, with a look of sincerity in his prominent dark eyes, "thank God I can prove all that. At the time I was mad enough to strangle those spies who followed me. It has been said of one of your English judges, Mr. Curtis, that he has 'no sense, no learning, no manners, and more impudence than ten carted harlots—'"

"Which judge is that?" inquired Bencolin, with interest.

"Nobody you know," said Curtis. "M. De Lautrec is referring to a man named Jeffreys, who has been dead over two hundred years."

"Well, I read it in a history book, and I remember it impressed me," argued De Lautrec, with smiling earnestness. "I can't think of a better description of those two men who followed me. Still, they did me a good service. They suspected *me* of—! Never mind. In any case I shall have to resign my post as secretary to M. Renoir; but, just between you and me and the bedpost, I always hated the job and only took it to please my father. What did you want to ask me?"

"About Rose Klonec. I understand she has been living with you for nearly a year?"

"Yes, that's right," agreed De Lautrec, in the same fluent, abrupt, clipped tone.

"Did you get on well with her?"

"Oh, so-so. Say about as though we were married."

"Were you in love with her?"

De Lautrec considered this, as though he were

140

watching a scales. "No," he decided. "I was only jealous."

"We have also heard that on Thursday, May 14th, you rang up Mr. Ralph Douglas and offered to buy the Villa Marbre from him at a good price. Why did you make that offer?"

Another change came over De Lautrec: his affability shut up like a closed book. He sat holding to the edges of the counter, looking oddly supercilious.

"I have nothing to say."

"You refuse to answer?"

"Yes."

"But you don't deny that you made the offer?"

The other smiled a little. "I suppose you've got an informant, so I can't very well deny it. But what has this got to do with the question in hand?"

"Now, my friend, I don't state any very deep secret when I say you have been in very bad straits financially—"

"Is that a crime? We all have reverses. But the luck is back with me now. I'm in a winning streak—"

"—and the Villa Marbre, with its furnishings, would have been a very expensive proposition, enormously expensive, three or four hundred thousand francs at the least. Therefore your offer could not have been genuine, could it?"

"I've told you I have nothing to say."

"One very harmless question then," said Bencolin, expanding now that the battle was joined. "You also told Mr. Douglas that you could not see him at the moment because you were going out of town for the week-end. Why did you tell him that, when your intention was merely to go to the house of Mme. de la Toursèche for baccarat?"

De Lautrec examined this critically. "Excuse me, old boy, but I can't see that this is any of your business. I didn't kill the woman. You know I didn't. So why bother me with this? Perhaps on Thursday I did mean to go out of town, and I changed my mind."

"Or perhaps not. Come now, my friend, that's unworthy of you! Surely the secretary of a cabinet minister can think of a better excuse than that?"

"All right. There's no harm in it. I almost invariably went to Mme. de la Toursèche's on Saturday, and when I went there I played all night. The only reason I broke off before half-past two last night was because I was winning, and I knew to the tick when I had come to the end of my winning streak for that night. Mind you," said De Lautrec, opening his eyes and pointing two fingers at Bencolin, "I'm not one of those fools who make blind plunges and expect to win. I *know* when my luck is in. I can tell it. It's like a fine horse under you...Wait, you were asking me something. Well, since I stayed away all night, and since Rose and I lived in adjoining flats in the same building, the 'going out of town' served as a sufficient excuse—"

"Did she know of your visits to the gambling house?"

"No."

"She wouldn't have approved?"

Several times, in his attempt to reply, De Lautrec's tongue was twisted over a word. He gave it up, and spoke in French, as though attacking an interesting problem.

"Monsieur, it was a curious thing about Rose in that respect. As a rule, women of her sort are mad on gambling, and yet it never interested her. It gave her no thrill to win. She comes, you understand, of good peasant stock—she has a father and mother in Provence now, to whom she used to send a little remittance each month—and I think at bottom she considered the hazard not worth the practical risk. She used to say that she would gamble with anything except money."

Bencolin leaned his elbow on the counter.

"Ah, now that's what I wished to ask," he said. "When you were searched during the unfortunate affair last night, there were found on you three very valuable pieces of jewellery. Is it likely that Rose Klonec, shrewd, practical, disliking gambling, and (excuse me) not too fond of you, should have 'handed over' those jewels to you to gamble with—as you said she did?"

During this De Lautrec had been shaking his head with a strange and fishy smile. His reply was fired back so quickly that Curtis suspected it had been prepared in advance.

"No, no. That cat won't jump. She would not have given them to me to gamble with; not Rose! She only thought I was going to have them reset for her. You see, my 'week-end trip' was to be to Brussels. The greatest jewellers in Europe, Pelletier et Cie., are at Brussels; that was why I selected the city. Therefore I could offer to take them with me, and have them reset. You see?"

"You make it very clear," replied Bencolin gravely. "When did she give the jewels to you?"

"On Saturday evening, just before I left this building."

"You were suspiciously late in going for your 'week-end,' weren't you?"

"No, I was to take the night express from the Gare du Nord, and not return until Tuesday night." He stopped quickly, as though he had made a slip of some kind; his prominent, snapping eyes remained fixed on Bencolin. "I told her my bag was already packed and in my car."

"Not until Tuesday night? Did you expect to remain at Mme. de la Toursèche's for three days?"

"I am getting tired of this," snarled De Lautrec, smacking his hand down on the counter. "There's the truth, and you may believe it or not, as you like. And be damned," he added in English.

"Easy!" said Bencolin with sharpness. "How did you spend Saturday? I mean, before you left on your 'journey.'"

"During the day? We went on a picnic. You look surprised. Yes, on a picnic! Rose had moods exactly like that. She wished to take a basket of food and float in idyllic fashion down the river, dreaming of nature—or Ralph Douglas." His expression grew dark. "That was the reason why I could not get my hands on her jewellery until the evening. We were never off the river between noon and dark; and I still have blisters on my hands from pulling the oars of that accursed boat. If you do not believe me, ask Annette, Rose's maid. Annette followed in another boat, with a professional boatman who was ogling her so much that the boat went broadside down the river after us like a shying horse. Oh, it was a pretty party. Look at my hands."

"Annette. That is the present maid? Is she here now?"

"No, the journalists were so thick that I smuggled her out and sent her to her parents in Montmartre. But I can give you her address. Very well: are you satisfied?"

"I am satisfied that you are lying to me, M. De Lautrec. I may add that you are one of the worst liars it has ever been my privilege to encounter."

In the warm basement there was a faint whirring noise as the white-painted figures at the end of the shooting-gallery, jerking endlessly on their mechanical belts, moved along against a black wall; and the wheels of rabbits endlessly dived. De Lautrec looked very thoughtful. He slid off the edge of the counter. Absently, his hand groped to the right and found one of the cardboard boxes of .22 cartridges piled there. He opened the magazine of the rifle and with quick gestures of his sinewy wrists began to flick cartridges inside. Except for the whirring of the figures, and a faint sound of voices from the direction of the gymnasium, there was no sound until De Lautrec closed the magazine with a snap.

"That is a strong statement, my friend," he said calmly. "I suggest that you be careful."

"I suggest that you be truthful. Do you know what Rose Klonec was?"

De Lautrec smiled. "Excellently well, monsieur!"

"But did you know, for instance, that she was an agent of Masset of the secret police, and that she has been watching all your movements for some time? Who do you suppose set those people on you last night? Do you think she wouldn't have noticed these mysterious 'week-end trips' of yours, that lasted until dawn? Do you think she didn't know quite well where you were going on Saturday night? Do you think she didn't know quite well what financial straits you were in? Do you think, therefore, that she would gladly hand over three valuable pieces of jewellery for you to toss across the tables at baccarat, or believe for one moment that you were taking them to Brussels to be reset? You talk like a four-year-old child."

The muzzle of the rifle, which De Lautrec was holding casually, was within two feet of Bencolin's chest. Bencolin looked down at it and laughed. *"Salaud,"* he said. He turned round to the shooting-gallery, whipped his cheek to the stock of the rifle, and fired three times. Three white figures of policemen vanished as though they had been sponged from a slate. De Lautrec fired again, and missed.

"Try the rabbits, old man," said Bencolin. "I find them easier game."

De Lautrec put down the rifle.

"So you think I stole her jewellery," he observed. "How do you think you can prove that?"

"I don't want to prove it. As a matter of fact, I don't think you did steal it: Rose Klonec was a clever woman, and would have outwitted you. (Aim for the center of that target on the left, now.) The real story is more interesting, and that's what I want... The facts are these. You were ready and even eager to discard Rose Klonec, if only because you could no longer afford her. That is the first point. Rose Klonec, as we have heard, specialized in getting her admirers to buy her jewellery. She had a remarkable collection of it, so much so that her former maid, Hortense, this morning swore she must have been murdered for it; though the few trinkets she took with her to the Villa Marbre appear to be intact. But you saw no reason why you should not get back some of the great sums you had spent on her, especially since a few good items out of that collection would put you in a position to redeem your luck at the Marquise de la Toursèche's. That is the second point. Finally, you have a reputation for violent jealousy, insane jealousy—in which Rose Klonec thoroughly believed."

"This proves?" inquired De Lautrec, from the depths of his throat.

"It proves nothing. I am too old a crow to believe that a random deduction of mine is necessarily true," acknowledged Bencolin, shaking his head. "But I suggest it, my friend. I *suggest* it. And unless you can satisfy me that it is not the truth, I am going to make matters warm for you. Very well."

He leaned both hands on the counter and looked steadily at the other.

"In some fashion (and this is what I want to know) you learned that Rose Klonec was preparing to take up her old affair with Ralph Douglas. You learned that she was thinking of meeting him at the Villa Marbre on Saturday night. You probably learned this as early as Thursday. And therefore, I say *therefore*, you telephoned to Ralph Douglas. You wanted these two former lovers to meet; you were eager for it. The whole purpose of that telephone call was to assure Ralph Douglas —as you did—that you were leaving town on Saturday and would not return until Tuesday, so that the lovers might not be made hesitant by any lurking fears of your homicidal jealousy. Perhaps

147

you flattered yourself, although I acknowledge that to have you on the other end of a duelling-pistol might be a serious matter. But you did not know Douglas at all well; you could not telephone him out of a clear sky and drop the information that you were going away; you had to have an excuse for speaking to him at all. The offer to buy the villa was merely the pretext for telephoning him, a pretext which, I think naturally, jumped into your head from the first. And there was another reason as well."

De Lautrec was so furious that, as the man's quick eye roved round, Curtis wondered whether he might not be meditating cutting loose with a shot at the electric light, by way of relieving his feelings. It had almost reached a point of the comic; yet there was a dead, dull color in De Lautrec's face which seemed to indicate that there might be something behind this.

"You appreciate the next reason," Bencolin told him. "You thought it possible that Douglas might pass on the information to Rose Klonec. If it had the effect of reassuring him, it might give her a germ of wonder as to whether that curious request to buy the villa might not mean that you—the violently jealous one—were suspicious. It would not prevent her from meeting Douglas; no, she would gamble with anything except money, and she was burning to pick up the old affair again. But it would prepare the ground for the little coup you meant to effect when you effected it. Of course, where your calculations went wrong was that Douglas had never made any arrangements with her, and your telephone call merely puzzled him.

148

"And now we will deal with your coup. You waited until Saturday afternoon, probably during that idyllic little excursion on the river. She was happy. She was looking forward to the night. The sun was very warm. Then suddenly you uprose and acted a part as Coquelin never acted in his best days. You were the Outraged Lover who has discovered All. You raved like a maniac. You were betrayed. You swore to kill Douglas; you even, it is likely, indulged in some such scene of threats as the one with which you tried to impress me a moment ago—"

"I still warn you to be careful," said De Lautrec.

"—and she believed you to the core. That is the one thing she did believe. She must have been considerably upset. It was not merely that her pride was salved at the prospect of getting Douglas back again; but your money had nearly run out, whereas Douglas was still rich; and above all things Rose was severely practical. If you even so much as sent a challenge to Douglas, to say nothing of killing him, the publicity would make Douglas dart back into the brush. Oh, she was in a fine mess. At length, however, you allowed yourself to be—persuaded. For a consideration, your wounded honor would be healed and you would promise not to make trouble. You had, you admitted, lost heavily at baccarat. If she would turn over to you a few good pieces of jewellery, you would nurse your anguish in secret.

"I call your attention," said Bencolin absently, "to the first words uttered by Rose Klonec to a certain Hortense Frey on arriving at the villa last night. Says Hortense: *Madame had expected to be her own maid over the week-end, eh, since the*

149

poor M. De Lautrec is so jealous and madame cannot trust her own maid?' Says madame, looking as black as a pit, *'Yes, he is jealous enough, curse him; you don't know what this week-end has cost me. It is droll.'* And again, in refusing to discuss the matter, *'I hope he enjoys his week-end.'* Which may refer to the fact that madame, in retaliation, had sent two Foreign Office men to make the night unpleasant for you, though she knew you were innocent of treason. She had reason to be furious, even if she saw the practicality of your conduct. She had to pay up. She was benumbed. She was caught in her own kind of practical trap."

"And a ruddy good thing too," Curtis muttered.

De Lautrec merely shrugged his shoulder. But a little bead of sweat ran off his forehead, and down between his rather bushy eyebrows.

"It is not criminal," he pointed out.

"Certainly not."

"At the same time, you—you realize that this story, told on the boulevards, would not improve my reputation. They would laugh at me."

"I am afraid so."

"Then why are you sticking pins in me?" De Lautrec asked between his teeth. "It cannot help you to discover who killed her."

"You admit the truth of my idea, then?"

"Yes. Why not?" asked De Lautrec in surprise. "She had got enough out of me. Why should I not get a piece of my own back from her, *voyons?*"

Bencolin leaned on the counter. "Will you never see light? You have been led along the path so very gently, my friend, so very gently. *Some-one*, an impostor, communicated with Rose

Klonec in the name of Ralph Douglas. You knew that. Well, what do you know of it? Remember, this was no simple question of sending a typewritten letter and a hundred-franc note to Hortense. When you are recapturing the old passion of a love-affair, you do not send a typewritten note directing her to be at such-and-such a place at such-and-such an hour: you would not even make a business-appointment as curtly as that. You must see her. At the least, you must telephone to her. How and where was this appointment made? How was the impostor able to deceive Rose Klonec, and make her think that it was Ralph Douglas—when she knew every line of his face and every tone of his voice? That is one of our most difficult problems. And only you know the answer."

"I see," said De Lautrec, with a breath of relief. "That is fine. That rouses my admiration. Well, monsieur?"

"If I tell you all I know in that respect, will it be necessary for you to mention the other—you understand?"

"I give you my word that I will not mention it."

"The word of M. Bencolin is satisfactory," said De Lautrec, with a sudden stateliness and deepness of tone. Its effect was somewhat marred by the fact that he kicked one of the spent cartridge-cases lying on the floor, and followed it across the room to kick it back again. When he looked up he was calm, even on the edge of a smile.

"Very well. Here, then, is my true information. I knew about the resumption of the affair because I overheard a telephone conversation. That was late on Wednesday night. You know that Rose and I

151

had suites of apartments that adjoined—so. There is an extension of the telephone in each. I picked up the telephone in my own study, intending to speak with a friend; and instead I found Rose in the midst of a conversation on the wire. I found it interesting."

"A conversation with whom?"

"I don't know. But the other party to the conversation was a woman," answered De Lautrec with broadening amusement. "You like to make sport with my intelligence. Did you know that you were a dull dog? Hadn't you guessed that this crime was certainly committed by a woman?"

Smiling, he took up the rifle again and turned his back to them. The flash of the shot merged into the clang of the iron bell.

11

The Criminologist of *L'Intelligence*

That De Lautrec had scored there could be no
doubt. Curtis would not have believed that Bencolin could be so taken aback. As though he
wished to be sure the rifle was not yanked out of
his hands, De Lautrec put it down and faced them
with such an expression of sincerity (over this one
point, at least) that there could be no doubt he
thought he was telling the truth.

Bencolin cleared his throat. "You have reasons
for believing that?"

"One moment," said De Lautrec. At his long
stride he crossed to the door of the gymnasium,
and returned with a tweed coat; from his pocket
he took a folded newspaper. "If you will glance at
this," he added, wagging it in the air, "you will
see that—"

"A newspaper. Good God, the man brings me newspapers!" said Bencolin. "Every amateur of the press sits on his behind at Chez Francis, and drinks his vermouth-cassis, and tells me what I ought to do. We were discussing a telephone call to Rose Klonec, and you say the person who called her was a woman. You are not trying to tell me, are you, that a woman could pretend to be Ralph Douglas? Or that Ralph Douglas would make his appointment with her through another woman?"

Now that he seemed to have dodged under his own troubles, De Lautrec was talkative; his long, mobile face seemed to express every thought.

"Still, hadn't you better look at it?" he suggested, wagging the paper invitingly. "Most of these journalist-detectives, I admit, are not good: but this is 'Auguste Dupin' of *L'Intelligence*, and he is a stimulating fellow ... You were saying? Yes, of course. I am not trying to tell you anything, except the exact truth of what I heard."

"That Douglas, or rather the impostor, made an appointment through another woman? Or that Rose Klonec would have believed in the genuineness of it?"

"I still think you had better read this," insisted De Lautrec, and slapped the paper down on the counter.

Bencolin bent over a remarkable first-page splash.

OUR SPECIAL CORRESPONDENT
SOLVES THE MYSTERY OF THE VILLA
MARBRE!

———

THE BRILLIANT EXPOSITION OF
AUGUSTE DUPIN!

MM. THE POLICE, TAKE NOTICE!

L'Intelligence here has the honor to present the first dispatch, from the actual scene of the ferocious crime at the Villa Marbre, written by our famous correspondent M. Auguste Dupin. The name of 'Auguste Dupin,' as all Paris knows, conceals the identity of a celebrated criminologist—

"His name is Robinson," said Bencolin out of the side of his mouth, "although he is French. He is actually a briefless lawyer who hangs about the courts. The devil of it is that the fellow, who is as shallow as a spectacle-lens, takes a jump at the truth and is often right. He really did put Durrand on the track about that strangler in the Bois de Vincennes. Also, for sheer persistence in bothering the police, I know of nobody who can match him. Well, let us see."

—who, not six hours after the discovery of the body, has by pure logic discovered the solution of this terrible mystery, to which we proudly call the attention of the police. But we will not longer delay the reader from the perusal of this remarkable document, whose truth we predict will speedily be demonstrated. It begins (we now quote M. Dupin) with the startling knowledge that

The man in the brown raincoat and black

hat is really a woman!

Villa Marbre, 6 P.M. Sitting here under these stately trees, smoking my pipe and composing the notes for my article to *L'Intelligence*, I reflect that—

"We don't give a curse what he reflects," snapped Bencolin. "But the housewives like this philosophizing and the men feel that it ought to be even if it isn't. How did he get his facts? Ah, I see; here it is. 'A conversation with that doughty champion of the law, M. Hercule Renard, at the wineshop of—' That finishes it. Hercule will be black-drunk and speechless now. Let's get to the center."

I need not trouble to report in detail the facts as I found them; these facts the reader will have studied in other journals. But my conclusions? That is another matter! For fully an hour, I confess that I was completely baffled—

"Modest sort of chap, isn't he?" observed Curtis.

—and then, suddenly, I saw! I saw what was, mathematically speaking, the only possible solution. I had got hold of the right end of my judgment! Let me put down the points as I gathered them from my notebook.

1. The man in the brown raincoat and black hat is seen by the maid, Hortense Frey, stropping a razor on a rough whetstone block. Not only that, but the stropping is done so badly that the razor, when examined afterwards, is found to be nicked and

blunted in several places. No man would strop a razor on such a surface, nor would he get such results. But it is precisely the sort of thing which might be done by a woman.

2. From here my mind flashed back to the first entrance of the mysterious "man in the brown coat" at nine o'clock, the occasion on which he broke the woman Frey's glasses. What is the testimony of Frey on this point? She states that the visitor slipped, stumbled, and almost fell, so that she had to catch at him. She descants on the extreme *realism* of the stumble. Of course, it is reasonable to think that the visitor would find some excuse for breaking the glasses of the near-sighted Hortense. But to go to such lengths as nearly to sprawl on the floor, and to do so with complete conviction, would be dubious and difficult. Now, what else do we know of the visitor's appearance? "He" wears Oxford bags—those past abominations of a vanity truly English, which, with careful walking, would entirely conceal the shoe. Suppose there is another reason for this stumble? M. Ralph Douglas, I have ascertained, is 5 ft. 11 inches tall. Not many women could pretend to a height like that. But suppose these antiquated trousers were worn to conceal the shoe, because it was some such footgear as a surgical boot, which would add inches to a woman's height, and at the same time be difficult to manage without danger of falling?

"The whole thing is fantastic!" said Curtis, forgetting that he was not supposed to understand

French. He saw De Lautrec eyeing him, but De Lautrec made no comment. "It is almost funny. The idea—"

"You were thinking of your little friend Miss Toller?" mused Bencolin. "Set your mind at rest. Mr. Douglas, as this states, is five feet eleven. Miss Toller is at most five feet two. To suppose that she added nine inches to her height, to suppose that she went reeling round the villa on stilts—no, that is beyond the farthest stars of disbelief. Besides, there is the question of the voice. But I find this account very suggestive. M. De Lautrec, you were quite right: Dupin, however misguided, is a stimulating fellow..."

"You mean the point about the Oxford bags?"

"No, in my view that is unimportant and our friend Auguste even misses the point of what he says. I mean the point about the razor. *There* is something, definitely. Let's see. Ah, now he warms up and his meerschaum is drawing well. Listen."

3. Afire with this new certainty, I proceeded to a minute study of the apartments, permission to examine which was given to me by the courtesy of Brigadier Jules Saulomon. The core of my search, obviously, was the dressing-room. On another page of *L'Intelligence* the reader will find photographs of these rooms. Let him study them as I explain.

The belief of the police is that Mme. Klonec had undressed herself and put on her nightgown. Their belief is based on the fact that the evening-gown, stockings, and shoes which Mme. Klonec had worn were all put away neatly in the wardrobe in a fashion peculiar to madame herself. I DENY THIS! I say that she was certainly undressed by the murderer, after being either drugged or stunned, so that she could be put into a warm bath and thus increase the flow of blood from the severed artery to kill her before she recovered consciousness. I say this, and I will tell you why.

If Mme. Klonec undressed herself, and put on her own night-gown, why did she not put on her negligee and slippers? Married men, bachelors of sporting habit, confirm it! In the wardrobe I found hanging up a peach-colored negligee of lace—obviously the companion of the nightgown; and just as obviously uncrumpled and untouched. No slippers were in evidence. But it cannot be thought that Mme. Klonec would walk round even the dressing-room (which has, I observed, an uncovered marble floor) in her bare feet.

What happened, it is clear, was this. The assassin stripped her of clothing and left her in the bath to die. Afterwards the assassin dressed her in a nightgown and thrust her into the bed. And this in itself is significant, when seen through the right end of the judgment! Who would have done this? A man would not have taken such pains. A man would have left her where she lay. Only a woman, for the look of the thing, would have covered her decently before leaving. Who, also, could have put away those other clothes in the wardrobe exactly as though Mme.

Klonec had done it herself? A man? No. Ask yourself the question.

4. The final point of my examination put the matter beyond all doubt. I asked myself the question: the assassin, whoever it might have been, could not for five seconds have hoped to deceive Mme. Klonec into thinking that "he" was M. Douglas. Once she saw him, madame would be aware of the trap. Once inside that room, the assassin must strike at once. Why, therefore, does the assassin encumber himself by carrying upstairs a heavy table laden with food and drink? Even if madame is not already drugged, it will interest neither of them. They will not eat; they will not drink, except with death. Why does he open a large bottle of champagne on that serving-table, and so conspicuously leave dregs in two glasses? Readers of *L'Intelligence*, readers everywhere, I will tell you the answer! *The assassin was really a woman, who arranged these things like properties on a stage to indicate that Mme. Rose Klonec was having an intimate supper with a man.*

It was very warm in the basement, faintly tinged with the smell of powder-smoke, and quiet except for the whirring of the figures in the gallery. Curtis whistled.

"Wow!" he said, unconsciously adopting the classic style of M. Auguste Dupin. "That's a corker. Say what you like about jumping to conclusions, the fellow's got a whacking good case. There may be gaps in it—he says nothing about the missing bottle of champagne, for instance, unless that was how the woman was drugged—but it's the most probable-sounding one that's been advanced so far."

Bencolin did not seem pleased. He rapped his knuckles on the counter; he picked up the paper and flung it down again.

"Yes, he uses his head, confound him! But I should hate to think that I was indebted for ideas to that—that *petit morceau*, Jean-Baptiste Robinson. Basically he is wrong; he must be wrong. But there are times, I imagine, when he almost burns his fingers on the truth. I had considered that same idea myself; you may remember how I battered at Hortense with the question as to whether she was certain Rose Klonec had undressed herself? I have told you not to place too much reliance on Hortense's positiveness. On the other hand, there are extra indications which to me make it sure that she did undress herself. Above all, it would be a fastidious murderer who, after dispatching his victim, carefully hung all her clothes up in the wardrobe.

"Yes, I have skimmed over many fantastic theories, like our friend in *L'Intelligence*. I even considered the possibility that the brown-coated man might have been none other than Mrs. Benedict Toller herself: a notion so staggering, to any-one who has seen the lady or knows anything about her, that I treated it with some reverence."

He turned to De Lautrec.

"Jean-Baptiste Robinson has put us off. I want to know more of your story, in which a woman speaks to Rose Klonec on the telephone, and makes an appointment in the name of Ralph

Douglas. Frankly, you don't sound as though you were lying, and yet—"

De Lautrec chuckled. Throughout the reading of the article, there had been a look about his eye which Curtis could not decipher and did not like; but now he was at ease.

"Many thanks. What else can I tell you? It was a woman's voice: I don't know whose. So far as I can swear, I had never heard it before."

"Did the voice speak in French or English?"

"In French."

"Can you recall the exact conversation?"

"You may well believe I can! It was very important to me. Evidently I took up the 'phone either in the middle or towards the end of the talk. The voice of the unknown woman was saying something of this sort: *'You understand why M. Douglas cannot communicate with you in person? His fiancée and her mother are in Paris, and the girl is very suspicious.'*" De Lautrec stopped, evidently reflecting. "To me that answers all your objections. That is to say, your objection as to whether Rose would have believed such a message, and fallen into his arms, if he had acted so casually. Under the circumstances, what is more natural than that he should have acted through a third party—or, at least, wouldn't it seem quite natural to Rose?"

"Yes, it is possible," admitted Bencolin. "One moment, though. You say that you believe the man in the brown coat was a woman. In short, you believe this?" He tapped the paper. "That makes the situation simple, at all events. The mysterious woman telephoned Rose Klonec in the character of a woman, a go-between for Ralph Douglas, because La Klonec could not have been deceived by any other pretense. The same woman pretended to be a man before Hortense...Is that how you see it?"

The other shrugged his shoulders. "Why not? The correspondent of *L'Intelligence* has all the proof on his side. It seems that the same woman acted in both cases."

"I see no actual proof. But go on."

"About the conversation? There was not much of it. Rose tried to end it; she said, *'Yes, yes, but you were a fool to ring me on the telephone; M. De Lautrec is here; come and see me.'* To which the other voice said: *'Can I tell M. Ralph that you will meet him on Saturday night at the Villa Marbre?'* The last words were Rose's: *'Yes, yes; let us meet and you shall tell me about him.'* And that's all. Frankly, I found it almost too good to be true. You know what I did. Probably it was indiscreet to get in touch with Douglas the next day; but I wished to assure myself, and to hear his response, as much as to assure him I was going out of town. Afterwards, as you have so elegantly outlined it, I set my trap for Rose about the jewels. But you were wrong about one thing: I did not spring my trap while we were on the river: I defy anyone to be dramatic in an open boat. So I waited until we had returned home, when she was eager to be gone to Douglas, and eager for me to be gone. I let her rise to that pitch of expectancy before I showed...but you have explained it yourself. That was why we were both late in leaving here, and probably why she was still in a temper when she arrived at the Villa Marbre. It was a fine scene, I can tell you. We were all alone;

it was Annette, her maid's night out, and Annette had left us before we returned; so—"

During the last few words so strange a change had come over Bencolin's face that De Lautrec hesitated, and then began speaking in a more rapid, harsh tone as though to batter down incredulity. Bencolin stopped him.

"M. De Lautrec, we have trespassed too long on your time," he said, with such an abrupt break that Curtis wondered what was wrong. "We will say good-night; it must be past twelve. I need not examine madame's apartments tonight. But two little things I must note, and one of them is a measure of precaution. Rose Klonec's famous collection of jewellery: is it kept here, or at a bank?"

"It is kept here, in her wall-safe. I don't know the combination. Her legal representative (yes, she had one) was here this afternoon to arrange such matters; but nobody knew how to open the safe." De Lautrec spoke with dignity. "He is coming tomorrow morning, with an expert, to get it open."

"I see. Now, this Annette, whom you mentioned a moment ago—you said you could give me her present address?"

"Yes. Annette Fauvel, 88 Avenue de St. Rouen, Montmartre."

"What sort of girl is she?"

De Lautrec looked puzzled. "Well...I don't know what to say. She is educated above her station in life; she was at one time a governess, I believe. She is capable enough, so far as I can judge. Certainly she looks capable. She is a big blonde, muscular, with a voice like—"

He stopped.

"Yes?" said Bencolin.

"The idea that came into my head just then," returned De Lautrec, staring at the gallery, "and doubtless into yours too, is absurd. Or so it seems; though, thank the Lord, I am no criminologist. It was not Annette's voice I heard talking to Rose on the telephone, and making an appointment. At least, I do not think it was. And why should she talk to her own employer in that way—unless, of course, she was pretending to be someone else? Yes; in that event, she would disguise her voice. I don't know. But, after all, why not? Why not? Of all the women I know, she could qualify most admirably in build and voice for the role of the man in the brown coat."

"And her motive?"

"I can't say. That's your affair."

"We will consider it. Again, good-night, and let me give you a word of advice. Don't be too hypnotized by the theories of M. 'Auguste Dupin.' Until Dupin can produce a piece of reasonable evidence—"

"Evidence?" repeated De Lautrec, regarding him with astonishment. "But that is the whole point of the dispute! There *is* evidence. Didn't I tell you there was proof of the fact that a woman committed the crime? Didn't you see it for yourself? Or is it possible that you did not finish the article, where it ends among the advertisements and the heart-cries? I see. You did not."

With a malicious pleasure he picked up *L'Intelligence* and ran his eye down to the corner of the page.

And now as I conclude, I hear some of my readers say, "Ah, he is clever! He is a veritable wizard, that Dupin, and he will show us the truth as he has done in the Paulton affair, and the robbery in the rue des Martyrs, and the stranglings of the Bois de Vincennes! But, after all, where is his evidence? What can he give to the police, that they may take before the President of the Tribunal?" Courage, little ones! Papa Dupin will not disappoint you. I have left my best plum, the pick of the basket, until last, and you shall have it now—

"I don't suppose he would ever have considered shoving the whole thing into a headline, and letting it go at that?" suggested Curtis. "He writes the whole story, and puts the most important part in a postscript. He may be a notable sleuth; but as a reporter he must drive news-editors to suicide."

In doing so, it may be that I must violate, to some extent, a little confidence imparted to me over a friendly glass or two at the wineshop of 'The Star of Boissy.' But truth must be served! And I am sure that the honest, intelligent, doughty champion of the law, M. Hercule Renard, whom I have mentioned before, will be the first to applaud my action.

Throughout my examination of the Villa Marbre, the behavior of M. Renard had struck me as peculiar in the extreme. For one so honest, he acted like a man with a guilty secret. He seemed to creep. It was very strange. When after my examination of the dressing-room I exclaimed aloud the words, 'It was a woman, then!' M. Renard's reflex action did not go unobserved by Papa

Dupin. I resolved to investigate. Seeing by his frank, open countenance that he was not averse to a glass of good wine, I invited him to 'The Star of Boissy' for refreshment. And presently he told me what had happened on the previous night.

On Saturday, at just midnight, M. Renard was returning home along the road past the Villa Marbre. He was pushing his bicycle, not riding it, since he believed one of the pedals to be loose. If he had taken a sip or two of cognac, is not that the privilege of Frenchmen and freemen? Was he drunk? No! Was he doing his duty? Yes! He had been instructed to keep an eye on the villa, and this he was doing. Seeing a light shining from the villa, he resolved to sink down covertly into a hedge, and watch. It was a long vigil. Here is his only dereliction: he fell asleep.

How long he slept he is unable to say, nor does he know what roused him. But he awoke with a start. He was able to see, by moonlight, the figure of a certain person come out of the gate of the villa, close the gate, and walk rapidly away along the road towards Boissy.

And now the irony! He sprang to his feet to follow. Unfortunately, he had forgotten his bicycle, which was propped partly against him. He stumbled, and fell so heavily that for a time he was unable to move. The intruder had gone. Bitter and chagrined, he thought it best to return home. Only this morning—when he hurried down to examine the villa again, and heard a woman, locked up in a ground-floor lavatory, screaming for help—did he realize. The news of the murder stunned him no less, for he knew he had seen the assassin. He could not bring himself to speak. He still cannot, though I assure him it is best. Courage, M. Renard! The law will know how to treat you.

But you, my readers, will wish to know who it was he saw going out on that swift, secret, evil journey from the Villa Marbre. At the moment, I go on to collect more evidence and prove my case beyond cavil. But I will tell you what he saw, and judge for yourselves how triumphantly the pure reason of Papa Dupin is vindicated:

It was the figure of a tall woman.

12

Bencolin's Mood

Sleep. A deep bed, fashioned with the epic comfort of France; the leaves of tall windows standing open, pushing up heavy lace curtains at an ungainly angle, with just an edge of street-light showing through, and just a rustle of breeze; the vast, high stillness that lies on Paris at night, broken only by the faint *whish* of a car passing in the street below; a fragrance of trees outside the window, and then a sinking into sleep. It was the one thing in the world Richard Curtis wanted most. It was also one of the things he seemed least likely to get. At a quarter past twelve he was stepping out of Bencolin's car before the Hotel Crillon in the Place de la Concorde.

"You'll never get to see Mrs. Toller tonight," he declared; "it's too late."

But Bencolin had been obstinate, not to say gloomy. He had insisted first on a brandy, which they took along the way; and Curtis never forgot him sitting at the pavement table under its awning, his long legs thrust out, his face grown Mephistophelian with ill-humor under the soft black hat.

"The mystery of Hercule," he said. "First blood is undoubtedly to Jean-Baptiste Robinson. I should have noticed that. I observed Hercule's behavior; but I laid it to other causes. It would seem that my wits are growing thick with inaction. So it was a tall woman, was it?"

"It's a strong theory, anyway."

"You noticed no flaws in it?"

"I noticed one flaw in Dupin's facts," said Curtis, taking the paper out of his pocket. "It may or may not be an important one; important, I should say. It concerns what he has to say about the clothes in the dressing-room. Now, he's quite right about the peach-colored negligee hung up untouched—so far as you can tell—in the wardrobe. But he's completely wrong about the slippers. He says there were no slippers anywhere, and bases one of his most essential deductions on it. Either he's falsifying the facts, or somebody took the slippers away. But, when I first looked into the dressing-room this morning, there was a pair of yellow satin mules standing under the dressing-table."

"*I* took them away," said Bencolin. "Keep your mind fixed on that dressing-table: with the slippers under it, and the jar of vanishing-cream whose lid is off, and the round wet mark made by the heel of a bottle, and the stiletto in the drawer

170

—where Hortense says she placed it. These things form the beginning of my case, which is somewhat different from M. Robinson's. I profoundly distrust these cases which are based on, 'only a woman would have done this,' or 'only a man would have done that.' All the same, that article in *L'Intelligence* is going to cause a stir. We had better go on to the Crillon and see Mrs. Toller."

Despite Curtis's prediction that they would not get in, they were welcomed. When they went into the foyer of the hotel, a harassed clerk at the Réception on the left was speaking with anxiety into a telephone. He clapped his hand over it at their approach, and hissed at them.

"We are profoundly grateful to see you, monsieur," he said. He pointed to the telephone. "That is M. Stanfield, speaking from the suite of the English lady, Mrs. Toller. Will you be so good as to go up at once?"

"Is there something the matter?"

"There is always something the matter," replied the clerk gloomily. He corrected himself, and resumed his professional manner. "Second floor, suite 3. The boy will—"

"One moment. Is M. Stanfield often here to see Mrs. Toller?"

The other was interested. "Well, that is only natural, monsieur. M. Stanfield manages madame's affairs."

"Do you know whether he was here at any time yesterday?"

"Yes, he was here early yesterday evening. I particularly remember it."

"Why?"

"Because madame's suite has a private lift, and her intimate acquaintances can come and go without passing through here, or without being seen by anyone. But yesterday evening M. Stanfield passed through the foyer both when he arrived and when he left. He arrived about eight, and left at just a quarter to nine."

"Admirable! How are you so certain of those times?"

"About the time of his arrival—no, I would not swear to that. But I am certain about the time of his departure, because he walked up to the desk here to look at the clock. He seemed in a disturbed state of mind, which was not usual. When he walked up here he dropped his top-hat, and it rolled across the desk, and I caught it for him."

"One thing more. Is any record kept of telephone calls to or from the hotel?"

"Of all outgoing calls. Naturally, monsieur, since they are put on the guest's bill."

"But incoming calls?"

The clerk hesitated. His voice grew frozen and colorless. "If monsieur is thinking of Mrs. Toller —in her case, yes, there is a record. Mrs. Toller is a lady of commendable prudence in money matters, which sometimes goes too far. On occasion she appears to think that the management credits her even with calls made to her from outside. Consequently, a complete record is kept for madame's convenience."

"This is real luck. Can you tell me what calls were made to her suite yesterday morning before one o'clock?"

The clerk went away for a mysterious conference, after which he returned with a ledger.

"With pleasure, monsieur. It is all the easier since there was only one call during that time. There is no record of its origin, of course, but the man at the switchboard believes it was M. Stanfield speaking to Mrs. Toller. And now if you will be good enough to go upstairs—?"

In the anteroom of the suite on the second floor, George Stanfield met them as though he were preparing their way into a shrine. There was evidently something on his mind, and he looked more paunchy in an ordinary lounge-suit. The shrine to which he led them was a large, florid room in pink and white, full of tassels, and with two windows opening out over the white forest of lamps in the Place de la Concorde. Bolt upright in a wing chair by the table sat Mrs. Benedict Toller: and Curtis understood many things.

Mrs. Toller was a large, lean, handsome woman, with a dry face, and brown bobbed hair permanently waved in such stiff ridges that it looked like leather. It is no exaggeration to say that you were conscious of a lowering of temperature when you met her; she was of such energy or intelligence that she carried her own atmosphere with her. Nor is 'handsome' the correct word, for complete good looks were spoiled by a large, long nose which flared out at the nostrils, and was a little tilted up. Curtis remembered Hunt's word, 'abomination.' It may have been this nose which wrongly gave her an unpleasant look; but Curtis thought that the real cause of it was her complete impassivity. You felt that if the chandelier fell or a bomb exploded she would scarcely blink a lid over those calm, shrewd, pale-blue eyes, and that she would have the utmost contempt for anyone who did more. Whereas Bryce Douglas's impassivity was assumed, hers was real. She was clearly a woman used to getting everything she wanted; and, if she did not get it, she would know the reason why.

The instant antagonism which sprang up between her and Bencolin was one of the most curious features of the case; it could be felt in the air before a word was spoken, while Mrs. Toller sat tapping her foot impatiently on the floor. At Bencolin she looked briefly, at Curtis with anger, while introductions were performed.

"The fact is," said Stanfield, "the fact is—"

"I see no reason for beating about the bush," Mrs. Toller interrupted calmly. "We have had a burglary." She looked at Bencolin. "Or what seems to be a burglary. I should be grateful if you would enlighten me about it."

Bencolin smiled deceptively. "I am afraid you must first enlighten *me* about it, Mrs. Toller. What was stolen?"

"Nothing."

"Yes. Well?"

"It occurred not ten minutes ago," she said, as though she were coming to a decision. "I heard a noise in my bedroom, like glass rattling. I went in immediately, and I was in time to see someone getting out through the open window on to the fire-escape. Someone had ransacked my desk and my dressing-table. It was an unusual kind of burglary. A purse on the dressing-table, with a considerable sum of money in it, had not been touched." Her foot stopped tapping, and she spoke more coolly still. "Why not tell me the truth?"

"The truth? Are you under the impression that I was the burglar?"

"I know that the police in France have liberties unheard of in England. The only thing in which the 'burglar' showed any sign of interest was an English firearms-license in a drawer of my desk. I believe that at the villa where that woman was murdered—we need not dignify her by mentioning her name—you found a .22 calibre automatic pistol with the number D3854 engraved in large numbers along the grip?"

"Yes."

"That pistol belongs to me," Mrs. Toller told him, looking him in the eye, "as I dare say you have by this time discovered. But I warn you: if you gain any nonsensical theories from the fact, or try to use it in any way, the consequences will be exceedingly unpleasant for you."

She broke off, for Bencolin was chuckling.

"I'm glad I have amused you," she added.

"No, no, it was a noise of admiration," said Bencolin, soberly and heartily. "I like the way you drive me into a corner. It doesn't surprise me to hear the pistol is yours; to tell you the truth, I thought Mr. Stanfield recognized it when I flourished it under his nose today. But see what happens. You have concealed vital evidence until it was dragged out of you. Mr. Stanfield has concealed vital evidence. And yet the moment the goose falls out of the larder you apparently threaten me with criminal prosecution if I have any curiosity about a weapon found on the very scene of the murder. In the graphic words of my friend Jeff Marle: Hot dog! It is the nuts."

"I refuse to answer mere impertinences."

"Dear madame, you refuse to answer anything."

She smiled bleakly. "And yet there will be a very unpleasant answer, I warn you, if I am compelled to enlist the aid of several of your Cabinet Ministers who are very good friends of mine. You see, I can prove that the pistol has not been in this hotel for over two days, and certainly not in my possession."

Bencolin grew attentive.

"In whose possession, then?"

"In mine," replied Stanfield. Stanfield had been fiddling with a handkerchief, as though wiping his palms. Now he put away the handkerchief with great nicety in his breast pocket; he faced the detective with an air of apology, but with great apparent frankness. "No, I'm not thinking of confessing to the murder," he went on humorously. "I've just remembered—and I'll admit it relieves me—that I left this hotel last night at exactly a quarter to nine. We've heard that the man in the brown raincoat and black hat appeared at the Villa Marbre at nine o'clock. Now I'll defy anybody without wings to get from here to the Villa Marbre in less than half an hour. So you may count me out as a candidate, in case it had occurred to you. But seriously: about that gun. Since Mrs. Toller is thinking of spending some time in France, I suggested it might be wise to have a French fire-arms-license as well as a British. You can't be too careful about these little formalities. Now, at our office we arrange for all such things: passports, identity-cards, car-licenses, and the rest of it. So I took the gun along with me, and dropped it into the drawer of my desk. But we've been fairly rushed with work, so I'm afraid I forgot it."

"You took it to your office when?"

"On Friday afternoon. I was here to tea, and I took it with me afterwards. So far as I knew, it was still there. You can imagine what a shock I got when, as you say, you flourished it in my face today."

Stanfield, his forehead wrinkled, was speaking with a light and humorous earnestness. Sincerity sat on him like a doctor's robe.

"I didn't mention the fact, I admit," he went on. "But I wanted to consult with Mrs. Toller first. Also, I don't know quite what you mean about 'suppressing evidence.' No such thing has been done. After all, the crime was only discovered this morning; and I had to make sure of my somewhat staggering idea that the two pistols were the same. In any case, I should have come to you to-morrow morning with the facts."

"Thank you," said Bencolin gravely. Curtis could not read Bencolin's look; but it was one he did not like, and the other two did not seem to like it either. There was a long silence, while they listened to the noise of traffic from the Place de la Concorde. "So we must assume that, whoever took the pistol to the Villa Marbre, or for whatever purpose, it was stolen from your desk?"

"Yes. I can only assure you that *I* didn't take it."

"You still don't seem to understand," pursued Bencolin, moving closer to him, "that this may be the most vital point in the case. You see how it narrows down our field of suspects?"

Stanfield looked startled. "Well . . . hardly that, is it? No, that's much too strong. Mme. Klon—that is, the woman to whom Mrs. Toller has referred— was not killed with a gun, and the gun was not fired or used in any way. You can't say that the person who stole the gun was necessarily the murderer."

"No. But we can say that the person who stole the gun was probably at the Villa Marbre last night? And consequently there is a strong presumption that it is the murderer? You agree?"

"I don't agree to anything," retorted Stanfield, with sudden asperity. "That's your business. My business is to give you the facts, since you insist on having them, and avoid poking fingers of suspicion at people—"

"*You* agree, Mrs. Toller?"

That lady did not bother to answer.

"Nevertheless, you will have to begin to poke," said Bencolin. "You have narrowed it down too much. Who could have taken the pistol out of your office?"

"Half the world goes through my office."

"Half the world is not concerned in this case. Very few people are. Who dropped in to see you between Friday and Saturday?"

Stanfield hesitated. "Well, there was Hortense Frey, of course. You knew that. I—"

"Yes, I knew that. But who else? Was Ralph Douglas there, for instance?"

Again Stanfield hesitated. His eyes slid sideways to Mrs. Toller, who had not moved or looked at him. Curtis felt under the tension a significance that just escaped him; Stanfield's lips were shaking, and he seemed trying to get over a barrier.

"I—" he said, and added with heat: "Take your hand off my shoulder. You try any of your third-degree methods on me, and I'll land you one that'll make your head sing, old as I am."

"That's the way to talk!" urged Bencolin, almost eagerly. "That's the way to talk. Now, then: was Ralph Douglas there?"

"No," said Stanfield.

The releasing of the tension was as though air had been given to a spent swimmer. Bencolin stepped back. During this exchange he had not been looking at Stanfield, but at Mrs. Toller; and, as he stepped back, there was on his face the shadow of a malicious smile. Whatever his previous look at Mrs. Toller had meant, it was evident that she had understood it. Mrs. Toller had now an air of complete boredom. You would not have thought the broad-nostrilled nose could have gone so high without absurdity, yet there it was: she remained only serene and unruffled, absolutely sure of herself.

"That will be all for tonight," she said. "Please get out."

"I quite agree, madame," Bencolin told her. "When I came here tonight, it was with the intention of troubling you with a hundred small questions. Now I hardly think I need ask them, for the present, at least. I have enough to think about. With your permission, we will say good-night. I must ask you and Mr. Stanfield to come to the Palais de Justice (say tomorrow morning at eleven?) for formal questioning on this point by the examining magistrate—"

"We will, of course, do nothing of the kind." She spoke without heat; she was even a little surprised.

"Madame," said Bencolin with ferocious tenderness, "you will be at the Palais de Justice tomorrow if I have to carry you there myself. Kindly make up your mind to that. A car will call for you at eleven. Until then! Thank you, Mr. Stanfield; you need not trouble to see us out."

He and Curtis went out through the anteroom, out of the suite, and into the dimly lighted corridor with the rich carpet. Once round an angle of the wall, Bencolin stopped and began to swear with such fluency and comprehensiveness that it was a minute or two before his remarks became printable. Curtis listened with critical approval.

"The old witch," Bencolin said at length, shaking his fist. "The yellow-eyed Bubastes with the thirty-nine tails. The swine-snouted polecat with the armor-plated hair," he amplified, defying the laws of zoology. "Gwouf! I was half tempted to unlimber my heavy artillery and blow her from here to the other side of Algeciras. And will I make it hot for her! You supply the response."

Curtis grinned. "Would you let your personal feelings—?"

"Certainly. For do you know what she was doing? I could see it coming; I could smell it." He looked thoughtful. "As for that little ghost story about Stanfield's taking the automatic to his office on Friday, it may or may not be true. We ought to be able to prove it one way or the other. But one point, one piece of embroidery, was meant to be added to that story; and it was not true. Don't you see Stanfield is under her thumb—like that." He pressed his own thumb on the wall and twisted it round. "She had him all primed and ready to swear that *Ralph Douglas* had called at Stanfield's office between Friday and Saturday; that he was the only one who had been there, and the only one who could have taken the pistol; thus putting him straight back under suspicion again. She is determined to entangle him in the business, either as murderer or as mere visitor, and break up that marriage if she can. She wants Magda to marry Bryce; and there you are."

"Look here, she must hate Ralph a devil of a lot."

"No, she doesn't hate him. She doesn't hate anybody; if she did I could find excuses for her. She simply wants her own way. She had never been baulked before in her life, until it came to the question of this marriage. She is going to show that no one can question *her* decisions, especially since the girl has broken away from her. Consequently, she cooked up this story of Ralph calling at the office. The trouble was that Stanfield hadn't realized, up until the last minute, how this was tantamount to accusing Ralph of murder. I made him see it. When it came to the actual pinch, he was either too cautious, or fundamentally what you would call too decent. He boggled."

"It strikes me," said Curtis, "that the whole story—about the gun being taken to the office—sounds fishy. Or does it? If it's true, the circle is as narrow as you say, and Stanfield becomes your most important witness."

"I know. He will be dealt with tomorrow."

"And what about this burglar who was after the firearms license? Was he one of your men?"

"No, not unless Brille or Durrand sent him, and they would hardly have gone about it in that way. I confess I don't understand the burglar. If—"

A mysterious voice behind them uttered the sound:

"*S-ss-st!*"

This time Curtis jumped and swore with the vigor of Bencolin. Just behind them, at the turn of the corridor, was a window curtained in dark velvet. Projecting between the curtains, with something of the effect of an ornamental plaque, there was sticking out a man's face. It was a round face of extraordinary intensity, having a little square patch of black moustache as high as it was broad, and a pair of eyeglasses with a gold chain: the resemblance to an ornamental plaque being lessened by the fact that the whole was surmounted with a bowler hat. After giving a sharp glance round the corridor, the plaque spoke amiably.

"Ah, my children! Good evening," it said.

"So it is you," said Bencolin with enlightenment. "Descend from there, and be quick about it!"

After a series of violent agitations behind the curtain, there jumped down the figure of a small man with a chest like a pouter-pigeon. He was dressed in black of shabby-genteel style; he wore a large pair of white cotton gloves, and had his breast pocket stuck full of pencils.

"Let me present," said Bencolin, "Mr. Curtis, M. Jean-Baptiste Robinson."

The newcomer thrust one finger between two buttons of his waistcoat, as though he were going to have his photograph taken, and spoke gravely.

"Auguste Dupin of *L'Intelligence;* a poor master of arts of the University; and a graduate of law from Strasbourg," he announced. "Now, as you see, engaged in the study of crime, like my great predecessor, Edgar Poe."

"That is another improving book," growled Bencolin. "I have yet to hear of Edgar Poe crawling about on fire-escapes and ransacking people's rooms after firearms licenses. It was you, wasn't it?"

"Edgar Poe made no difficulty about going to the moon, monsieur," said Robinson, with dignity. He addressed Curtis with a gleeful and confidential air. "Ha ha ha! I have the bulge on this old joker, and he knows it. He is jealous of me. In the old days I was the only one who could give him a run for his money. I had not his good right arm; I could not smack 'em over—so; and—so; but as for the intelligence, that was different. I see he carries my article in *L'Intelligence*. That shows you."

"You know I could have you thrown into jail for this?"

Robinson fired up, stung on his favorite subject.

"You dare not," he said. "The power of the press protects me. You dare not, I tell you! Besides (I do not wish to make a speech now) I have something to exchange. I have something that you very much desire."

He threw back his coat. Reaching into his inside breast pocket, he drew out and held up in his big white-gloved hand an empty half-bottle of Roederer champagne.

There was a pause, except for a noise from Bencolin. Very slowly Robinson turned the bottle round, and beamed behind it: his chest thrown out, his eyeglasses shining.

"You are not going to tell me," said Bencolin, "that you found *this* in the apartments of Mrs. Toller?"

"No, no. I found it buried in the grounds of the

183

Villa Marbre, where my wits led me to look for it."

"When did you find it?"

"Late this afternoon."

"Then why the devil didn't you bring it to Durrand or me?"

"I am a journalist, monsieur," answered Robinson proudly. "My first duty is to my editor and my public. I had first to take it to the editor of *L'Intelligence*, and let him inspect it."

"I trust he found the sight improving. You have never heard, I suppose, of fingerprints?"

"There you would be wrong, monsieur. Observe my gloves. In the offices of *L'Intelligence* there is a fully equipped outfit for the taking and developing of fingerprints. I persuaded the editor to buy it after that affair of the Sewers of Clichy. Unfortunately, too many cooks attacked that bottle, and we found, alas, that we were all taking each other's fingerprints on it; but it had been buried for many hours in the earth and I do not think we should have found a print anyway."

Bencolin took the bottle and turned it over in his hand. He sniffed at it. "Earth," he said; "no, wait," and sniffed again. Robinson watched, his pouter-pigeon chest thrown out, with the same air of dignified pride. Then Bencolin carried the bottle across the corridor to get a better light, where he studied it closely.

"Was there a cork?" he asked.

"There was no cork. But you observe what has been done to the bottom of the bottle, where there is the deep cup-shaped depression with which they cheat us of a full bottle?"

Bencolin stared at it. "Yes, it has been done very clumsily."

"Someone," Robinson explained to Curtis, "has cut out the bottom of the bottle and replaced it. One of our colleagues, who has worked in America, has explained that this was once the practice of the American bootleggers. This is the pronunciation, eh? The liquor was 'cut'—eh?—with inferior stuff. Afterwards the piece of glass was replaced, intense heat was applied, and the softened glass closed up the opening. But I have never heard of anyone doing it with champagne. Gin or whiskey, yes. But with champagne it is merely ridiculous, and I doubt if it could be done."

For a time Bencolin remained staring at the bottle. Then he turned round, with a growing surprise, and pleasure, and certainty.

"Excellent!" he boomed, slapping the bottle. "This goes beyond my hopes. Jean-Baptiste, you are the best fellow in the world, and if I am right you shall have the story for *L'Intelligence* in order to prove you wrong." He held it out. "Look at it. You see before you a bottle which has served as strange a purpose as ever a bottle did—"

Robinson regarded him with some apprehension. "Bah, you are only making mysteries. You don't tell us poison was put into the bottle, do you?"

"No."

"A sleeping draught, then. I guessed that. I mean, my reason said—"

"You are still missing the point and also the joke," urged Bencolin, spinning the bottle in his hand. He looked at Curtis. "Tomorrow, let us say at noon, I will give you a great part of the explanation—as I promised. But my promise will have to be revised. I told you this evening that I knew the name of the murderer, but that I could not explain all the circumstances. I now find the wheels shifting and my cosmos turned round. I can explain all the circumstances of the puzzle at the Villa Marbre; but (it is the best joke in the world) I do not know the name of the murderer . . . Shall we all go and take a bottle of champagne?"

13

Possibilities of a Picnic

Despite the fact that he was dead tired, and went to sleep as though he had been dropped down a chute, Curtis spent a troubled night. He dreamed incessantly. His dreams were not the too-scrambled fantasy always described in fiction; most of them were sensible enough, but faces kept moving in and out. Magda Toller figured in them, sometimes in strange ways. It was half-past ten when he awoke, a warm and dull morning on which little fresh air stirred.

He was having his rolls and coffee by the window when the 'phone rang to say that Ralph Douglas was on the way up. Ralph, on poking his head round the door, showed a subdued manner. He sat down and twirled his hat in his hands.

"Well, how goes it this morning?" asked Curtis.

"Feeling more cheerful?"

He felt that he had better not overdo the doctor's bedside manner, but Ralph did not notice.

"No," Ralph admitted.

"What's wrong?"

"I don't know." He spoke gloomily. "Oh, I suppose it's Magda, in a way. She—she's not like herself, exactly. Restless. Fidgety, or something. When we were out at dinner last night, and I was telling her a racing story, I could see she wasn't listening to a word I was saying; it was the best story I know, too. That sort of thing makes you uneasy. It's the ending of many a beautiful romance."

"Thinking about gratitude and her mother, probably."

"No, it isn't that. When Magda makes a decision, she sticks to it." He meditated this, turning it over as though a new aspect of it had struck him. Presently he began to grin. "Then there's something else. When I woke up this morning, I got a hell of a shock. Once when I was a kid, I woke up in the morning, or half-woke up, and a big snake stuck its head round the corner of the bedroom door and looked at me. I suppose it was actually a dream, though I could have sworn I saw that snake in real life. This morning's business was like it. I woke up, and there was somebody sitting in a chair at the foot of the bed. I don't know how he got in. Nobody seems to know. He was a little man with a round head and a moustache like Hitler—"

"Ho?" said Curtis. "So you've seen Jean-Baptiste? I know. Don't be surprised if he next jumps up out of the inkwell or the soup-tureen. He's beginning to haunt us."

Ralph's scowl gradually changed to amusement again.

"Anyhow, there he was, sitting as cool as you please and smoking one of my cigarettes. He said he was Auguste Dupin, criminologist expert of *L'Intelligence.* I asked how he'd like to be slung out of the window. Confound his cheek! But he's got such a frantic seriousness of manner, and talks so much the person he's interviewing can't get in a word edgeways, that you can't stay annoyed. I couldn't anyhow." Ralph scratched his chin. "Then, in some mysterious manner I can't remember, I found he was invited to have breakfast with me. Anyone who says the French can't eat our breakfasts has never seen J. B. Robinson sail into a plate of bacon and eggs. He wasn't eating; he was excavating. But that isn't the point."

Restlessly Ralph got up and stared out of the window. His big shoulders were slouched: he seemed to set them in order to approach the object he had in mind.

"What he really wanted was to find out what sort of theory Bencolin's got, and he seemed to think *I* could tell him. I pointed out that I was the last person in the world who would be likely to know. I said that, the last time I saw the gentleman, he gave me such a dirty look I expected him to produce handcuffs at any minute."

Curtis was conscious of a new apprehension. He put down his coffee-cup in some haste, but tried to make his voice casual. "Look here, I hope you didn't talk too much? You were non-committal, weren't you? Because if you weren't, you'll read all about it in this evening's paper. I don't quite understand the libel-laws in France, or even whether there is such a thing as a libel-law at all in matters of this kind; but what did you say?"

"Not very much," Ralph answered, after a reflection ending in relief. "As I say, the fellow talked so much himself that I didn't have a chance, but occasionally he'd stop and shoot out a question. It's odd, too, what he's got in his mind. He asked me what I thought of Mrs. Toller. I said she was an old bitch, of course—"

"*You said*—" roared Curtis, and stopped, appalled. "That'll do for a starter. It is technically known as slander. I must shut up Jean-Baptiste if I have to strangle him. Don't you know better by this time than to talk to the newspapers?"

"Well, the fellow said he was a criminological expert, not a reporter," grumbled the other. "Besides, they never get what you tell 'em right, anyway. Look at that business about the night-club. In any case I don't give a curse, because that happens to be exactly what she is, and if she wants to soak me for damages she can go ahead and try. I also said, in case you're interested, that all Mrs. Toller's crusades for Temperance and Anti-Gambling were probably masks for a trick to swindle honest people. She's a crook if I ever saw one."

"And Jean-Baptiste liked that, I suppose?"

"He loved it. But here's the odd thing. I actually did the old gal a service in spite of myself, and Jean-Baptiste can print that if he likes." Ralph bent forward, full of an incredulous excitement. "Do you know what he's got stuck in his mind? He thinks Mrs. Toller is the murderer."

"H'm."

"Believe it or not, he does. The idea is that Mrs. Toller is sweet on Bryce, and since she can't marry him herself (at least, not without tying up Bryce with clothesline, and giving him ether before the arrival of the clergyman), she's determined to hand Magda over to him."

"And is Miss Toller—" Curtis began slowly.

"Why Miss Toller? Why the formality?"

"All right, is Magda fond of Bryce?"

Ralph regarded him with a new and rather savage expression. "Oh, she likes him, I suppose, but perhaps not as much as Bryce thinks she does. So let's consider Mrs. Toller in the eyes of the energetic Jean-Baptiste Dupin, or whatever the devil his compound name is. His notion is that this whole thing is an elaborate frame-up directed solely against me, in order to discredit me in Magda's eyes and make such a public uproar that things will be broken off. I'm flattered. I'm very much flattered. What's more, I don't like Mrs. T., and nothing would please me better than to find out that she's a notorious killer who has been living a double life. But it's the ruddiest nonsense I've ever heard of in my life. Do you think anybody outside a lunatic asylum is going to commit *murder* just to discredit somebody? It's rubbish, when there are so many other ways. Do you agree?"

"I do," said Curtis. "It's what I've been thinking all along."

"And there's another thing," pursued Ralph, beginning to stride round the room. "Even aside from the fact that nobody is raving mad enough to do it, the person must have at least the sense to see it would have precisely the opposite effect on

Magda. If I'm supposed to have killed Rose, it's to get rid of her, to shut her mouth, so that Magda doesn't know. Now, that's exactly the thing that would make a girl say, 'You did it for me,' and collapse on your neck, and hold tighter to you than before. Follow me? Of course, if the purpose of the trick is to get me convicted of murder, then it's simple. In that case—"

He brought the edge of his palm down across the back of his neck, and made a gruesomely realistic ducking motion of his head. Then he looked grim.

"—in that case, my head's separated from my body, and I admit I'm in no condition to marry anybody. But it seems much too drastic. Besides, if the real murderer has gone to all this terrific trouble to compromise me, why the blazes has he neglected the one part of his scheme that was most necessary to him? I mean, making sure I couldn't prove where I was at the time of the murder? That alibi of mine pips the whole business. Why wasn't I lured away by a decoy telephone call, or something, the way they do it in the detective stories? Yet the murderer did nothing whatever about it. No, my lad. It won't work."

"Here, you're inspired this morning," said Curtis, staring at him. "What's up? Everybody seems to be inspired, except Bencolin. It's time he showed what they say he can do."

Ralph paused, looking a little shamefaced.

"Er—yes. But the thing has got us going, and you'll admit I'm pretty closely concerned with the outcome. No; my point to Jean-Baptiste was that nobody would plan all that *solely* to incriminate me; and that what we wanted was a list of Rose's past lovers, because there's where we should probably find the murderer. They say De Lautrec is now out of it as a serious suspect. Is that true?"

"Definitely out of it, it seems."

"Then I wonder what our friend Bencolin has up his sleeve? Look here, old boy." Ralph hesitated. "Here's what I've been so long about getting at. Jean-Baptiste says that Bencolin asked you to come to his office today for a little demonstration or outline of this business. Jean-Baptiste says he himself would give an ear to be at that conference, but that Bencolin misunderstands his motives and won't let him in. He says he frequently assumes disguises when digging up his facts, but if he tried to walk into the Sûreté Générale in a false beard they would only throw him out on the seat of the pants. Well, do you think *I* could possibly get in; or would they only throw me out?"

"It's worth trying," said Curtis. "Come along."

They were not thrown out. In the lobby of the hotel, as they descended, Curtis found (to his surprise) that Magda Toller had been waiting for them all the time. She did not look worried; she looked pleased and impish, and she wore one of the most elaborate white dresses he had seen.

"I've moved into a flat off the Rondpoint, but it's a dead secret yet," she explained, as they got into Ralph's car. "It's glorious; I feel like a *poule-de-luxe*."

Under a dull, warm sky they drove across the Pont Neuf to the Ile de la Cité, where trees masked the gray buildings. There was the usual crowd round the law-courts. Some distance further on, Curtis, who was on the alert for Jean-Baptiste Robinson, could have sworn he saw

Robinson talking to a woman who looked like Hortense Frey. But he was too late. When he tried to catch up, Robinson gave one look and darted away, clutching his bowler hat to his head, his little legs going like a wheel. Curtis was left jostling people, swearing, and feeling certain the crime-expert must be up to some devilment. It was possible that Bencolin might be able to do something about this. They entered the building in the Quai des Orfèvres by a low door, and an agent took them up through a dusky, rambling building (past the door of a great laboratory, which for no apparent reason made them all stop talking) to a room on the top floor. The place had a faint humming noise, and was filled with an even fainter smell like disinfectant. In the top-floor room, Bencolin sat at a desk across from a strongly built girl with dyed blonde hair. The girl was weeping quietly.

"Come in," Bencolin said, getting up from behind his desk. "Yes, you are all very welcome. I must apologize for the state of this room. It is not customarily used; but then I don't know where I stand in this affair. M. Brille, the chief of the Sûreté, is at present out of town; the examining magistrate is now questioning Mrs. Toller and Mr. Stanfield," he jerked his thumb, "down along the line; and I stand between the two departments, as a sort of buffer. But there seems to be a general wish that I should take charge. Giraud!—some chairs. Ah, I forgot. This is Mlle. Annette Fauvel, formerly Mme. Klonec's maid, who is just finishing her deposition."

The sturdily built blonde, whose sobs were less like weeping than like a crooning singer, drew herself up with an effect of massiveness and tried to adjust reddened eyelids. She was well dressed, and spoke with the precise intonation called "Comédie Française": which is as much of a jest in France, and for the same reason, as the thicker forms of accent are in England.

"Monsieur," she intoned, evidently to defend her position before the newcomers, "I have told you all I can. I do not know of what you suspect me. I can produce a character, I assure you, from employers far more distinguished than Mme. Klonec. For some reason you appear to suspect me of having designs on madame's jewellery." She clapped a very small lace handkerchief to her nose, and got up. "By this time you know, or should know, that this morning madame's lawyer opened the safe in her apartment, and not so much as a rhinestone had been disturbed. There."

Bencolin reassured her.

"But just before you go, mademoiselle, let me make certain you know what you have testified. I repeat, then, a part of it. On Saturday you went for a picnic with Mme. Klonec and M. De Lautrec."

The large blonde heaved out an assent.

"You left her apartment at ten-thirty in the morning, the three of you driving in M. De Lautrec's car. You drove to Auteuil, where M. De Lautrec engaged a boat for the river. During this time M. De Lautrec was not out of madame's sight, or out of yours. Is that correct?"

"Perfectly."

"From that time onward you were on the river between Auteuil and Billancourt. You followed in another boat, with a hired boatman. During that time Mme. Klonec and M. De Lautrec did not leave the river—"

"Not exactly, monsieur. Once, for two hours or so, they put the boat in among some willows at the foot of a hill to eat their lunch, and lie and talk; but they did not leave the river because they did not leave the boat. I could see them."

"Still, if the boatman were your 'flirt,' are you certain that you would have—?"

"Monsieur!" shouted Annette, outraged.

"I wished to make sure," said Bencolin. "Very well. You returned to the city with them at about dark; and, since it was your evening off, you asked to be dropped off at the Métro station by the Ecole Militaire. So far as you know, they then went home. Is that correct? Thank you, and good day. No, that is the lavatory door, mademoiselle; this way out. So."

He closed the door after her, but not before she had turned a good, hard, unwinking glance at Douglas, who stirred uncomfortably. Then Bencolin sat down and contemplated his three guests. In the small room he looked enormous. Today he seemed to have a length of chin, a twirl of ragged eyebrow, which gave him angles of mockery and a touch of grim caricature that the boulevards knew well. Curtis again experienced the feeling he had known yesterday at the Villa Marbre, of the completely foreign mixed with the sinister.

"So you wish to know about champagne-bottles?" he began, amiably enough. "Yes, Mr. Douglas, I know about Robinson's visit to you this morning. You must be well versed in the facts. Whatever else Jean-Baptiste told you, I presume he did tell you about the champagne-bottle and the .22 automatic. Also, I should think Miss Toller has heard of them. So we can begin at scratch.

Will you smoke?" Bencolin held out a box of cigarettes. "In the luggage of Pierre Voisin, whom we caught and executed two months ago, there were a thousand Turkish and Virginia cigarettes; and they have been supplying the chief's office ever since. No, don't draw back; they are perfectly good; Pierre was a throat-cutter, not a poisoner. Turkish this side, Virginia that."

"*I'll* have one of the things," said Magda, with an expression which matched his own. "They tell me (let's face it) that the automatic you found at the villa yesterday is supposed to belong to my mother."

"You saw it yesterday, Miss Toller, as well as Mr. Stanfield. Didn't you recognize it?"

"No, and that's just the trouble. How on earth can George, or anyone else, recognize a particular gun simply by looking at it? They all look alike; or at least they do to me."

"Mr. Stanfield's eye is trained," replied Bencolin, with a judicial air. "The point had occurred to me. Still, you don't deny that your mother owns such a pistol; you knew that?"

"Oh, everybody knows that. But what I mean is—well, I mean this awful nonsense about her— you know what I mean. It's so silly that I can't even get mad over it. I start to giggle every time I think of it."

"It is Robinson's theory. Not mine."

"What is your theory?" Ralph asked quietly.

Bencolin opened the drawer of his desk and drew out a large buff container. He had lighted a cigarette which he put down to smoulder on the edge of the desk; but he did not pick up the container.

"As you came in here," he said, "you noticed our laboratory. Do not get excited. It is not ultra-mysterious, or even ultra-modern. Aside from toxicology, it is mainly based on the camera and the microscope: or, in a combination of the two for the courts, the photo-micrograph: a painful concentration on things too small to be seen by the naked eye. I think (though Mabusse must correct me on this point) that the process of photographing through a microscope was first used in the Eustachy case over fifty years ago. Now, my business is to direct the director of the laboratory; to decide who the criminal might have been, what the criminal might have done; and then to tell him where he might find indications of it for a jury.

"Let us begin the story of Rose Klonec's murder, starting out at a little more than a quarter past eleven on Saturday night when she arrived at the Villa Marbre. Since Hortense Frey is our only witness to the happenings there, we must accept her story unless our utmost examination can find a flaw in it. So far, Hortense stands the test remarkably well.

"We have heard from Hortense how Rose Klonec arrived at the villa in a sulky mood and flaming temper. Naturally—since she had just been compelled to part with some valuable jewellrey to M. De Lautrec. That fits. We have heard how she was disappointed and angry that Mr. Douglas was not there to meet her. That fits, very well. To get to this meeting, for which she had been eager all day, she has suffered embarrassments and nervous shocks, and she has parted with a good round sum to M. De Lautrec. Yet *he*,

Ralph Douglas, is not there: and he has not even left any excuses.

"This is her state of mind at eleven-fifteen. She bathes; she is dressed and bedecked; the time crawls on to midnight; and still he is not there. We have Hortense's statement that by this time madame was dangerously near an outburst. She orders her half-bottle of champagne, and sends the maid to bed. The champagne is left, to reach the proper degree of chill, in a cooler on the table of the sitting-room. From the sitting-room, Hortense goes out by a door into the hallway, which is then unlocked.

"If the time passed slowly before, how is it for madame now? Remember, she has no watch. And still he is not there.

"When I first looked at those rooms yesterday, my belief was this: At some time between twelve-fifteen and one o'clock, madame made a decision. She is going to teach her lover a stinging lesson! She will not rush away to Paris: no, Rose Klonec is a careful soul who cannot afford to miss the patronage of Ralph Douglas, and in any case such a gesture is not to her taste. She knows a better gesture, a more effective one. She will lock every door by which he can get into the suite. She will prepare for bed. She will even take a large dose of sleeping-tablets so that, no matter how much trouble there may be during the night, she will sleep peacefully; she will neither waken nor weaken. Then she will take her champagne nightcap, and turn in. When the sluggard at last gets there, let him try to get in. He needs to be taught a lesson, and, by the horns of passion, he shall have it. I can see that red-haired charmer sneer."

During this time Bencolin had been speaking with a solemnity which Curtis much suspected, because it was too much like his 'oratorical' style; and now Curtis saw a gleam of amusement in his eye. His mood shifted for a moment. He nodded. He said:

"I see. You think I am talking too much like Jean-Baptiste Robinson, eh? Well, let us see if we can prove it.

"Take the first point, the locking of the doors. Here you will say I land on my ear before I have jumped the first hurdle. The door from the sitting-room into the hall was locked: true. The door from the dressing-room into the hall was also locked: true. But the door from the bedroom into the hall, by which you who discovered the body entered on Sunday morning, you found unlocked —though the key was in the door on the inside.

"When you three had left the villa yesterday, and Mabusse and I got down to work, I considered this key. It was an ordinary sort of key, powdered with a light coating of incipient rust like most keys, and dusty from its long presence in the lock. Under Mabusse's pocket lens, the flange of the key at the tip of it showed some odd horizontal scratchings like a band round the tip, for this rust is a good surface; but at the moment the marks were too faint. I looked round the bedroom, and one of the first things I saw was a pair of pliers.

"Most pliers, as you know, have inside their jaws a horizontal series of tiny indentations like ribs, so that the jaws might get a better grip on a smooth surface. I thought it might be as well to have photo-micrographs of the key and the pliers side by side."

From the container he took out a big sheet of photographic paper on which stood up a great black shape which was vaguely distinguishable as the flange of a key; but it was spotted in such fashion that the only distinct markings were five horizontal and parallel bands in white. Three of them were shaky and blurred; two were comparatively sharp.

"It is magnified only five times," said Bencolin, "but these markings are fresh, and photograph well. On these next sheets we have the pliers, taken apart and separately photographed, and finally the other side of the key. In the distinct markings, the ridges in the jaws of the pliers exactly correspond to the scratches on the end of the key. Measure them with callipers, and you will find not a millimeter of difference.

"Now here is something definite. Rose Klonec *has* locked that door on the inside. But someone outside the door—we begin to see the man in the brown raincoat again—has taken a pair of pliers, has gripped the end of the key from the other side of the keyhole, and has turned the key so that he can open the door."

Bencolin put aside the photographs.

"That is a fact worth storing away in the mind while we go on. It is not only a key to the locked doors; it is also a key to the whole mystery. You understand what I mean?"

14

The Three Locked Doors

Nobody spoke. Bencolin picked up the cigarette he had lighted, which was smouldering nearly against the edge of the desk, and put it in an ashtray.

"Next, we have the point that, after locking the doors, madame proceeded to undress herself and prepare for bed. I conjecture, since she intended to go directly to bed, that her first gesture was to swallow three tablets of the chloral hydrate in a glass of water in the bathroom—so that the chloral might have time to make her drowsy, you understand, while she undressed. She then returned to the dressing-room, leaving her fingerprints on the glass in the bathroom.

"Now we look at the evidence for her decision to go to bed. There is already good presumptive

203

evidence of it in the fact that her clothes are hung up and folded in a way peculiar to herself. But that is not all. You all looked at her dead face, and you saw that she wore no cosmetics, despite the array set out on her dressing-table. The only thing showing as used on her dressing-table was an open jar of cold cream, vanishing cream, with the lid lying beside it.

"Being in my younger days what Mr. Robinson elegantly calls, 'A bachelor of sporting habits,' I could draw certain inferences. I ask Miss Toller to confirm them now. That is the sort of cream which women, particularly women in the middle thirties, smear on their faces before going to bed as an aid to beauty next morning. But tell me, Miss Toller: if you expected to meet a lover that night, particularly one you had not seen for nearly a year and were anxious to impress, would you remove the cosmetics and bedaub yourself with the cream?"

Magda shook her head. "I most certainly would not! But—"

"Yes?" prompted Bencolin quickly.

"It probably isn't anything. I—that is, I was only thinking—"

"Nevertheless, let us hear it."

"Well, I was only wondering why she didn't put the lid back on the jar after she'd finished with it. That stuff cakes and hardens quickly if you leave the lid off; and if it's exposed too long it becomes no good at all. Putting it back is an automatic gesture, and you say she was a tidy soul."

"Good!" said Bencolin, still with a twinkle in his eye. "We will return to that in a moment, for there is another bit of evidence in connection with it. So Rose Klonec undresses, puts on her nightgown, and sits down at the dressing-table. Here we touch on the hilarious business of the untouched negligée. You notice that before using the cold cream she puts on her slippers; but she does not put on her negligée. Help us again: why not?"

"Of course she wouldn't," Magda told him, rather testily. "If you mean that heavy fancy lace one that was hanging up in the wardrobe, she wouldn't want to take the chance of smearing it up with her hands all over cream."

Bencolin sat back in his chair.

"Very well. We now have her sitting in front of the dressing-table, in her nightgown and slippers, either applying or preparing to apply the cold cream. She is not yet quite ready for bed, because she has not yet closed the sitting-room windows giving on the balcony and the pleasant night— which she ultimately means to do, for (remember) there is an outside staircase to that balcony, and locked doors will mean nothing if her laggard lover can simply walk up through a window. At this point she remembers the nightcap half-bottle of champagne, still standing in its cooler in the sitting-room. She goes and fetches it. Up to this time it has not been touched.

"Ah, say you, but there's a Papa Dupin jumping-at-conclusions! Why are you so sure of that? How do you know she hadn't opened it, and been nibbling at it, ever since Hortense left at a quarter past twelve? Well, even on our examination of the rooms so much was at least indicated. You saw on the right-hand side of the rosewood dressing-table a round scar, the scar of a half-bottle, staining the wood. That sharply defined mark had been made by alcohol, not water. A great deal of creamy stuff had poured down the sides of the bottle to form it, as Mabusse discovered; and it was an indication that the bottle had been opened there on the dressing-table, where Rose Klonec poured out a glass for herself as she sat down to finish her toilette.

"And then she was interrupted."

"Interrupted?" repeated Ralph sharply.

"By the entrance of someone. Concentrate your attention on that dressing-table, for everything centers round it. Don't you see how the tempo changes, the scene is fixed in mid-air, the woman's traceable movements come to an abrupt stop? She is interrupted in putting cold cream on her face—for she has not put the lid back on the jar. She is interrupted after opening a creaming champagne-bottle—for she, the tidy soul, does not make a move to clean up the spilled mess on an expensive rosewood dressing-table. The next day her slippers are found unused under the dressing-table—though, as has been pointed out, she would not walk about on a marble floor in her bare feet. The big windows in the sitting-room are not locked or shuttered—though she would have barred that entrance, too, against the tardy arrival of a lover who had angered her. There by the dressing-table everything suddenly *halts*. If she did not walk away from the dressing-table in her slippers, how did she leave it? And what did she do in the flash of that stopped interval?

"There is only one indication as to what she might have done. Round the handle of a stiletto belonging to her we found a fine, sharp set of her fingerprints, showing that she had gripped the handle tightly. I think I can tell you what happened. As she stood before the dressing-table, she saw or heard something that struck her with terror. As the only means of protection she had, she reached out and snatched up the stiletto, which was lying in the dressing-table drawer under her hand."

As Bencolin made the appropriate gesture, everyone in the room stirred a little. It was his first sign of showmanship, and Curtis did not like it. During the pause Ralph Douglas spoke.

"I know," said Ralph, who was sitting on the edge of his chair. "She heard the murderer coming up through the house, of course. He had come in downstairs, and sharpened his razor, and now he was coming up. Those halls at the villa are also bare marble; and he must have made a lot of noise carrying or pushing a loaded serving-table of dishes—"

"No," said Bencolin.

"That will not do," he continued reflectively, in his slow and heavy voice. "I admit that the halls are of bare marble, and that it would be next to impossible to carry a table piled high with articles expressly designed to rattle, without making a noise. Above all, even if our brown-coated figure has been prepared for all the locked doors, I defy him or anyone else to open a door with a pair of pliers without difficulty, and without a noise audible in the suite. See those blurred marks where the pliers have slipped! But there is where we flounder. Why should hearing anything of that sort strike Rose Klonec with alarm? Why should it make her snatch up a weapon, and almost upset a bottle of champagne which stains the table? After all, it was only what she expected to hear. She might feel grim satisfaction, a sense of pleasure in her determination. But that sudden stoppage, so that she is spirited away from the dressing-table without her slippers? Remember, she could not see anything. For all she knows, it is only Hortense. Let me emphasize that she could not see anything: the doors were locked, the bedroom windows were locked and curtained, the dressing-room windows were locked and shuttered. In fact, there was only one direction from which anyone could have approached her *suddenly*."

Curtis sat up. "I see," he muttered. "The open windows giving on the balcony in the sitting-room."

"Yes. And now we see it creeping closer as it crept up on Rose Klonec. You will have noticed that the dressing-table is so placed that its mirror faces sideways towards the door of the sitting-room. I observed yesterday, when I looked into the glass, that I could see you reflected from where you stood in the door of the sitting-room. Remembering still that we are only theorizing, I ask you to imagine that gilt shell of a dressing-room, with its black-and-white marble floor, and in both rooms the crystal chandeliers illuminated. Someone has come up the outside stairs to the balcony. Someone has walked across the sitting-room, very softly. But more than softness of foot is necessary. Rose Klonec, putting down her bottle and glass, looks up; and sees another face reflected beside her own. Someone is standing in the doorway, carrying an automatic pistol—a firearm, the only weapon in the world, we have heard from Mr. Stanfield, that Rose Klonec feared."

"The man in the brown—" began Ralph, but Bencolin held up his hand and stopped him.

"No," said Bencolin again. "Cigarette, anyone?"

"Look here, this is cat-and-mouse," Curtis interposed quietly. "Do you enjoy it?"

"It is merely an interval for reflection. Take it. Don't fall into the abysmal error (as I did yesterday) of believing that the person who came up by the balcony, gun in hand, was the man in the brown raincoat and black hat. It is what makes the mirror blur and all the lines grow crooked. It caused a great part of my trouble. For my situation was this: I had to assume—and I still have to assume, since it is true—that Rose Klonec was attacked immediately after that figure of X stepped through the window with his gun. She was in some fashion dragged into the bathroom, and that cruel gash was made across her arm with the stiletto, so that she should bleed to death.

"It was only natural to think that the brown-coated man might have crept up by the balcony and the windows. Why not? If he went round to the back of the house, the driveway would take him directly under that balcony with all its open windows. He could creep up there even if he only wished to look and reconnoiter. Very well; he goes up—and he kills her, as I have indicated.

"But *afterwards*, if we try to swallow this theory, his behavior becomes the wildest farrago of nonsense I have ever encountered.

"He has killed her with the stiletto. Afterwards, leaving all the hall-doors of the suite locked on the inside, he descends by the balcony staircase. He goes to the rear of the house, he enters by the rear door, and he rouses Hortense. He lets Hortense obviously see him sharpening a razor—which he does not mean to use on Rose Klonec, because he has already killed her with the stiletto. Here again we stumble over the rich profusion of weapons. This man came to the villa provided with both an automatic pistol and a razor: and he used neither. Instead of cutting her arm with one stroke of a razor, he chose the clumsy and uncertain method of digging at it with the stiletto. Then he goes downstairs and sharpens the razor.

"If so far his behavior has been eccentric, it now becomes dancing mad. To the filled serving-table, which Hortense has set out, he adds still another big bottle of champagne. He carries this upstairs. Instead of opening the door of the bedroom when he was in that room before, he now proceeds to fool about with a pair of pliers to open it from outside. He—well, I don't need to go on. You see the incongruities pile up one after another.

"And then I woke up. I woke up because it became necessary to ask myself the question: Unless this man is ten times madder than a March hare, what do these actions denote? It was not very difficult.

"*There were two people concerned in the crime, each working independently of the other.* The man in the brown raincoat was one, X was the other. The first man intended to kill Rose, his weapon to be the razor, and he had set all this elaborate little trap for her. Just how he planned to work that trap you will see for yourselves in a moment; but I can assure you that, properly understood, his behavior was anything but insane.

210

The trouble was that X walked straight into the middle of his plan.

"While the brown-coated man was only preparing, X was acting. It was X, and X alone, who had the pistol. X came up by the balcony—probably at or before one o'clock. Then occurred the attack on Rose Klonec; the whole wild business was over, and the woman was dead, before our brown-coated man arrived at the villa. Now a great deal of what has seemed his weird behavior will gradually become clear to you. He was going through with the performance, not knowing his intended victim was already dead. I venture to think it gave him the nastiest shock of his life to find that Rose Klonec—whom he merely supposed to be lying in bed asleep, peacefully, with her night-gown on and the covers drawn up—was actually dead."

Bencolin paused.

"But it is X we are discussing. You know what X did—"

Magda Toller interrupted him. "What *who* did?" she cried, and her own gesture knocked her handbag off her lap. "They're right; this is cat-and-mouse. You can't do it. It's—it's not fair. You can't do it. Who is this X? If you know, can't you tell us? Who did all these things, and cut her artery open?"

Bencolin leaned his elbows on the desk. He spoke very mildly.

"You did, Miss Toller," he said.

15

The Alchemist's Bottle

We are not so quick to understand as we think; we hear only what we may reasonably expect the other person to say; and, when something of this sort occurs, the brain turns like a gramophone-record before the needle takes hold. Or so it was with Curtis, although he realized it perhaps a second before Ralph Douglas.

He turned to look at Magda. She was sitting back in her chair, her shoulders a little lowered and hunched as she pressed them there. Her head was also a little lowered. Her black bobbed hair hung forward nearly to her cheeks. And all the while she was looking up at Bencolin from under the brim of a tilted white hat, with that same stealthy quality Curtis had seen just once yesterday at the Villa Marbre. Then the dimples showed in her cheeks as she began to smile.

"How utterly ridiculous," she said.

If he had not heard her voice at that moment, Curtis would have laughed. But he heard her voice, and he knew Bencolin was right. There was not time to think of anything else.

"Oh, my *God*," whispered Magda, and her eyes brimmed over.

There was no explosion of any kind from anyone, since even Ralph did not seem to understand what was going on. He expressed himself first in a series of sputters like disjointed profanity which ended in, 'Don't talk rot,' spoken with such hollow and ghostly incredulity that it sounded like a distant wind. The first thing that impressed him was that Magda was shivering. Then he, too, woke up.

"Now, look here!" he protested. "This is going too far. This is a joke, and a ruddy rotten joke at that. If I thought for one minute you did mean it, I'd—I don't know—I'd—"

Bencolin had not moved. He was sitting with his elbow against his table, his chin on his fist, looking quietly at Magda. Now he roused himself at Ralph's roar, and frowned.

"Kindly lower your voice," he said. "Remember where you are; you are in a police station. Some of my colleagues do not regard murder with the same tolerant eye as I do. Oblige me by going over and locking the door. I don't necessarily want to keep you in; but I do want to keep the others out while we decide what is to be done about this."

Magda was trembling so quietly and horribly that Curtis wondered what *he* could do about it.

214

He must get her out of this somehow; and, though pitting himself against Bencolin was likely to prove a futile business, he meant to have a shot at it. Bencolin had taken a tumbler and a bottle of cognac from his desk. He spilled several fingers of the spirit into the glass; after looking at her, he put in still more; then he held it out to her without a word.

"You know," Curtis said to Bencolin, "I've been wondering whether you yourself believe in this nonsense any more than the rest of us. Miss Toller," he said, now turning to the girl, "having an accusation like that pitched against you in the midst of all these police trappings is apt to upset anybody. If I were you I wouldn't say anything, or it may be misunderstood."

"Oh, what's the good?" demanded Magda fretfully. She added with great intensity: "In my effort to break away from restrictions, I certainly took a most marvellous first step, didn't I?"

"My God, Mag, you didn't!" said Ralph.

"I did, though. And you ought to see your face at this minute. I never saw anything so funny in my life. Boo!" Making an extraordinary face, she raised her fingers like claws and wiggled them in the air. Her volubility was nearly on the edge of hysteria. "You're sitting beside a self-confessed murderess. Don't you get gooseflesh? Don't you want to run away? Why don't you run away?"

"Take it easy," Ralph told her with dignity, though he looked apprehensively at the door to make sure it was locked. "Nobody's going to desert you. The only thing is—well, this is a devil of a business to have sprung on you all of a sudden, isn't it? I can't get used to the idea that somebody won't say, 'Now we've all had a good laugh, let's forget this and get on to real business.' If anybody can say that, for the love of Mike speak up. Murder! The worst—what I mean is—"

"Why should you be so shocked when she tells you, wrongly," Curtis's caution had nearly slipped in his bitterness, "tells you wrongly, that she did this to Rose Klonec because she loved you? Was she so shocked when she heard you were accused of doing the same thing because of her?"

"No. But then she had no reason to be," said Ralph. "She knew it wasn't true."

The thrust was so unexpected and so deep that Curtis blinked. Ralph was infernally right, no doubt: the sanctity of the law must be preserved, or no clichés could be read or sung again; but in this case all his fighting instincts rose up against it. The three words, "I have killed," altered astonishingly little. In his state of bedevilment, seeking for a way out, he glanced at Bencolin. Bencolin had returned to his chair, and was watching matters with the same look of critical interest.

"I didn't do it because of Ralph," Magda said in a rapid burst, over the rim of the glass. "At least, it wasn't more than a tenth that. I don't know why I did it. I don't. Maybe because my father was hanged by the neck, and it's bound to come out in you. I didn't *mean* to do it, even, when I went out to that villa to see whether Ralph was really carrying on with her as mother said...But I saw her standing there in that dressing-room, with her great, white, cold face; drunk as Davy's sow; with the cold cream on her hands; and I thought of all the things she'd been able to get away with, Lord knows why, when I couldn't see how she was able to get away with anything. Then she came at me with that stiletto, and—"

Magda could not finish the brandy. She put down the glass on the desk.

"Ever since then I've been trying to imagine what came over me. It was the most horrible idea that ever came into my head, because I didn't even think of shooting her with that gun in my hand. But she had drained the blood out of everyone she'd ever met. I thought she ought to have the blood drained out of her for a change. I'm not saying anything in my own defense, except that I found I couldn't go through with it. Once she was hanging over that bath, I couldn't go through with it. All of a sudden I got scared and sick; and I grabbed the towel and tried to stop the blood, because I meant to revive her and show I didn't mean it. But there wasn't as much blood in her as you men seemed to think. I was too late. Just when the brainstorm had passed off me, I saw she was dead." She put her fists up against her eyes. "All I want to know is, how on earth did you know I had done it? I was horribly careful. I didn't run away. I had even handled that dagger in a towel, and I wiped everything where I might have left those fingerprints they talk about. Only, and this is what is so funny, I took care of all the little things; and I walked right out of there and forgot that automatic, and left it lying bang in the middle of the floor."

She began to laugh.

"Look at me!" said Bencolin sharply. He caught her scared eye, and held it; she could not look away, and not a person in the room moved. "This

217

is someone else's case, you understand? It is not yours. You are looking at it from the outside. I am going to tell you exactly what happened, and why it happened, and in the meantime you will not have another brainstorm.

"You left traces, Miss Toller. It is no credit to me that they were found. You shall hear about them to keep you away from hysterics." His voice had grown mild again. "These traces were apparent from the briefest examination of the suite yesterday. Rose Klonec had been dragged from the dressing-room into the bathroom: a laborious process, the discarded slippers being left under the dressing table. She was not actually put into the sunken bath, but she was dragged beside it and left there with her right arm hanging over the edge.

"So much, of course, was clear from the indications. In the soiled linen hamper of the bathroom Durrand found three towels. Two were still damp, but unstained; the third was quite dry, but had in one place small traces of fresh blood. But if a person is put into a filled bath, when the blood flows from a severed artery to dye the water—or even lies in an empty tub with water flowing past —then the body will be stained with diluted blood when it is removed from the bath. No such stains were on the body of Rose Klonec. On the other hand, she had not been dried off: for the two damp towels were not in any way stained, and the fresh-stained towel was bone-dry.

"There had been, in fact, another use for that stained towel. Mabusse told you all what it was yesterday. To avoid fingerprints, the murderer had handled the stiletto in that towel, and had gripped it half-way down the triangular blade. There were no prints; but on the side of the blade, which is nowhere more than half an inch wide, someone had brushed a part of the hand. A similar indication from the palm was on the edge of the bath, where someone had leaned. Someone, after wiping the automatic pistol, had left part of another handprint on the back of the grip. All of the marks were very small, the largest being not much more than half-an-inch in any direction, and might reasonably have been considered harmless. They are not. They are dangerous."

Ralph interposed huskily. "That won't do. There's nothing identifiable about the hand; I read that. It hasn't got distinctive markings like the fingers—"

"The hand has pores. Don't look at me, any of you. It is nothing new. It is a discovery of Dr. Locard,* and was used as long ago as the trial of Simonin at Lyons in 1912. I am only the layman looker-on; it is Mabusse who does the work. You know, however, that under the microscope the sweat-pores of the hand are as distinctly visible, and set far apart, as holes made by so many pins? A photo-micrograph shows them in that fashion. Impressions can be identified by counting the number of pores in any given area. Just as the ridges on the fingers vary, so the number of pores varies with each individual. Here, for instance," he opened the container, "we have four photographs in each of which is marked out the same

*Dr. Edward Locard, Director of the Police Laboratory at Lyons. *L'Enquete Criminelle et les méthodes scientifiques*, Edmond Locard, Paris, 1929.

given area. The ridge-markings are dead white, separated by black lines, and on the white lines each pore shows black the size of a pin-head. In addition to some distinctive ridge-markings, each has eight hundred and four points of agreement."

"But whose—?"

"They are yours, Miss Toller," said Bencolin. "The first three are from the stiletto, the edge of the bath, and the automatic; the fourth comes from the handle on the door of your car.

"Your behavior at the Villa Marbre yesterday was such as to rouse our curiosity, and at least to look for possible confirmation when the first three marks were discovered. Yesterday at noon you appeared at the villa with startling unexpectedness. I saw you come in. You drove in, you came hurrying round the side of the villa—and you saw Mr. Douglas walk out of the back door. There has seldom been anyone more astonished than you were when you saw him. You had to ask twice whether you were seeing correctly. When he asked you what *you* were doing in that locality at noon on Sunday, you made the hasty reply that someone had telephoned you that morning, to say that Ralph Douglas was in trouble at the Villa Marbre. If that were true, why should you start with surprise when you saw him there? It was not necessarily significant, but it was worth following up. Even if the identification of the prints had not been conclusive, it was worth asking the clerk at the Hotel Crillon whether any telephone calls had come to your suite on Sunday before one o'clock. There had been only one call, from Mr. Stanfield to your mother; and therefore you could have received no such message.

"With you as the person who had used the stiletto, the main outline of the business was easy to follow. Deceptively easy. You were drawn into it through the fact that Hortense Frey took to George Stanfield for translation a letter purporting to come from Ralph Douglas. This letter said that the old affair with Rose Klonec was being picked up again. Stanfield took the news to Mrs. Toller. He chose a time when you were out, having dinner with Mr. Douglas. We heard, from the clerk at the Crillon, that Stanfield came to the hotel at eight o'clock on Saturday evening. He left at a quarter to nine, in such a state of agitation that he could not hold his hat. You returned at half-past ten, and met your mother.

"I pass over any emotional states. We have had enough of that. But I think what most rose in you was that you had to know, you had to see for yourself whether this was true. When everyone was in bed, it would have been easy for you to have slipped out of the hotel unseen by your mother or by anyone else: we know that the suite has a private lift. You had your car. You took the automatic from the table in the drawing-room. Mr. Stanfield's story that he had taken this pistol to his office on Friday was so obvious a lie that we scarcely needed pay attention to it, especially since we knew your marks were already on the pistol. The interesting thing was why he should have told such a story. It may be—as you doubtless think—that your mother suspected or knew what you had done, and therefore contrived this story to throw suspicion away from you. It is not impossible; but I don't believe it. I think there was another reason.

"In any event, you drove to the villa and parked your car some distance away. It was easy to tell where any occupants of the villa might be, for there were lights blazing from a line of open windows over the balcony. You went up. What happened then was bound to happen. At the end of it you did one thing more, which was the only thing you could do: you put a dead woman to bed."

Magda spoke with calmness.

"You had better hurry up," she said. "The drug is wearing off, and I shall be making a most awful fool of myself in a minute. No, Ralph, don't come near me; I'm a murderer, remember.—Anyhow, it's convenient we're already in the police-station. Where do you take me now? What are you going to do?"

Bencolin sat back. The atmosphere of the room subtly altered: it was as though some of the life, some of the vitality, had washed out of him, and left him a mild elderly gentleman with a taste for pedantic speech.

"Nothing," he said.

"Nothing?" repeated Magda stupidly. Ralph got up and took two steps towards his desk.

"Last night,'" he went on in the same reflective tone, "I was in no mood to dance jigs. I knew by plain evidence who must be the murderer. And at the same time I did not believe it . . . Miss Toller, I am too old a crow to preach sermons, even if I felt any taste for them. There is not a real criminal instinct in you. You are a product of Mrs. Benedict Toller's school for ladies; and, if I did not dislike Mrs. Toller so much, I might like you less than I do. How many times you have been reminded of your tainted heritage I should not like to guess. It is not surprising that you broke out violently. You have had a shock that will do you no harm, and now you had better know the truth. It is no wonder you tried without success to repair the damage. It is no wonder you could not quite credit your own guilt…The fact is, you did not kill Rose Klonec."

There was a silence of such bursting quality that to Richard Curtis even images in the room seemed blurred. He did not look at Ralph or Magda, though he heard her draw in her breath with a sound such as a woman makes in sleep. For in Curtis's mind the puzzle was fitting itself together, and coming just to the edge of clearness.

"I did not believe it yesterday, though I could do nothing until the report came from the medical bureau," Bencolin said. "In the bathroom of that villa there was an amazing situation. The victim had not been put into the bath, but lay beside it with her arm hanging over. The (apparent) murderer bent over her with a stiletto swathed in a towel, the murderer's hand gripping the blade half-way down. An artery had been severed with a long wound: an artery, from which blood not only flows, but *spurts*. Yet on that towel next to the long wound there was only one small stain of blood."

He paused and looked at Magda.

"Now tell me. No, you must brace up! That's better. A little while ago you told us that, when you went into the dressing-room and faced Rose Klonec, she was 'drunk as Davy's sow.' Why did you think that?"

"Well—because she was. Or at least that's what

223

I thought. She was standing there by that dressing-table with her great ugly gooseberry eyes looking all queer; and she'd been opening another bottle of champagne and gulping the stuff out of a glass, so as not to waste a drop of it when it started to fizz. When she tried to take a cut at me with that stiletto, she lurched round and went over as drunk as I ever saw anybody. There was a smell, too, that made me half sick—"

Magda stopped abruptly. It was Curtis who spoke.

"I think I've got it," he said.

"Well?"

"It's the first solution," said Curtis, "and the real solution. It's that damned champagne-bottle again. Listen! There really was a sleeping-drug in it after all: say a big dose of chloral hydrate. The real murderer had prepared it in advance, and got it palmed off on her since it was the only half-bottle of Roederer in the house, so that she should be asleep when he got there. She had to be asleep when he got there: it was the man impersonating Ralph. *But* what he didn't know was that Rose Klonec had already swallowed three twenty-grain tablets of chloral hydrate, of her own accord, before she took the champagne.

"That's sixty grains she takes herself. There must have been much more than that in the champagne-bottle, to ensure sleep: but say it was no more than sixty grains. To save the champagne when it spurts, Rose Klonec gulped down a couple of glasses in a row. On top of the original sixty grains, she had then swallowed sixty more—or easily enough to kill her. No wonder she went down in a heap! No wonder there was such a small amount of blood when her arm was cut! She was killed by an overdose of chloral hydrate, and dead before the stiletto was used at all."

The stimulus of his inspiration carried him forward to the desk, where he was leaning across and poking his finger at Bencolin with each word. Wrinkles of what might have been amusement deepened round the other's eyes.

"No," he said.

"But it's got to be! There's no other—"

"You see, you have touched on one of the major problems of the case. How was she so *instantly* overcome, so that she could be attacked without a struggle? I will lead you through the maze, since I groped through it so confoundedly myself. Even supposing that she had previously taken three tablets of her own accord, there is no sedative drug powerful enough to strike like a pistol or a knife. Even supposing she had gulped down three hundred grains from a champagne-bottle, it would have been minutes before the full symptoms came on, still longer before she was helpless, and at least an hour before she was dead. It is impossible."

"Then—you mean to say it was some swift poison like cyanide? Look here, you agree she was dead before her arm was cut? Then it must have been that, although you swore no poison was put into the bottle."

Bencolin shook his head. "No, for in that case the puzzle grows worse. Whatever was put into that bottle, it was put there by the man in the brown raincoat and the black hat. But if we imagine cyanide, or anything designed to kill the woman, his subsequent behavior again becomes dancing mad. What about his sharpening of razors, his strange tricks with pliers and serving-tables?"

"All the same, something killed her. I don't suppose it was witchcraft?"

"No," said Bencolin. "She was killed by what you call the innate perverseness of all human events, before the man in the brown raincoat came to complete one of the most unpleasant and ugly murder-plots in my experience."

Reaching down to pull out the lower drawer of his desk, he produced an empty half-bottle of Roederer champagne.

"Jean-Baptiste Robinson was illuminating last night. He was particularly illuminating because he told an untruth. You see that someone has cut out and replaced the bottom of this bottle, in order to put something into the contents. Jean-Baptiste is under the impression that, in the great days of the liquor traffic in America, the bootlegger cut his liquor and resealed the bottle by the application of intense heat to the glass at the bottom. Now, the method is possible; but it would be expensive and unhappy, for in seven cases out of ten you would merely burst the bottle. A light adhesive cement, of the transparent nature of fish-glue, is what was actually used. But a good many people seem to be under Jean-Baptiste's impression. The man in the brown coat was. That is the method he used, the application of heat. He is a remarkable fellow with little knowledge of anything, including chemistry, but of a striking ingenuity which he thought could overcome all difficulties.

"The first difficulty came of putting anything at

all into a small champagne bottle. But he had to choose it because it was the one drink which Rose Klonec, when alone, would be certain to take. If champagne is taken out of its bottle, and tampered with or transferred, it goes flat. How flat depends on the length of time it stands. Our brown-coated man thought that he must introduce into his prepared bottle an artificial 'sparkle,' the sort formed by carbonic acid gas in the original. And what he used was sodium bicarbonate, ordinary baking soda, a strong alkali."

Ralph had been looking at him queerly, with his arm across the back of Magda's chair.

"Yes, but what of it?" he demanded. "I shouldn't imagine it was a very pleasant compound; but you could drink a gallon of champagne and bicarbonate of soda without being killed, couldn't you?"

"Certainly. But that was not the important ingredient, the one he put in next. And that was,"— he looked at Curtis,—"as you correctly say, three hundred grains of chloral hydrate. It is an enormous amount, which would easily have killed the woman had she drunk the whole bottle. But he knew she would never drink the whole bottle: it has a distinctive taste, and a glass of it would tell Rose Klonec that it was bad, even if she did not know why. Therefore he must see that in the first glass she had enough to put her effectually asleep. He wished her asleep: and that is all he wished.

"Whereupon it is the devil of the perverse who juggles the bottles. It is the devil of the perverse who has been moving all through this case. Don't you see what happened? You saw exactly the

227

same experiment performed yesterday by Mabusse, in the bedroom of the villa. You saw it in miniature. Here," he opened the container, "are the notes. In this case you have a tablespoonful of sodium bicarbonate, $NaHCO_3$. You have 300 grains or over two-thirds of an ounce, of chloral hydrate, $CCl_3\text{-}CH(OH)_2$. To these, when the bottle is sealed, you add intense heat..."

Bencolin threw the notes on the desk. He sat back with a broad and evil grin, which altered the whole aspect of his face.

"The man in the brown raincoat is a great poet," he said enthusiastically. "He is a mighty and unconscious poisoner. In this alchemist's bottle, completely unknown to himself, he has brewed a drug as deadly as cyanide, and almost as swift. When the shaken bottle began to erupt under the influence of the sodium bicarbonate, Rose Klonec —being a thrifty soul—gulped down as much as she could so as not to waste any. Therefore she failed to notice the fiery taste in her throat, from what had accumulated on the surface of the liquid. Pistol, razor, stiletto, and drug tablets: there were four weapons in the case, and all of them are false. Rose Klonec died of being practical. A minute or two before Miss Toller walked into that dressing-room, she had swallowed over two hundred grains of pure liquid chloroform."

16

What Happened at the
Dressing-Table

He grew more sober. "That was the smell which made you half sick, Miss Toller. The smell did not remain noticeable the next morning, since there was a line of windows open in the room next to the dressing-room, and even from the first there would have been little odor about the body itself. There is, I think, only one other recorded instance of poisoning by swallowing liquid chloroform—the death of Thomas Edwin Bartlett in London in 1876, the celebrated case in which the wife was tried for murder and acquitted. In the Bartlett affair the symptoms, or rather lack of outward symptoms, exactly resemble those of Rose Klonec. Bartlett's physician found," he ran his finger down the notes, "that *'the mouth had no odor, the face was pale, but the expression natural; there was no appearance of convulsive action.'* At first he thought death due to an aneurism, as we in Rose Klonec's case thought it due to loss of blood.

"Outwardly there was little to contradict this view. But once we had reason to suspect something else, an analysis of the stomach last night gave back traces of every ingredient that had been in the merry bottle of champagne. Still, Rose Klonec was fortunate. She had a quick and merciful death. Even the burning sensation of the chloroform going down her throat was light compared to what the man in the brown coat had in store for her afterwards. He must have cursed plentifully when he found out what had really happened to her."

"What was he going to do?" demanded Ralph.

Bencolin looked thoughtful. "If my notion is correct, something a little more unpleasant than has entered your heads. I say now, as I said before: we want that fellow, and we want him badly."

"Being," grunted Ralph, "no nearer to finding him now than we were before."

"You think not? I am not certain of that." A slight film had come over Bencolin's eyes. "However, our way is clear towards him now, and at least free of red herrings. I have gone into all this in great detail because you needed time to cool off. Miss Toller may be able to help us a good deal."

Magda spoke softly. "What *I* did," she said, "was rather unpleasant too, wasn't it? No, Ralph,

I'm not going to look round at you, so you needn't keep your eyes on the floor. I know you're all trying to be frightfully decent about it, and the great Terror of a detective, with horns and a tail, has been ten times more decent than I deserve; but—"

Ralph was clearly trying to pump up cheerfulness as you pump air into a tire, but he was just as clearly uncomfortable. A thought seemed to come back to him which he had kept away for a while.

"Rubbish," he growled. "Absolute rubbish, my girl. You've got nothing whatever to worry about: nothing. The whole point is, you didn't actually do it after all, did you?"

"Oh, darling," she said with great dreariness. "I'm not going to the guillotine, if that's what you mean. The whole point is *not* that I didn't do it. It's the part I did do, or tried to do. I know what you're thinking, all of you. I've been sitting here writhing every time anyone mentioned...arteries, and arms, and blood, and things like that. The odd part is that I don't feel any guilt at all. I only feel horribly humiliated, as though I'd done something mean instead of that. And what you've been thinking is, 'If only she had taken that gun and shot the woman—a good clean shot, since she had to go mad—that would be a whole lot better than this business. This business is only sticky.' Ugh!" She brushed her hands together and threw them outwards. "That's what you're thinking. I wasn't even a good violent murderess, who would have the nerve to go through with a crime and then look up at you sweetly and swear I didn't do it. I say, Papa Bencolin, you don't happen to have one of those veils they used to wear at funerals in France hanging about, do you? I don't even want to go home, or get out of these four walls. It would please me a whole lot if nobody could look at my face for a long, long time."

"Now, it's all right," Ralph urged. "But you'll have to admit—I mean—well—"

Whereupon Mr. Richard Curtis lost his head.

"Who gives a damn what you did or didn't do?" he asked. "Looking at your face is the one thing a sensible man would want most to do for the rest of his natural life."

These sentiments, coming from the person they did, and spoken with such furious sincerity, caused a startled pause in which they all looked at him. They must have felt as they might have felt if a picture on the wall had said something. In the next second Curtis, in the phrase, could have bitten out his tongue: for he did press it against his teeth, and feel a warmth flood up from his collar. Magda gave him one swift glance before turning away.

"Ha, ha," said Ralph uncertainly. "These lawyers know how to turn a compliment, don't they? Where were we?"

On Bencolin's face was a beautiful expression of serenity. Magda answered after picking up the half-emptied glass of brandy again.

"You wanted to ask me some questions. I'm quite ready. I don't think I can produce any good reason for being backward or untruthful now." She hesitated. "Also, I—I think I can give you a bit of help, if I can be detached enough about it, though I don't suppose I ought to want to help."

"Why not?"

"Do you honestly think that I'm out of the

woods? Or that you could get me out of them even if you liked? No, this is all very nice, and I'm terribly grateful to you. But when you find out who really did kill her, you will have to explain to the world how she got that cut on her arm. As I say, I may not go to the guillotine, but what will happen to me otherwise I can guess. I'm not complaining, mind you. I'll take my medicine. But as for tampering with the law—"

"My dear young lady," said Bencolin very gently, "I can tamper with the law when, where, and how I like. I have tampered with the law when, where and how I liked; and I will do it again. For the moment forget this as a personal problem; and, if you feel up to it, tell me what you have to tell me."

"In the first place you're quite right about that smell, now I come to remember it. It was chloroform. But it never occurred to me at the time, because I thought she was 'using' ether. You know? Inhaling it to get herself drunk, as some women do; and it was another thing I had against her. In the second place, since everything seems to depend now on a question of time—I mean, the time Hortense told you the man in the brown coat got there—"

"Ah! You understand that." Bencolin could not quite control his impatience. "Well?"

"Well, the funny thing, the ludicrous thing about all the times Hortense gave you—"

"They were all wrong?"

"No, the funny thing is that they were absolutely right," replied Magda, nodding in a somnambulistic way. "For a woman with such bad eyesight, Hortense is marvellously alert or else she's an inspired guesser. I mean that the murderer really did arrive at that villa at ten minutes past one, just as she said. Whoever had an alibi before, this De Lautrec man or even poor Ralph, the alibis are ten times stronger now. I know the murderer arrived then, because I was keeping track of the times myself; and I—I saw him."

Bencolin brought the palms of his hands down flat on the desk, and straightened up. The noise of the hands was one that made them jump a little. Looking at his face then, Curtis thought that he would not like to be there to hear the quarry squeal when this man pounced.

"It would be very unwise, Miss Toller," he said, "to lie to me now."

Magda faced him with pale determination. "I was afraid you were going to say that. But it's true. I swear it's true! Why should I lie to you, of all people?"

"That remains to be seen. We will alter this a little. I will ask questions, and you shall answer them. At what time did you leave your hotel?"

"At about twenty minutes past twelve."

"Where was your mother then?"

"Asleep and snoring. I listened outside the door, and I know. You're not still thinking of that ridiculous—?"

"Across the road from the gate of the villa, a conscientious policeman was lying drunk in the hedge. At some time in the night, not specified, he woke up long enough to see a woman come out of the gate and walk away. It can be argued that Hercule was much too soaked with cognac to give testimony of any value. Nevertheless, he swears this was a tall woman; and nobody could possibly mistake you for that. We can return to the point. At what time did you arrive at the villa?"

"It must have been under half an hour. There wasn't a tremendous lot of traffic, and I drove very fast. Say I got there at a quarter to one."

"You had no difficulty in finding it?"

"No." Her mouth moved as though she were biting at her lip. "I had been curious about the place, do you see; and one day a month or so ago I drove out alone and looked it up."

"Where did you leave your car?"

"In a lane a little way off from the villa."

"Towards Boissy?"

"No, in the other direction."

The mildness had gone from Bencolin now. He was asking the questions in a monotone, but very rapidly.

"And you went directly up to the balcony when you saw the light?"

"Yes. I tried to go in quietly, but she must have seen me in that mirror over the dressing-table. She had just drunk a lot of that stuff, and the smell was something awful. When she saw me, she started screaming at me in some language I didn't understand. It wasn't either French or English—"

"Polish?"

"Maybe. I don't know. As I say, I thought she had been drinking herself silly and taking ether as well to make her raving drunk. No sooner had she got that stiletto out of the drawer, then over she went right beside the dressing-table, with her great thick arms and legs all sprawled out in that peach nightgown. I leaned on the dressing-table and looked down at her. The bottle was on it then, I remember, and a champagne-glass. Then I spoke to her out loud. I ended up by saying, 'Do you know what ought to happen to you? You ought to be put in a bath, and have all the blood drained out of you...' Then was when I began to feel mad and giddy. They talk about going slightly mad as though it weren't a physical thing. I mean, as though you know what you were doing even if you can't stop yourself. But you don't. Do you know, I have no recollection of dragging her into that bathroom? I didn't even know there was a bathroom. The next thing I remember is leaning over her on the edge of the bath, with the towel and that stiletto in my hand. Then was when—as I told you a minute ago—I began to feel sick; and tried to stop the bleeding. But it was too late."

To say that Bencolin was following her with interest would be to understate the case. He had bent forward eagerly with what might have been approval, relief, or the realization of a theory verified.

"I'll spare you the grisly details," she added abruptly.

"No. No, that is exactly what you will not do. You may not realize how important those grisly details are. Go on."

His tone startled her. "Nothing much, anyhow. I—I went to the washstand and sloshed some water on my face. Then I got as cold as ice, because I knew what I'd done. Everybody knows about fingerprints, of course. I started to clean up that bathroom with a towel, so that I would be sure not to leave any. I looked at my wrist-watch and saw that it was five minutes past one o'clock. I nearly went out of my mind at that, because I couldn't think where all the time had gone..."

236

"Where all the time had gone?"

"Yes. It couldn't have been much more than a quarter to one when I got to the villa. And, somehow, I'd been nearly twenty minutes at—you know. I went through the suite looking for places where I might have left fingerprints. I even wiped off that automatic pistol: why I don't know, because I intended to take it away with me: and again, for some feeble-minded reason I can't understand, I left it behind. This must sound like the most awful rot. You would think a child must have more sense. But I know that's how people act because it was the way I acted.

"And now, do you see, the time seemed to go more slowly instead of more quickly. I got done all I could stand doing by ten minutes past one. I turned out all the lights in the suite, and went down the balcony staircase again. Then was when I saw him."

"Him?"

"Our famous man in the brown raincoat," she replied wearily. Leaning back in her chair, she gripped the arms of it and looked at a corner of the ceiling. "Of course, I didn't know who he was. I was afraid he might be someone coming to investigate, maybe a noise I had made or something that was suspicious. But I didn't like the look of him, whoever he was.

"I had just got to the foot of the staircase. It was bright moonlight, so bright that it looked bluish. But I was in the shadow of the villa, which extended about halfway out across the sanded driveway. On the other side of the driveway there's a strip of grass bordering the driveway, and then a line of tall trees. The man was approaching the villa from the direction of the driveway gates, walking on the strip of grass under the trees. First I saw his coat, and then his hat, and then an ugly long jaw. One thing I am sure of: it was nobody I had ever seen before."

"Even in disguise?"

"Even in disguise," Magda told him positively. "He had a different way of walking, a different way of carrying himself altogether. He was about as tall as Ralph; he was clean-shaven and had a look like dough about him, if I can describe it in that way. Why I thought there was an ugly, evil look about him I can't tell you, because he wasn't malformed in any way. Otherwise I can't describe him. The brim of his hat was pulled down. He went past without looking at the place where I was standing, and I—I *ran*. But you know why I came back to the villa next morning. I had to know, even if they caught me then and there. Now I've told you everything I know. May I go home?"

Bencolin pushed his chair back and got up. He went to the window, where he stared down at the swift river flowing round the Ile de la Cité. When he turned round again he was holding his nose as high as Mrs. Benedict Toller, and he rubbed his hands together with relief.

"No," he said, "you shall not go home. I will tell you what to do. You shall go to the Restaurant Larue; you will order the best lunch that the house affords. I will join you there as soon as I can, and I will pay for the lunch. You have taught me a great lesson. You have taught me not to distrust my intuition and my common sense."

Ralph, his face black with doubt, had unlocked

the door; and now he turned back.

"I've had about enough of this," Ralph said. "Do you think anybody's in a mood to celebrate? Haven't you trusted your intuition and your common sense too far already?"

"No. For instance, these things told me, against all the known facts and the neat patterns of science, that the young lady you see there was incapable of carrying out such a scheme as that of digging open an artery in a woman's arm. I could not believe it when the facts indicated it. I could not quite believe it even when she admitted it herself. The scheme might occur to her. She might threaten Rose Klonec, as indeed she did. I would call your attention to the fact that she made this threat *aloud*."

"But what of it?" cried Ralph. "Rose Klonec couldn't hear her."

"No," said Bencolin; "but someone else could. I refer to the real murderer.—Miss Toller, you must endure one exoneration after another. It may startle and even shock you; but you did not cut the artery in Rose Klonec's arm. Are you under the impression that you set about your work as soon as she tumbled over in a stupor by the dressing-table?"

"Yes, of course. I—I wouldn't wait, would I, if I hated her as much as that?"

"Presumably not; and therefore she would not have had time to die. Liquid chloroform is very rapid in inducing a stupor. It is even very rapid in causing death, since it takes only ten to fifteen minutes. But had you flung on her as you say you did and as you think you did, she would have died from bleeding to death after all. She did not; she died of chloroform poisoning. There is that curious and inexplicable gap of nearly twenty minutes, for which you can give no account at all. You are not even conscious of what you were doing. Believe me, such a gap is the result of no brainstorm. It does not come to those who lose their heads and butcher. It does come to those, of frail physique and nerves exhausted by family troubles, who stand in a small room soaked in the fumes of chloroform; who lean over a dressing-table bearing two receptacles for chloroform while they talk to an unconscious woman. The fumes will quickly pass off if—say—you are removed to another room, where you find yourself with a stiletto in your hand, kneeling beside the body of a dead woman whose arm is badly gashed.

"That gash was made by the ingenious phantom we want, whose coat and hat are now notorious. He had unintentionally killed Rose Klonec with chloroform, when that was not his intention. He arrived at the villa to find one woman dead and another on the edge of unconsciousness from inhaling the fumes. He saw an opportunity for fastening the crime on you even in your own mind. That was why he stole away the damning bottle and buried it deep in the grounds. And then he was ready to perform the added little flourish with a razor and a serving-table: if you will think for a moment, you will realize that this apparent insanity with the razor is really the key to the whole case. It took me until the last ten minutes to understand it." Bencolin now turned to

Douglas. "You, Mr. Douglas, spent many hours at 'The Man Who Was Blind.' I am the man who was blind. You, Miss Toller, may go out and drink with a good conscience. You never laid a finger on her. We return in a long circle to a certain person in certain clothes; and, when I have finished with him, he will wear a red collar as well."

Magda, Ralph, and Curtis went down in somewhat dazed fashion to the street. They were surprised to find the street full of warm sunlight, and a rush of everyday cabs.

"Look here," muttered Ralph, staring at his watch, "it's only five minutes past one."

"I know," said Magda. "That's what *I* felt like on Saturday night, you know. We've been under intellectual chloroform to have our brains removed, and I don't want it to happen every day."

"I say, Mag—" Ralph began, and grew a little red. As he said the words, a thick silence descended on them all; each knew what must be in his mind, and each fought against it.

"You don't like scenes, do you?" she asked calmly. "Then not one more word. Don't dare say a word more, or you'll hear me weeping and screaming in the street. Just come along, and we'll have a lunch with all the wine in Paris, as that grand old terror suggested. Then I want to go to sleep." She never once looked at Curtis, who was feeling oddly depressed; but he could feel the force of her personality as plainly as though he had touched her hand. "All the same, there's just one good thing. We're inured to shocks now. We've been through the worst; or at least I have. We've tasted all the possible bitter water or laughing water. Nothing could startle any of us now."

This was not quite true. She was unaware, for instance, of the hand grenade then being prepared by M. Jean-Baptiste Robinson of *L'Intelligence*.

17

"By the Hill of Acorns"

Just as twilight was setting in, with the pink after-glow fading, Curtis sat among the trees at the Pavilion Dauphine in the Bois. He was feeling depressed, and, it must be acknowledged, a little lonely. He had not gone to lunch with Magda and Ralph. Under the circumstances, he thought that they would prefer to be alone; and he admitted to himself that he was thinking more of that girl than was good for him. Furthermore, he had work to do. It consisted in tracking down Jean-Baptiste Robinson, and making sure that no indiscreet word of Ralph's about Mrs. Toller appeared in that evening's edition.

He at length ran Jean-Baptiste to earth in, strangely enough, the office of *L'Intelligence* it-self; and even then not until he had satisfied the outer guard that his purpose was not felonious assault. On the occasion of Jean-Baptiste's last logical analysis some weeks ago, it appeared that the office had been invaded by a gentleman with a revolver. "And when we convinced him that M. Dupin had departed precipitately for China, what does this grimy type do? He takes aim at the water-cooler and lets fly. It is a sad business to serve truth."

But Jean-Baptiste had sworn, with what seemed clear sincerity, that he had no intention of quoting M. Douglas with regard to Mme. Toller. It was impossible not to believe him. He even seemed surprised. He pointed out that even in England it was surely not hot news when a man expressed decided opinions as to the character and antecedents of his future wife's mother. Curtis had left the office still wondering what the little blighter might have up his sleeve; but reassured nevertheless. Subsequently, even despite a good meal, his spirits sank to a depth of depression he would not have believed possible. The Parisian venture, which two days ago had seemed romance, was now merely flat and foreign; and he thought with a contempt amounting to self-hatred of his dreams of a mysterious Personage with a mysterious mission. The face of Magda Toller obtruded itself wherever he turned. He even thought with affection of London.

In this state of mind, with his glass of coffee untasted on the table under the trees, he looked out sourly on the Bois. It was not yet quite dark. The skeins of electric lights overhead had not yet been illuminated, to give each leaf a theatrical green; and the terrace was so empty that the few waiters, standing motionless with folded arms among vast rows of tables, had something of the effect of Plainsmen in a desert. At this point Curtis got the shock he needed.

"I'm seeing things," he said aloud. "It can't be."

But it was. Craned round the edge of a tree, a bowler hat and a part of a face were being stealthily withdrawn. Curtis made a peremptory gesture. The figure hesitated. Then it popped out as though with decision, and advanced with brisk little pigeon-toed steps.

"Good evening, M. Curtis," said Jean-Baptiste, removing his hat with great courtesy, and making a bobbing motion of his stern rather than a bow.

"Good evening, M. Robinson. Will you allow me to say," observed the other, "that, if I were a theatrical manager, I would cast you for the role of somebody in *A Midsummer Night's Dream?*" He felt his spirits a trifle on the rebound. "With your ability to be in two places at once—Tell me: you didn't commit the murder yourself, did you?"

Jean-Baptiste was evidently taken aback. "Ah, that is a joke," he said, after a slight pause. "You will do me the honor of drinking, monsieur? Good. Waiter! Two whiskey-sodas."

"No, you must drink with me. But will you tell me this: why have I become a center of interest?"

"A center of interest?" repeated Jean-Baptiste, even his moustache wrinkling with hideous perplexity and guilelessness.

"Good journalists, like yourself, go only where there is news. And I am not news. To anyone, unfortunately."

"You have not seen M. Bencolin this afternoon?"

"No."

"Or returned to your hotel?"

"No."

"Without doubt there was something on your mind. There were two reasons why I searched for you, M. Curtis," Jean-Baptiste told him, with explosive pride. "The first, to show you the copy of *L'Intelligence*." He whipped it from under his coat. "It is this evening's edition. Now read it, and judge for yourself whether I have kept my word. Judge for yourself whether there is one indiscreet word of M. Douglas concerning Mme. Toller. What he may think of Mme. Toller, and (between ourselves) what I may think of Mme. Toller—that is another thing. For that I refer you to my analytical article, which contains the account of the champagne-bottle and of a certain firearms-license to which readers are invited to direct their attention. But here, you will see, is the popular news of the day. Eh?"

Curtis glanced at the headlines, and could hardly stifle the beginning of a howl.

It was popular news. It said:

M. RALPH DOUGLAS NAMES
the
ASSASSIN OF THE VILLA MARBRE!

———

A VIOLENT DENUNCIATION!

———

ONLY L'INTELLIGENCE CAN GIVE THE COMPLETE LIST OF MADAME KLONEC'S LOVERS!

HERE IT IS!

M. Leon Considine, President of the Paris branch of the Great-Midi Bank of Marseilles. (1929–1930).

Señor Enrico Torredas, the noted bull-fighter. (1930–1931).

M. Henry T. Witherspoon, President of the Mammoth Hotels Corporation of America; banking interests, etc. (September, 1931–May, 1932).

M. George Stanfield, Director of MM. Toller's Tours at Paris. (May, 1932–November, 1932).

M. Georges Foulard, no occupation, since believed in prison. (November, 1932–January, 1934).

M. Ralph Douglas. (June, 1934–August, 1935).

M. Louis De Lautrec, Private secretary to M. Jean Renoir, Minister of the Cabinet. (August, 1935–May, 1936).

"It was one of those scoundrels who did it; seek him out!"

His eyes flashing, his voice vibrant with passion, M. Ralph Douglas arose in his apartment in the Avenue Foch, and pointed dramatically to the above list. He continued—

Jean-Baptiste checked off the names proudly on his fingers. "Two bankers, a bull-fighter, a noted businessman, the secretary of a cabinet-minister," he announced. "That is not bad, eh?"

"No, it is not," said Curtis in a hollow voice. "You could not find an ambassador and a couple of clergymen, could you? God's light, there's a million pounds' worth of damages in it."

"Most of the information came from Hortense Frey, who put me on to other maids." Then Jean-Baptiste seemed to realize. He broke off, appalled. "You do not like it?"

"It would be difficult to express my full views. Would you like me to put the paper on the ground and dance on it?"

Jean-Baptiste stared. "But, monsieur, this is terrible! I had hoped—what is wrong with it? Continue to read. Read M. Douglas's magnificent and eloquent defense of his mother-in-law (which, after all, is news) against any charges! I thought it would please you. That is why I wrote it."

"Has any formal charge been made against her?"

"Not exactly, of course, but—"

"If I publish in *Paris Minuit* or *Le Drapeau de Napoléon* a statement saying, 'I most firmly DENY that M. Jean-Baptiste Robinson is a liar, a thief, a coward, and a traitor,' without doubt that will be pleasing to you? Also, what do you think these other gentlemen will say when they see their names bracketed as both lovers and murderers?"

Jean-Baptiste's chest came out. "If they have any complaint to make, monsieur, they can seek satisfaction on the field of honor."

"Satisfaction from whom?"

"From M. Douglas, naturally. He said—"

"Exactly. What did he say? Can you look at me and swear he ever in his life talked like that?"

"Well, it is possible that I may have made it a very little bit more dramatic. After all, we must do these things or often the news would be as dull as it usually is. But that in general was his talk, and the waiter who served our breakfast will testify to it. I may not have had the complete list. But I had something, which the waiter will swear was the list in case of difficulty." He paused. He dropped his air both of blandness and outrage. Then he made an appealing gesture. "Now see! I drop my defenses! I am uncovered. I invite a kick. But I came here hopefully to show you that paper, and to ask a favor—"

"I am uncovered too. A favor!"

Jean-Baptiste leaned forward.

"A moment ago I told you I came here with two pieces of information. I am desolated that my poor effort has not pleased you. But my next piece of information you will be eager to get. I have a letter for you."

"A letter? A letter from whom?"

"I have reason to believe that it is from M. Bencolin, who has been looking for you throughout the afternoon. Sergeant Giraud left it at your hotel. I persuaded the hotel people, who know me, that I knew precisely where you were and would deliver it. I also used other persuasions. Now see how tirelessly, how determinedly, I have searched for you! It is not for me to say it, and yet but for my friendship you might never have received the letter. You might have gone off to Montmartre with a poule. You might have gone back to England, for all I know. And now, even when you use boiling words, do I resent it? Do I attempt to withhold the letter from you? No. And here it is."

Curtis was now past speech. He took the letter and tore open its envelope, which had evidently not been tampered with. It was from Bencolin. He would have expected Bencolin's handwriting to be large, hasty and scrawled. This was large, but it was of an unusual copperplate fineness.

You seem to have disappeared, and I hardly wish to send out a police alarm. You can, if you wish, assist me in a little game tonight, provided this finds you in time. Ralph Douglas has been persuaded to assist me as well. The two questions are, are you fond of cards and are you well supplied with money? If the answer is no, pay no more attention to this. If it is yes, and you wish to see something interesting, take the enclosed card, which will serve as your introduction. About half-past ten go to the home of the Marquise de la Toursèche—say to the chauffeur, "by the Hill of Acorns at Longchamps," and he will know where to take you. Others you know will be there; but particularly M. De Lautrec. Whatever game M. De Lautrec plays, play it yourself as high as you dare, and wait.

Enclosed was a visiting card engraved, "M. le Comte de Maupasson," and written across it in bright blue ink were the words, "Dear Deidre: This is to introduce Mr. Richard Curtis, of London, who will play for whatever stakes you name. I hear you are preparing a surprise for your guests on Monday night. I wish I could be there."

Curtis sat back. Up over his head the great skeins of lights flashed into a blaze among the trees; and they met his mood. It was exactly the fillip he had needed. Quite suddenly he found himself glowing with it. It was the mysterious Personage whisking back with the mysterious mission. At the same time that such a situation out of sensational fiction occurred to him, there occurred its inevitable corollary: that this was the sort of note which lures away impetuous young men to get knocked over the head by Burmese dacoits. He did not believe it. Also, he could test it. Nothing more in keeping with his mood ever warmed his heart. He was carrying about ten thousand francs. The hotel, who knew his firm well, would probably cash his cheque for as much more as he asked.

Then he became aware that Jean-Baptiste was speaking.

"Monsieur?" Jean-Baptiste said, like an urchin approaching to ask for a cigarette-card.

"You would like to know what is in this letter. Is that it?"

"To be frank," said the other, quivering, "—yes. After all, I think I deserve it. You remember that the old fox promised me the story. But what has he done since then, I ask you? I have a right to know what the old fox is up to!"

"Very well. You may see the letter on one condition: that you write a retraction of that story, denying Mr. Douglas ever said any such things—"

Jean-Baptiste cried out with agony. "But it might be managed," he admitted.

"—and that you write two copies of it here and now. One for me."

More bouncings ensued, while Curtis called inexorably for pen and paper. There was no harm that could be done even if his companion knew his destination; for, without a card, Jean-Baptiste could not penetrate those locked gates of the Marquise de la Toursèche. But he saw that the other was disturbed, and wondered why.

"You think that the old fox is up to something?"

"I am sure of it!" said Jean-Baptiste, giving the table such a whack that the whiskey-sodas spilled over.

"You have, then, no longer your deadly suspicions of Mrs. Toller?"

"I am seldom wrong, monsieur. That I can truthfully say, and I have true inspiration. But he who acts on inspiration has much to explain afterwards, as my friend Pepi said when he tried to write a detective-story. Besides, I know what the old fox suspects. You might not believe it, but we have ears even inside the Sûreté. And do you know whom he suspects? He suspects a woman."

Curtis was instantly on his guard. He was afraid this might be some more excellent acting, to draw him with regard to a hint that might have slipped out concerning Magda Toller; for handling a greased pig was a simple matter compared to dealing with M. Robinson. Evidently his companion saw what was in his mind, and spoke dryly.

"No, my friend. None of your English ladies, alas. Otherwise it might be easy. I mean a Frenchwoman."

"A Frenchwoman! Who, then?"

"Who?" said Jean-Baptiste.

Five minutes later, Curtis was speeding through the Bois in a taxi, with the letter, the card, and a document signed by Jean-Baptiste in his pocket. The latter had made no move to follow him. He had not even commented, or shown elation or disappointment, when he read the letter. Curtis left him sitting with some concentration at the table, and twisting round his finger a piece of black thread which, with a pin or two, he evidently carried in his lapel.

To return to his hotel, to get something to eat, to change into evening kit, and to draw a cheque: this, Curtis estimated, would leave him enough time to reach the home of the Marquise de la Toursèche not much late for the hour indicated. He was in such haste that he had scarcely time to think. But he telephoned the Sûreté, found Inspector Durrand, and assured himself by cryptic questions that the appointment was genuine. What was up, Durrand could or would not tell him. All the while that he was driven to that address, "by the Hill of Acorns at Longchamps," he turned over in his mind certain words equally cryptic.

To find that there were such bleak spaces on the environs of Paris, running to high wall and blank streets, surprised him. The Hill of Acorns itself, with the great house on a crest across from it, was woodland. His taxi-driver seemed to know the place well, and shouted directions while he negotiated the last path on foot. Then he stood on a flat place by a fringe of trees, with the great wall in front of him; and tonight there was a light in the concierge's lodge.

His rattling at the gate brought out an old man with a Homeric moustache and a lantern. His card was examined by the light of the lantern, without comment; the gates were opened and locked with a clash behind him, still without comment. In the same somnambulistic way he was directed by a nod up a path between the oak trees. He had no sense of alarm or even uneasiness. It was merely a feeling that the positive locking of those gates shut him into a new place, as a man might go into a room through veils: though he knew that this was foolish. Behind the closed shutters of the house ahead, he knew exactly what he would be bound to find. The Marquise de la Toursèche would be a brisk, alert, handsome woman of middle-age, who had founded a paying concern. Despite the fact that only a dozen people were ever supposed to come here, there would be croupiers with little black bow ties. There would be a lounge, there might even be a bar.

He was wrong.

Even allowing for this, he was not prepared for the dingy and stuffy magnificence of the hall into which he was led. It was lighted by a pyramid of white gas-globes, which contrived to suggest gloom. No article of furniture, no massive carpet or curtain, had altered from the fashion of sixty years ago; and, though each was scrupulously kept clean, you might imagine that no stick of gilt, no bounding expanse of plush, had even been moved since then. The effect was like that of being shut into a tent or a richly draped pavilion, except that it was a little too dark. Whenever he moved he expected to knock something over. But most of all he noticed the silence of the place.

Though it was muffled away from the outside world, that silence was the silence of concentration. He gave his name and card to a major-domo, who took him into a drawing-room towards the left of the hall. There he was greeted—not to say pounced on.

Before the empty fireplace of a room much like the hall, his hostess came forward to meet him. She was a little fat old woman with a baggy skin, a baggy neck, and a painted face, wearing a low-cut gown of black lace. Yet she conveyed no impression of the comic, and no impression of anyone but the Marquise de la Toursèche. Any other lasting impression lay, probably, in the extraordinary snap and sparkle of her dark eyes; the sense of ferocious and yet amiable gusto with which she pounced on everything, so that even her fingers crisped and unclenched as though she were concentrating. Beside her stood an old man with dim eyes and a short square of beard.

"You are Mr. Curtis?" she said, pouncing. She pronounced the name in the English way; then she presented the man with dim eyes by some title Curtis did not catch. "We are always glad to welcome any friend of Philippe de Maupasson. I have seen you at Le Touquet?"

"No, madame."

"Or at the home of the Marquise de Bourdillac?"

"I fear not, madame," said Curtis, a little disturbed at all these great names, and also at the way she was firing out her machine-gun questions.

"You are English?"

"Yes."

"From London?"

"Yes."

"I am Irish," said Madame unexpectedly, in English; and she laughed. Her laughter was a part of the same gusto. Yet her speech had a rusty and disused note, more foreign than French, and seemed to jar her like the works of a clock. "You see my name on the card—Deidre, though poor Philippe takes liberties there. The O'Dowd was my father, more years ago than you would guess. I am one of the lost seven hundred and seventy-seven tribes. No, let us speak French. Tell me, then: you take Chance seriously?"

"Chance compels us to take her seriously, madame," said Curtis, whose highest play so far had been a mild flutter at Monte Carlo for a pound or two. But he saw that he had pleased the old lady.

"That is a good answer! That is a very good answer! I love it. That is what I like. Did I ever tell you of my friend...no, I will not mention names, which would be indiscreet, but did you ever hear of him?"

"No, madame."

"Well, it was a long time ago, and I will not name the casino, either. But he had just been married. He was passionately devoted to his young wife. Passionately! But also passionately was he devoted to the little cards. He had one run at the table which was ruining them; but he would not leave off and wait until Chance returned to him; he clung to the table; he could not be moved from it; he had his food there. And still he lost. His wife, who did not understand, was desperate. She thought of the only way of removing him. On a card she herself printed, 'Your wife is deceiving you! If you do not believe it, go to the house of the Comte de N'Importe and you will find her there in his arms,' and she had it sent to him. He read it. His face grew like a storm-cloud, and he uprose with his fists clenched. Then he stopped. The croupier heard him mutter, 'Unlucky in love, lucky at cards.' He quadrupled his stakes and won a million. And the next day the Comte de N'Importe, who had never even met his wife, received the present of a large bottle of brandy bearing a card merely labelled, *Merci*."

The old man with the dim eyes stirred.

"Yes, that is all very well," said the old man quickly. "But it is not so good as the story they tell of Talleyrand. Who was the lady (I have forgotten her name) who was so devoted to him that, when she died, she ordered her heart to be put into an urn studded with jewels, and delivered to him for his eternal keeping? The delivery of the urn found this redoubtable man at the table, losing heavily. Without hesitation he seized the urn and pushed it across the table as his stake." The old man regarded Curtis with the animation of a wheezy chuckle. "As you would say, that is strip-poker *par excellence*, eh?"

Curtis smiled dutifully, because it seemed to be expected of him, though both anecdotes struck him as a trifle grisly. He began to look round and wonder. These might be stock-stories with which madame encouraged prospective guests. But on madame's face he had seen an eager expression, which was familiar. He had seen it last night on the face of Louis de Lautrec when De Lautrec spoke of his luck. Again he looked round him; and wondered, in this overdressed room with its dim white gas-globes, what drums had begun to beat.

"I cannot hope to compete with such men, madame—"

"Well, we shall see," said madame, her face wrinkling into one smile.

(Here! How much money have I got?)

"—but may I ask what is the game madame and her guests usually play? Baccarat, I believe?"

This was the question for which she had evidently been waiting. She pounced.

"But you have read Philippe's card? You see he speaks of a surprise?"

"Something different?"

"Something special," said madame.

"Then I only hope, madame, that I know how to play it."

"You do not know how to play it, monsieur," she told him gravely. "But you need not apologize for that. There is no person alive who has ever played it."

He contrived to look at her without surprise. She was evidently not in the least mad; on the contrary, she was a very sharp-witted old lady crushing the last essence of pleasure from her favorite passion.

"Listen to me," she went on, wagging a finger at him in such a way that the wrinkled skin crawled up and down the back of her hand. "And judge why I am excited! We are to play a game which no one has played for two hundred and fifty years. It is a lost game. Its very rules are known to few except one or two scholars who poke and prod among the dusty records of the past, where so much sparkle of life is imprisoned if only we knew it. Eh, my professor? Eh?" She glanced at

Dim Eyes, who was appreciative. "If we hear the cry of Soissant* et-le-va! tonight, it will be the first time it has been heard outside the rooms of the Grand Monarque. Yet once, they tell me, it was the rage of the earth. Its fascination was such that it ruined even the families at the court of the Grand Monarque. In one respect it is the perfect gambling-game, for not an ounce of skill is used or can be used in it: it is governed by the laws of pure Chance. We shall see whether M. De Lautrec's luck can challenge the past. I refer, monsieur, to Basset, the royal game of the kings of France."

At one end of the room double doors were opened, and heavy black portières were pushed back, by the major-domo.

"Your guests are waiting, madame," he said.

*The old French spelling of "soixante" has been retained from the original rules.

18

The Corpses' Club

The murky room to which Curtis was taken, and to which Mme. de la Toursèche led the way with her hand on the arm of the man she called the professor, was pierced by a shaft of brilliant light. It poured down on a longish table covered with green baize, from dead-white inverted gas-lamps. There were very few people present: the exact number Curtis could not tell, because the edges of the room were dim. In contrast to the comparative austerity of the table, the chairs about it were deep and thickly padded with bunched plush after the fashion of the house; and the walls seemed to be lined with weapons. The complete absence of noise may have been due to the thickness of the carpet, or to the atmosphere of the place which was hushed in expectancy as before a contest.

The first persons Curtis espied in the group were Magda Toller and Ralph Douglas, Magda wearing an evening-gown that showed off her shoulders. He thought he saw an expression of relief cross Ralph's face as he entered; but none of them gave an obvious sign of recognition. At one side of the green baize table (built low, so that guests could sit back in easy chairs to watch the play) there sat bolt upright a mild, stocky, elderly man making notes in a little book. On a divan some distance back sat two elderly women, muttering in low tones. Still further back he thought he could make out a figure which looked like De Lautrec; but he could not be sure.

While Mme. de la Toursèche swept round the room giving greetings, each with a pounce, Curtis made his way towards Magda and Ralph. They were standing by a sideboard. He did not know whether he was supposed to be acquainted with them: it depended on what plan of devilment the old fox meant. But he had received no instructions not to know them; if anything, Bencolin's note had hinted at the opposite. There was a slight and stuffy odor from the gas-lights, which sang faintly. A stray beam shone across Ralph's shirt-front.

It was Ralph who spoke, almost like a ventriloquist, without opening his mouth but with the uneasy air and curious swinging motion people fall into when they attempt the trick.

"What's up?"

"I don't know," said Curtis, swinging beside him: "That's what I was going to ask you; I don't know anything. Where is Bencolin?"

"Can't tell you, except that he's not here. Or doesn't seem to be, although I could have sworn a while ago—" Ralph stopped. "Something's on the way, that's certain. All the instructions I got were to play, and if possible to play against De Lautrec. He's here, by the way, though he hasn't spoken to us yet."

"Yes, I thought I saw him over in the dark. He thinks his luck's in, and he's out for blood. Have you ever been here before?"

Ralph's eyes strayed. "No. It's not what you'd call younger people's style. But I'll tell you this, my lad, from what I've heard: this is the shrine of the devotees and plungers. The more rheumatic and desiccated they are, the more they plunge. Johnny Sainclair calls this the Corpses' Club; but it seems that when the corpses get jolly well under way they play games that would make your hair curl." Again his eyes moved, pointing out another guest. "You see that mild-looking chap making marks in the book? That's Paul Jourdain, about the seventh or eighth richest man in France, who can't afford to be seen going it in a public casino. Of course, you can set your own pace; this is only an ordinary little social club. I don't know who one of the two women is, but the other is a professional card-player who makes a good living at it on the Riviera. In most games of skill she would have her own way, but I understand that tonight there's a game of plain chance. Well, that suits me." He shifted, his hands on the edge of the sideboard, and Curtis could see a big vein beating in his temple. "I don't want to have to think or concentrate; I want somebody's shirt

...And I say, Mag: don't urge the need for caution."

"You haven't said hullo to me, you know," Magda interposed to Curtis, and looked him steadily in the eyes. He greeted her with casualness. "I'm not urging the need for caution. Do what you like. It's in the air."

"Where do we change our money here?" asked Curtis. "We use counters, I suppose?"

"Yes. See the butler or whoever-it-is. Stop a bit!" said Ralph. "Our hostess has the floor."

The Marquise de la Toursèche had come to the head of the table, and was standing with two fingers on it. The short dumpy figure did not now look as though it might pounce on the green baize; it had a sort of greedy dignity.

"*Mesdames, messieurs*," she said in a measured voice, crow-harsh. "With your consent we are about to attempt the revival of a game which, I think, ghosts will approve. Of the last great occasion on which Basset was played, I do not wish to speak. Like all seventeenth-century card-games, it is of an extreme simplicity, and you will understand it in two minutes. I wish to explain the manner of the play, and to warn you of the great advantages which lie with the bank."*

*"This game, amongst all those on the cards, is accounted to be the most courtly, being properly, by the understanders of it, thought only fit for Kings and Queens, great Princes, Noblemen, &c. to play at, by reason of such great losses, or advantages as may possibly be on one side or another... Here the dealer that keeps the bank having the first and last card at his own disposal, and other considerable privileges in dealing the cards, has a greater prospect of gaining than those that play. This was a truth so ac-

She snapped her fingers. The major-domo placed beside her several opened packs of cards; and a rack of round counters which were painted silver, gold, and black. Madame's raddled face was very distinct in the hot, hard light: everything round the green baize was gloom.

"First, *mesdames, messieurs,* I call your attention to the fact that in Basset the various suits do not enter into the scoring at all. You are to cease to think of clubs, hearts, diamonds, spades. You are to think only of the pips—ace to ten, knave, queen, and king.

"Let us suppose that I am the *talliere,* or banker. I have before me one complete pack. I put it on the table face downwards—so. As many as choose may play against me. Each of the persons who plays against me has a book of thirteen cards, composed of all the cards in one suit. They are taken from another pack; and they are (of course) the ace, deuce, trey, four, five, six, seven, eight, nine, ten, knave, queen, and king. They are laid face upwards in a row before him—so."

From another pack she extracted thirteen diamonds, and put them carefully in order before the stocky little man with the diary.

"We imagine, then, that M. Jourdain is playing.

knowledged in France that the King made a publick edict that the privilege of a *Talliere,* or one that keeps the Bank at Basset, should only be allow'd to principal *Cadets,* or sons of great families, supposing that whoever was so befriended as to be admitted to keep the Bank, must naturally in a very short time become the possessor of a considerable estate."

—Charles Cotton, *The Compleat Gamester,* 1721.

(Others may play their own hands against me at the same time. M. De Lautrec, say, has the thirteen spades; my friend André the thirteen hearts.) For the sake of simplicity we take M. Jourdain's cards. It is now his business to place a bet on any card or cards he likes in his own book—as others do with their own books, each playing simultaneously against me. He may bet as much as he chooses, anywhere he chooses. It is pure Chance. Usually he will elect to back more than one card. But for easy example, let us say he chooses the ace alone. He takes a louis, or twenty francs—the lowest coin for which we play here—and he places it on his ace.

"Once the game is made round the table, no more bets can be placed until this round is finished. Well! I now begin to play against him.

"I therefore turn up the first card in my pack. Remember, the first card is always the banker's card, and wins for the bank. I turn it up—so. It is a six, you see. Well, no one has backed the six. Therefore, although that is my winning card, I can collect no money. But (as would probably happen if several persons were playing) suppose someone has backed it I win whatever money anyone has put upon it.

"We continue! The next card I turn up from my own pack is the *players'* winning card, for which I must pay out the sum that any of them has happened to place on the card that appears. I turn it up—so. It is a three. Well, M. Jourdain has not backed the three, so he collects no money from me. But if any of the other players has backed it, I pay.

"Thus we continue alternately through the

pack: to the bank, to the player; to the bank, to the player; each in turn, until the cards are exhausted. So far, there is nothing. So far, it is commonplace. But now we come to the great hazard. Ah, here it is! On the player's trick, I turn up an ace. M. Jourdain wins. And the true game commences.

"When a player's card wins, he may do one of two things. He may receive his money from the bank, and remove all stakes from that particular card. Or he may let his first stake rest there. If he does this, he receives no money from the bank. There is still only one louis. To signify that it remains, he reaches out and twists up one corner of the card, like a little horn—so. He has made the *paroli*. He is now betting that out of my pack an ace will appear for a second time for him.

"We continue dealing. Now let us suppose that an ace does turn up for a second time! If so, he receives from the bank seven times as much as he has placed on the card to begin with. This is called the *Sept-et-le-va*. (If we may freely render archaic French terms, we may call it, 'Seven and she's still going!') At this time he may withdraw, taking his winnings. Or he may let it rest once again. He twists up the next corner of his card to signify this. He is now wagering that an ace will turn up for him the third time. On *that* card are now staked seven louis, or 140 francs.

"And now, *mesdames, messieurs,* I think it becomes interesting. We go on. We suppose that for the third time the ace appears for the player. When it does, the player receives fifteen times the amount then lying on the card; the *Quinze-et-le-va*. Again he may withdraw: for his winnings now amount to one hundred and five louis, or 2,100 francs.

"But with gambler's pertinacity (we say) he does not retire. He wagers it instead on the appearance of the fourth and final ace. Again he crooks up a corner of the card to signify it. If he is right, and the ace appears for him he has made the *Trente-et-le-va*. He receives from the bank thirty-three times the amount then on the card—or 69,300 francs. It mounts, eh? For during one round of the game, during the space of time in which it is possible to deal out fifty-two cards, and starting with the lowest possible stake, he has won just under seventy thousand francs.

"But that is not all," said Mme. de la Toursèche.

A sudden rustle, in the gloom beyond the table, was stilled. It was very warm in here. The gas-lamps sang thinly. Glancing towards the other end of the room, Curtis saw the flame of a cigarette-lighter spring up, and above it the lantern jaws and high color of Louis de Lautrec: seeming more lantern-jawed as he bent over a cigarette. But De Lautrec was smiling.

Mme. de la Toursèche smiled as well, like a gargoyle.

"Should the player thus attain *Trente-et-le-va*," she went on in her harsh voice, "the bank must allow him one last and tremendous hazard. I warn you, this next hazard seldom happens. Even *Trente-et-le-va* itself must seldom appear. For remember! In the dealing out of a pack, all four aces must (of course) appear. But if one of them is turned up by the banker, as his own winning card, the bank immediately sweeps up everything the player has staked so far. The same goes for any other card which is being built up. Again, the first card dealt is the banker's; and (I now tell you) the last card is always the banker's. But if the intrepid player has won four times, he can then demand of the bank his final throw. He can ask for the cards to be reshuffled. He can ask for one more deal, with all the aces again in the pack. He is then wagering his seventy thousand francs that an ace will turn up for a fifth time—as his winning card. That, *mesdames, messieurs,* is the *Soissant-et-le-va.* And the banker must pay to him sixty-seven times what he has placed on the card. I hesitate here. My mental arithmetic becomes cloudy. But the sum then received will be something over four million six hundred and forty thousand francs.

"*Mesdames, messieurs,* shall we play?"

There was a dead silence.

Curtis had expected some outburst, some comment at least, as at the end of any explanation. There was none. The stocky little man sat and looked thoughtfully (hungrily, you might have said) at the edge of the green baize. The two women across the room were very still; but he heard the click of a purse being opened. Curtis himself felt like making some comment. He realized by a little hazy arithmetic that the last-named sum, at the current rate of exchange, would amount to over £35,000 in English money. He felt very small as well. Beside this merry little invention of the court of Louis the Fourteenth, the stakes of even the greatest present-day gamblers looked like pennies. It was a long chance, of course. It was an almost inconceivable chance. But that is what makes Chance itself.

He turned to Ralph.

"Are you getting into this?"

"Yes, he is," said Magda. "I love people who take chances. Everything's queer tonight, somehow."

Ralph was considering, his eyes narrowed. "Yes, but I'm going out to buy the bank. That's where you'll strip 'em. This win-four-times-with-one-card-and-then-break-the-bank-with-the-fifth is only bait. You'll see. They'll win once, possibly twice—and then the bank will scoop up everything. It will go on just like that. Of course, if somebody starts out with a really good first stake —say a hundred francs instead of one louis—and the inspired lunatic really managed to pull off *Soissant-et-le-va*, the banker would go down to the tune of a hundred thousand pounds. But it couldn't happen. Better go and get your money changed, Dick."

Curtis did so. The major-domo led him to an office where he received a rack of counters: the silver-colored ones for twenty, the gold for fifty, and the black for one hundred francs. On his way back, where the others had now gathered round the green baize, De Lautrec stopped him.

"Good evening, old chap," said De Lautrec in English, with his precise and gusty intonation. The cigarette hung from the corner of his mouth; the burning tip of the cigarette in the gloom had the same pallor as his own earnestness. "I see you're here with your friend Mr. Douglas."

"Good evening, Mr. De Lautrec. Yes, that's right. You know him, don't you?"

"Yes, yes, fairly well. But I don't want to—talk, and spill my head, tonight. I feel as though I'm walking about with a pail of water on it. Look here, I'll give you a tip. Don't play against me tonight if you value your pocket. I can't lose. Besides, there's money about and lawyers never have any. You see the two women over there. One is a professional (card-player, I mean—ha ha ha!), but the other is Mrs. Richardson, the wife of the American soap king or leather king or something." He stopped abruptly. "Where is your friend Bencolin?"

"I haven't seen him tonight."

"Possibly not." He blew smoke sideways past the cigarette. "But they have been pestering me again. There is some ridiculous talk of my having taken some of Rose's jewellery and substituted paste ones. But Rose's lawyer (damn lawyers!) opened the safe today, and what did he find? Annette says—" He stopped. "Why are you here? It can't be chance of either kind. Wait, they're beginning."

They had gathered round the table, with Mme. de la Toursèche at the head of it. On her right the mild gentleman was sandwiched in between a lean, elderly Frenchwoman and a very fat elderly American woman with sleepy eyes surmounting a jovial smile. Ralph and Magda were on her left.

"I observe," continued De Lautrec, raising his voice, "that our friend M. Douglas has bought the bank. I have no anxiety to take it; I prefer it the other way. And what now, Mama de la Toursèche?"

Their hostess pounced round, and gave him a black look at the familiarity. "Without doubt M. De Lautrec has no anxiety," she said. "He knows when to stop, and when to take a breathing-space from the table even when his luck runs high. Now, M. Douglas, you will sit here at the head of the table. You will deal your own cards from this 'shoe.' I sit beside you as croupier. Mme. Richardson, from America, has chosen a suite of thirteen hearts. M. Jourdain has chosen a suite of thirteen clubs."

She glanced round inquiringly; but Magda and Curtis, on Ralph's bank, elected for the moment to stand out. De Lautrec sauntered to a chair on the left-hand side of the banker, and sat down with a kind of slap. Though he and Ralph nodded to each other with restrained politeness, Curtis did not like the expression of either.

"Diamonds," De Lautrec decided. "Oh, without doubt, I will have diamonds."

"Since this is an experiment," said Madame, "I remind you again that no stake can be added or altered once the banker has begun to deal. Place your bets, *messieurs, mesdames*—"

De Lautrec's opening gun was to place fifty francs on the deuce of diamonds, a hundred francs on the seven, and two hundred on the king. There was a clicking sound from his rack of counters; and a pause. Across the table Mrs. Richardson and M. Jourdain hesitated. Apparently they were used to old rules and honored custom; this newness and unorthodoxy disturbed them, no less than De Lautrec's decisiveness. They seemed to be meditating moves at chess. What cards they backed Curtis scarcely noticed, except that the choice was very cautious. Then Mrs. Richardson spoke.

"Undoubtedly," she said with a sleepy smile, and in excellent French, "you wish to pursue your luck of last Saturday night, monsieur. I wish I could have seen that. Unfortunately, this is the first time I have had the pleasure of coming here."

The stocky little man hesitated. It was his only sign of surprise; or, in fact, of any animation at all.

"Nor I, madame," he said. "It is the first time I—"

"The stakes are laid," sang their hostess. *"Nothing more goes—"*

Instantly a dead silence fell on the table. Ralph, with a new and shuffled pack face downwards in the little open-faced box, began.

"Card to the banker—four. Mme. Richardson loses."

Their hostess, though insisting on acting as croupier, delegated elsewhere what might be called the menial work. It was her major-domo, André, who collected the losses or delivered the gains.

"Card to the players—ace. M. Jourdain wins." She pounced inquiringly. *"Will you continue to Sept-et-le-va?"*

Jourdain shook his head. He scooped across to himself the twenty-franc counter he received from the bank, and took both off his card.

"The Corpses' Club," observed De Lautrec, just audibly.

"Card to the banker—deuce. M. De Lautrec loses..."Card to the players—king. M. De Lautrec wins. Sept-et-le-va?"

De Lautrec reached out and twisted up one corner of the card which bore two black hundred-franc counters. *"Sept-et-le-va,"* he said.

A faint billow of cigarette smoke began to roll

up into the overhead lamps. There was a feeling that they had drawn closer to the table; the high gloss of the cards, and the bright colors of their markings, against green baize, were beginning to have a somewhat hypnotic effect. The next turn-up was a card on which no stakes had been placed, an eight. On the following, Mrs. Richardson won with a ten. She turned up the corner of the card and let it remain: only to lose it again immediately afterwards when the bank itself drew a ten.

"Card to the players—king. M. De Lautrec wins." There was a slight pause. *"Quinze-et-le-va?"*

Without removing his eyes from the card, De Lautrec nodded and twisted up its second corner. He was smiling slightly. There was now in front of him the sum of fourteen hundred francs.

"Card to the banker—three. No stakes . . .

"Card to the players—five. Mme. Richardson wins. Continue?"

"It is the last card I've backed. Good luck to it. Yes."

"Card to the banker—queen. M. Jourdain loses."

The queen was the last card Jourdain had backed, and he folded his arms. Two non-stake cards ran in quick succession, after which Mrs. Richardson won again. In her excitement this buxom lady, who was over seventy, flushed. She let it remain for a third try, while the cards went on turning and glistening. The thin and sallow Frenchwoman, who up to this time had not uttered a word, now began to hiss advice:

"No, no, no. It is not orthodox. It is not scientific. It is not possible, madame, that you should—"

"*Card to the players—king. M. De Lautrec wins,*" said their hostess, her eyes snapping now. "*Trente-et-le-va?*"

Richard Curtis felt a slightly queasy sensation, which was going round the entire table as they realized the nature of this game. With three kings, De Lautrec had now won twenty-one thousand francs from the bank. Most of all Ralph Douglas, the banker, must have realized it. But he did not show it. He leaned one elbow on the table, easy, handsome, and a little supercilious (always the mask of his family), while he tapped the fingers of his other hand on the box. What driving notion had got into him tonight Curtis could not imagine. Ralph took up their hostess's question.

"*Trente-et-le-va, madame asks you?*"

"No," said De Lautrec curtly, and swept his winnings to one side. "I retire. The king will not come up again for me."

"*Card to the banker,*" intoned madame, as Ralph dealt again, "*—king. No stakes.*"

"The damned game's bewitched," Curtis said to Magda, out of the corner of his mouth. He felt rather than saw her nod. She was standing close beside him, which was disturbing in itself, and she was holding on to his arm. The cards seemed to flash now in a run of no-stakes, while De Lautrec lost his hundred-franc bet on the seven. Sevens turned up rapidly. Mrs. Richardson was brought down by the bank while making her third try for a five. At the end of the hand Mme. de la Toursèche chuckled.

"There is a little sample," she announced complacently. "Shuffle, shuffle; deal, deal—if it pleases you. The faster go the cards, the faster go our hearts. They are the poetry of old women. You have shuffled? So. We stand no casino ceremonies here. Now—"

M. Jourdain spoke with a thoughtful air.

"Madame! A point of the rules, if you please. Are two persons allowed to back the same card in their respective hands? If M. De Lautrec, for example, should decide to back an ace; and at the same time I should decide to back an ace—"

"I can find nothing in the meagre seventeenth-century rules against it. It is, we presume, a matter of taste."

De Lautrec regarded him with a bony face of sarcasm. "By all means cling to my coat-tails if it pleases you, monsieur," he said. "M. Jourdain's millions are safe on my choice, and—"

"Z-zz-z!" cried their hostess, making a noise like a blue-bottle fly in protest. "M. De Lautrec, this is intolerable. This is insufferable. Remember, please, that we are only a group of friends gathered together in a private home for—"

"I was only about to observe," said Jourdain imperturbably, "that I have taken rather a fancy to that ace. I like it. It was used first in the illustration as my card. In the next hand, I should like to back it for a thousand francs to begin with. However, I wondered whether several persons with high wagers and high winnings might not be against the rules. As for clinging to your coat-tails, monsieur, do not be alarmed. Forgive the prosiness of an old man; but at a time when you were clinging to your father's coat-tails I was shaving the necks of the great Russian punters at Trouville. Shall we continue?"

A new game was bringing out some odd sides to its players.

"I beg your pardon," said De Lautrec, and roared with mirth.

"It is nothing," the other assured him. "I was curious about your method. For instance, I heard Mme. de la Toursèche say that you sometimes broke off play even when your luck was running high, and left the table, and returned to it. That's unusual. I remember my old friend—"

"Yes, yes, it is a method. Let's get on with the game!"

"But a new method, M. De Lautrec," put in their hostess, pouncing with interest. "And it surprised me on Saturday night. Though that was a great game, eh? And we could not be bothered with much for long. But why you should have such an earnest conversation with M. Ledoux the jeweller when you went to drink...you know him, M. Jourdain; I had hoped to have him here tonight; but he is in Amsterdam today...and then why you should absent yourself for a whole hour—"

She threw out her arms. Possibly she did not understand why Ralph Douglas suddenly put down the little box, and why three people turned round to stare at De Lautrec.

19

Trente-et-le-va!

De Lautrec crushed out his cigarette and sat up straight. His prominent eyes had acquired a new fixity.

"Take care, madame la marquise," he warned humorously. But he did not address her as "mama" now; and he had a weighty courtesy. "You may be surprised at the effect it has. But make yourself clear. When you say that I 'absented myself,' you merely mean that I did not sit at the table, don't you? I did not leave the room?"

"But of course, of course, of course!" She fussed. "You did not leave the room: what of it? Unless you went to get yourself something to drink in the other room, and you were remarkably abstemious, my child."

"Still, I did not leave the house?"

"Assuredly not."

"You see, a situation is now agitating Paris," he explained, his long face growing malicious, "which, as you have read in your newspapers—"

"You are not *that* M. De Lautrec?" Mrs. Richardson was beginning explosively, and opening wide her cherubic eyes, when their hostess interrupted.

"I have not read it in my newspapers," she said grimly. "I have not read a newspaper for thirty years. That is the privilege of the old: we are not obliged to know what is going on. *Tiens*, there is an epigram, isn't it? I remember when it was fashionable to make epigrams. We used to lie awake at night torturing ourselves by thinking of old proverbs and then turning them the wrong way round in order to make them sound better. I remember once at Trouville, now you mention it, M. Jourdain—" She stopped, as though to give point to her next remark. "And whatever *is* printed in the newspapers, my child, I do not wish it discussed here. You understand?"

There was a silence. Curtis felt that a dangerous wing had brushed that room, briefly, and that it would return again.

"Our toast grows cold," complained Jourdain.

"Place your bets, mesdames, messieurs! Pah, I have been a professional hostess for so long that I have begun to talk like a croupier. *Place your bets, my friends—"*

Ralph brought the box down on the table, and took only one puzzled glance at Magda and Curtis: for he was occupied. It was the right time of night. The next few hands of Basset went with a swing that promised something to come. They

280

were not as compelling as the first, but they were working up to something greater. Jourdain and Mrs. Richardson had now settled down: the first with mildness, the second eagerly; and they were steadily increasing the size of their stakes, after the ghost of the *Soissant-et-le-va* which once agitated Versailles. Three times. Mrs. Richardson went at it like a bull at a gate, with original stakes of over a thousand each, but she got no nearer than Jourdain. Both lost with great profit to the bank—and at the same time De Lautrec's winning streak only grew better. It was partly excellent judgment, where the others seemed to use none in a game demanding judgment if not skill. But that could not be all. He turned up a corner at the right moment, he stopped at the right moment. Never yet had he got as far as the *Trente-et-le-va*, the winning of the fourth card. He had tried it once with his favorite card, the king of diamonds, but it failed and he had not tried again. Yet at the twentieth hand, by this phenomenal run, Curtis estimated that he must be well over a million francs to the good.

Curtis itched to get into the game, but at the same time he would not do it. He would not do it because Ralph was in difficulties. With the swift passing of the money back and forth, it was impossible to make out the exact status of the bank. But he knew that the bank must have lost heavily. In any but a world of cloud-cuckoo-land De Lautrecs, the bank would have won by a succession of steady pluckings that would have left the punters bare. Ralph knew that; and his temper was going.

"I say, Mag," he protested, "can't you make yourself useful and get a fellow a drink? Madame says there's whiskey here, and the butler can't leave. Out of a door down there, and straight across the hall. Damn it all—"

"I'll get it," said Curtis briefly.

He groped down to the end of the room where Ralph pointed, and out into a hall which, despite its dimness, was brighter than the card-room. Across the hall was the partly open door of another room, showing against the wall a sideboard with bottles.

"May I come along and help?" said Magda's voice, trailing him.

He never forgot her at that moment, in the hall with its pyramid of white gas-globes, and its tasselled hangings like a tent. Her silver slippers moved across the dark gray carpet. She looked at him curiously.

"It's all right. I can manage."

"What is the matter with you?" she asked.

"I know," she went on. "It's What a Fella Does and What a Fella Don't, isn't it? In case it's of the slightest interest to you, Ralph has made a flaming discovery. Perhaps after this afternoon he's right, but he has discovered that he and I were making a terrible mistake, and that we really weren't suited to each other after all."

Curtis felt he had to push the words away from him, like a man putting a heavy shot. "What did you think of it?"

"Oh, I like him as much as anybody I've ever met, and he's worth it. But I had already made the same discovery. Oh, Richard, *how* much more have I got to say: or aren't you the person I think you are?"

Unromantically, Curtis let drive with a curse

that was rich in religious fervor. In a mood of real exaltation, he stood in the hall and lifted his fist and swore.

"That's it," she said breathlessly. "That's just what I want to hear. You're a little like me. Now I *know.*"

"Come here," he commanded. "I've got something to say to you."

He took her by the wrist (she did not seem unwilling), he took her across the hall, he almost dragged her through the door of the room on the other side—and they came face to face with Bencolin, sitting near the sideboard and smoking a cigar.

"Ah," said Bencolin, removing the cigar from his mouth. "I am very pleased to see that nowadays young people run hand in hand after the cocktails like Jack and Jill. You will find the buffet well supplied."

It was like having the breath driven from your body: their acute embarrassment was equalled only by Bencolin's amiability. Had it been only Bencolin who was in the room, neither of them would have minded. But also sitting there, with glasses and cigars, were a startled Mr. George Stanfield and an even more startled Mr. Bryce Douglas.

"What the devil—!" Curtis exploded, and trailed off. "How did you get in here?"

"How do the police get in anywhere? But close that door, please."

"Does Madame know you're here?"

"Naturally," said Bencolin, raising his eyebrows. "Now listen to me. At present there is no time to explain." He pointed toward the cardroom. "We are closing in on him now—"

"I tell you it's no good," said Bryce wearily. "He did *not* leave this house on Saturday night, and—"

"You don't understand." Bencolin gestured with some savagery. "How is the game going in there?"

"De Lautrec, you mean?"

"Yes."

"He's sweeping the board," said Curtis. "There's nobody who can stand against him. He couldn't lose if he wagered that there were five aces in the pack."

Bencolin rubbed his hands together with such pressure that the hands shook. "But they are still playing?"

"Oh, yes. They—"

The door opened, and Ralph Douglas came in. If he felt any surprise at seeing Bencolin, especially with the other two, he did not show it. There was a handkerchief protruding from his side-pocket, as though he had been mopping his face; but he was very calm. He went to the sideboard, poured himself out several fingers of whiskey, and drained it neat.

"I've had enough," he announced, leaning against the sideboard and turning the glass round in his hand. "Even with all I picked up from the other two, I've dropped several thousand already —pounds, not francs. Oh, yes, I can easily afford to lose it; but I'm no fool. There's a kind of green baize lunacy that catches you if you're not very careful, and it's ruddy well not going to catch me. I've given up the bank."

"Who's got it now?" asked Curtis.

"De Lautrec. Now will somebody kindly tell me—?"

He stared round inquiringly. What thoughts were in their minds, what was going on in this muffled dining-room, Curtis himself did not know. He was looking down at Magda beside him, and reflecting that he was going to break De Lautrec's luck. He had no animus against De Lautrec, nor did he wish any gain for himself: it was oddly abstract, as though they were playing only for those little gilded counters. He would break De Lautrec's luck simply as a quiet outlet for his feelings—just as he had written the *Lawyer's Ode to Spring* only three days earlier as a means of relieving an attack of boredom. He glanced at Magda, and he suddenly realized that she was feeling the same thing. Gravely he held open the door for her, and she went out ahead of him.

It was several minutes before they regained the cardroom, and by that time De Lautrec had settled down with his bank. Mrs. Richardson and Jourdain sat in their former places. Madame was between Mrs. Richardson and De Lautrec at the corner of the table. The banker showed no sign of anything whatever; he sat bolt upright, slightly shading his eyes with one hand, and slowly pushing out the cards with the other. So intent were all of them on the game that when the two newcomers sat down they were not noticed until Curtis made a gesture to their hostess. No one talked. At their entrance into the game, Curtis with spades and Magda with De Lautrec's old suit of diamonds, De Lautrec inclined his head briefly to them: after which he shaded his eyes again.

Madame's voice, and the soft rattle of the rake, kept the game on edge.

"Place your bets, my friend. Place—"

It had become a mumble of syllables. Curtis, with the amateur's usual passion for backing court cards from a sense of greater value in winning with them, opened heavily on the jack, the queen, and the king. Magda liked the seven and the ten.

"Card to the banker—knave. M. Curtis loses...

"Card to the players—ace. M. Jourdain wins. Sept-et-le-va?"

"Sept-et-le-va," agreed Jourdain, who was each time making careful little notes in a book.

De Lautrec did not deal with Ralph's quick dash, but his very deliberation made each card seem more full of expectancy. But now the players were "plastering the board"; not a card remained without a stake of good value. Six hands passed, while the money moved across the baize to De Lautrec as though it were drawn thence by the force of gravity. In the seventh, when they were only halfway through the pack, Jourdain got as high as winning the third ace with a first stake of five hundred. For twenty-five following draws he waited without a sign, and without an ace appearing. When the fifty-first card had been exposed, they knew what the last one—always the banker's—must be. De Lautrec exposed the ace for himself; then there was a slight sigh from Jourdain as he pushed back his chair.

"I have finished, my friends," he said. "With your permission, I bow to you and retire. These things are much worse for the heart than for the wallet. When, as in the case of a business-man like myself, the two are the same thing, it is doubly dangerous."

At the end of the eighth hand Magda, who had brought the smallest stake, dropped out. She and Curtis had been speaking in whispers, but for the life of him he could not remember what they had said. He knew he could not beat De Lautrec—or, in other words, beat the world in order to show how much he had gained from a few words of Magda Toller—but he was continuing. In the first pleasure of the evening's adventure he had brought along with him four times as much money as he expected to use, and more than he earned at his homely job in the course of a year. Of this there remained at the beginning of the tenth hand just two hundred and fifty francs. Two hundred of this lay on the queen of spades; and he made *Sept-et-le-va*, the second win, very quickly. He turned up the corner to call for a third.

The evening was nearly over, and they all knew it. Ordinary conversation had come back again. Mrs. Richardson spoke gustily, in English.

"Well, people, this is my last hand. When that little nine of mine goes—as it will—I'm folding my tents. My husband is going to be furious about this; but, as Madame says, cards are the poetry of old women. I don't want to discourage you from your last stake, Mr. Curtis, but—"

"Card to the players—queen. M. Curtis wins." Madame, now hoarse from long singing, stopped and looked up at him.

They all stopped.

"Trente-et-le-va, M. Curtis?" inquired Madame. "Come, we can be informal and, between our-

selves, I am sleepy. As Mrs. Richardson says, this is the last hand. You alone play. There are twenty-one thousand francs for you, nearly four hundred and fifty of your English pounds, out of what you have lost. So if you care to pick up your winnings—?"

Curtis carefully crooked up the next corner of the card.

"*Trente-et-le-va,*" he said. "Thirty and she's still rising."

After a pause, De Lautrec removed the hand with which he had been shading his eyes. They saw what he had heretofore concealed: that his eyes were burning with a light behind the eyeballs, and his fingers handled the cards carefully so that they should not shake.

"Very well," he said with dry pleasantry. "I merely remind monsieur that the winning of the fourth card has not yet been done tonight. Are you ready, Madame?"

"*Card to the banker—six. No stakes . . .*

"*Card to the players—three. No stakes . . .*

"*Card to the banker—nine. Mme. Richardson loses.*"

Mrs. Richardson had not even glanced at her own hand. Two other persons who had been almost invisible all evening, the sallow woman professional and the old man with the dim eyes, had come up noiselessly to the table.

"*Card to the player—eight.* No stakes now remain on any card except the queen, so we will dispense with comment."

"*Card to the banker—ace.*"

"That is lucky for him," whispered Jourdain from the background.

"*Card to the player—seven*. Pah, I have a cold in my throat."

"*Card to the banker—deuce* . . .

"*Card to the player—queen. M. Curtis wins Trente-et-le-va.*"

Curtis sat back in his chair. Well, he had done it. He had done what had not been done here to-night, and in some fashion achieved the cloudy goal that was in his mind. Nor did he look up at Magda, who was standing behind his chair with her hands gripped round the back of it. He did not particularly care what happened now. About him he became aware that there was a sort of bursting pause, as though people were uncertain about whether they ought to give congratulations or merely nod approvingly. Stacks of counters came sweeping across the table. It was, he thought, a hell of a lot of money.

"Ho?" said Mrs. Richardson, somewhat inadequately.

"Yes, I once saw Dmitri of Russia do that," remarked Jourdain. "I had hoped to do it myself. I have already estimated in my little book what it would amount to. My figure is 693,000 francs."

De Lautrec had got to his feet. It had touched a spring in him: possibly of charlatanism, more likely of some mystic passion associated with his stars and his luck, which was a great deal of his life.

"I congratulate you, my friend," he said. "That was a good win. So I suppose we may conclude. For I think—yes, I am *certain*—you would not dare to challenge me again, and be so rash as to try for the final stake of *Soissant-et-le-va.*"

"No, I am not ambitious. You see, I only tried to

break your luck. Now that I have done that—"

"Evidently, evidently." De Lautrec smiled. "I warned you tonight not to play against me. You do well to heed it. Your own proverb that discretion is the better part of valor is applicable to your own prudent case. Again I congratulate you."

"But, look here," Curtis murmured, "you don't want to continue, do you? If you lose the next shot—"

De Lautrec's face went fiery, and he struck the table. "So you tried to break my luck? By God, I say that you have not the courage to see what my luck is."

"Well, if you put it like that—" said Curtis mildly. He reached out and twisted up the fourth corner of the card. "*Soissant-et-le-va.*"

Little M. Jourdain said nothing: he merely began to walk about the table in circles. Only his legs seemed excited, for he kept a calm face. More people seemed to have gathered round the table; Curtis found Ralph Douglas at his left hand, plucking at his sleeve.

"Don't be a flaming chump," urged Ralph in a fierce whisper. "I've seen this before. Take your winnings and get out while you've got the chance. That was only an accident. He's bound to get you sooner or later. It's like Doubles or Quits."

Madame's hoarse voice was upraised and quieted them:

"I am sorry. *S-ss-t!* all of you, and listen to me! I am sorry. By the head of my husband, I should have liked to see it. But, M. De Lautrec, I cannot allow it."

De Lautrec rounded on her. "So you say? We cannot allow it, eh! We cannot allow it! Why not?"

Madame chuckled. "For you it is a beautiful dream, but it is impossible. You have forgotten that you are playing the game of the Grand Monarque. I warned you what it was. I had, of course, prepared for this contingency on the part of the house: had I kept the bank, there is in my safe enough money to meet the loss if a successful player went to *Soissant-et-le-va*. You have won enormously tonight, I grant you: enough to keep you in luxury all your life. But you forget that, if the queen appears for the fifth time to M. Curtis, you will be obliged to pay sixty-seven times what has already been won. You know the rule of this house—cash. He does not insist on his right, or you might be in difficulties. If he should win, where would you get the money to pay him? Why, such a sum has not been played for since the days of the Bourbons!"

De Lautrec was aflame with that idea. "Has it not?" he asked softly. "Then we shall see. In the first place, I assure you that he will not win—"

"That is enough, eh?"

"Listen to me, mama! Do you want to drive me mad? Listen and let me speak. I *have* the money. It is you who forget how I won here on Saturday night. I borrowed one of the steel strong-boxes in your safe, didn't I, to put most of my winnings in? You advised it yourself, so that I should not take so much away with me through lonely country at that hour in the morning. I took only a comparative bagatelle away with me, didn't I?"

Penetrating slowly into Curtis's mind was a realization that he knew he should have fastened on long before. When De Lautrec had left this house on Saturday night (or morning), he had been taken and searched by the Foreign Office men. Curtis remembered the exact details of the money he had been carrying then: "one packet of twenty thousand-franc notes, and one packet of fifty hundred-franc notes." It was a good full-blooded sum, of course. But it was of no size compared to the stakes that were played for here—and yet all through the case De Lautrec had been constantly congratulated by everybody, had even congratulated himself, on his astounding run of luck. It could not be thought that the high-living De Lautrec would dream in bliss over a win of twenty-five thousand francs.

"I concede that," Madame told him. "You have my receipt for it, I think. I had thought of it, yes. Yes, yes, yes! But still it is not enough—"

"Suppose I gave you security, then?" he shouted.

"Security?"

"That's what I said. Security that would make all your beautiful conscientious scruples foolish—"

A curious expression had come into her eyes.

"What is it, M. De Lautrec?"

"Ah, that's of no importance. Something else that I put into that little steel strongbox—something you did not give me a receipt for, because you did not see me put it in. It makes you jump eh? Well, there is enough security to make your bank safe. Here, I have the key." He fumbled in his pocket. "Now take me to your office, and let me open my box, and—"

"I still ask, what is it?" insisted Madame quietly. "Besides, it is not I whom you will have to satisfy: it is the gentleman you must play against."

De Lautrec stopped. Already he had shuffled the cards, in a sort of frenzied abstraction, passed them to be cut, and jammed them into the box. Now the box fell out of his hand upon the table. His jaw opened as well; he checked himself, and, as he turned his head round, there was an expression of something like horror on his face. He had realized what he had said.

At the same time a hand and an arm emerged from the gloom beyond the blaze over the table. It was a powerful and somewhat hairy hand, and it fastened on De Lautrec's.

"I will have that key, my friend," said Bencolin. "So that is where you hid Rose Klonec's jewels, eh? Do not disturb yourselves, I beg of you," Bencolin added, turning to the others. "Madame la marquise, I am sorry this had to happen here; but I had hoped he would lead us farther afield than this. M. De Lautrec, I should like to have a word with you. Madame, we shall require your assistance, and I should be obliged if you would accompany us. M. Curtis, since you ought to know against what stakes you were to play, I suggest that you come also. The others will please remain here."

In silence they went out of the room, and into the dim little office off the central hall, where Curtis had changed his money before. Madame turned up the gas-jets, to show a roll-top desk, a deep iron-barred window, a small safe let into the wall. Bencolin closed and locked a door walled with iron.

De Lautrec's wits had returned. His momentary

touch of what Ralph had called green-baize lunacy was gone; his face had brightened like the gas-jets, with a vast look of relief.

"M. Bencolin, you accuse me—?"

"Of having stolen the greater part of the jewellery-collection of Rose Klonec from the wall-safe of her apartments at 81 Avenue des Invalides."

"It is a foolish charge."

"Why? We have only to open one strong-box with this key—"

De Lautrec shook his head. "Under the circumstances, to prove such a charge would be difficult. I borrowed some jewels from her, and I liked them so well that I decided to keep them. A week ago—even two nights ago, I acknowledge—I could not have paid for what I wanted, and then it would have been theft. But you don't seem to realize that I am now swollen with money. Why," his eyes narrowed, "why, consider what I offered Rose for them! Much more than she could get from the merchants. I am prepared to pay that value now...or, of course, to return the jewels."

"Without doubt," said Bencolin dryly. "Still, I think Rose Klonec's parents would prefer your very generous money offer. They are people in Provence, I understand, not too well off; and they would rather have a little over the value of the jewels than to see you in prison. In fact, I had already consulted her solicitor on this point. So if you will just sign this—"

Taking a folded sheet of legal paper from his topcoat pocket, he handed it to De Lautrec. De Lautrec read it, and his face went pasty.

"This admits too much," he said.

"Yes. It also promises you immunity. It is called

compounding a felony as well, but I have no objection to being a party to it, and to doing a little good by exceedingly crooked ways."

"There is no trick here?"

"None. It is a correct account? You will sign?"

"It is a correct account. I will sign," blurted De Lautrec.

He put it on top of the small safe, and signed with Bencolin's fountain-pen.

"After all," Bencolin went on reflectively, "admitting that it is a correct account is an excellent safeguard for you. It prevents your arrest on a much more serious charge than stealing Rose Klonec's jewels. It prevents your arrest for murdering Rose Klonec herself."

De Lautrec managed to get the cap back on the fountain-pen. "God above, you thought I was the murderer? You thought I was the man in the brown raincoat and black hat?"

"No," said Bencolin.

He was standing with his back to the door. He turned round now; he unlocked and opened it without haste, but in time for them to see a person who had been leaning close to listen outside. He drew this person inside and closed the door. It was a man slightly under medium height, with a long nose, a sandy moustache, and a supercilious but frightened eye.

"This is the man in the brown raincoat and the black hat," said Bencolin, with his hand on the shoulder of Bryce Douglas.

20

". . . That Walks a Crooked Mile"

It may have been dawn or still night; but you could not have told which in the closed house of the Marquise de la Toursèche, and it is not certain that anyone there would have cared. Four persons sat round the green baize table under the bright lights. Bencolin sat at the head of it. At one side of it sat Madame herself, her wrinkled hands folded and her eyes still gleaming. On the other side sat Richard Curtis and Ralph Douglas.

"He will go free?" inquired Madame.

"For a certain reason, he will go free," replied Bencolin.

It was like the sing-song air of a ritual. Ralph himself kept his eyes on the table.

"Monsieur," their hostess went on, "I lent you my house for your little trap. I enjoyed it and I should enjoy it again. I could make sure that none of my customary guests attended, to give us a bad reputation. Even when you provided all the actors except M. De Lautrec, I would not have them disturbed with talk of murders: for I think Mme. Richardson and M. Jourdain found us too exciting company not to return. But now you shall tell us about it. And you shall tell me also why you insisted that that magnificently beautiful little girl be sent home like a child."

"Because," said Bencolin, "so much of the story concerns her that it would not be good for her to hear. For the same reason, these two must hear it. But they must also promise me that on one point she never learns the truth."

He sat with his elbows on the table, brushing the palms of his hands together.

"The truth?" repeated Curtis.

"The truth of why Bryce Douglas killed Rose Klonec," said Bencolin.

After a pause Bencolin went on.

"This story is the story of two crimes—a robbery and a murder—each unconnected, entirely independent of the other and yet each serving to conceal and guard the other. They intertwine to such an extent that they cannot be separated, though it is in the murder that we are most interested.

"From the first we were misled by one fact: that no murder had been intended. It threw us completely off the track in searching for a motive. We were searching for a man who either hated, feared, or loved Rose Klonec. Rose Klonec was killed unintentionally, however, by a man who neither hated, feared, nor loved her: indeed, who hardly knew her except as one government agent knows another. He seemed, and was, a man of painfully circumspect professional life. He did not care for Rose Klonec. But he did very bitterly and also painfully care for Magda Toller. He made no secret of it. He was so abnormally sensitive on this point that he betrayed his emotions, and asked questions, even when a stranger's eye strayed towards her. He seldom concealed his belief that she was a young girl who was never genuinely in love with Ralph Douglas—and there, as in many things, he was correct. His grand mistake lay in his egocentrical certainty that he was *the* person, and that under the proper circumstances she would discover it. (She must not learn this: Miss Toller does not know her own potentialities for upsetting the lives and apple-carts of men. I am talking to two people who, next to Bryce Douglas, know it best.) And therefore Bryce worked out a curious plot. Murder had no part in it. He would have been shocked, then, at the idea of murder. He worked out this plot with a loving ingenuity, exactly in the style of his favorite detective fiction. His careful attention to detail—especially sensational detail—was like that of a Murder on Paper. He never lost his nerve, because he had meant it to be little more than a Murder on Paper. So far as my own belief is concerned, I should call it ten times worse than a real murder." Bencolin paused for a moment before continuing.

"But I had better tell you about it as I put it together. At the outset I was not suspicious of him, any more than I am congenitally suspicious of everybody, because there was no motive and because in one happening he led us ingeniously astray. Had there been a motive, or had it not been for this happening, he would have been one of the first to suspect; and I told him so to his face. The fondness for elaborate detail, enigmatic detail, was exactly like him.

"The first time a possibility occurred to me was during our interview last night with De Lautrec. We had just come, you recall, from an interview with Bryce, in which we got the story of De Lautrec's alibi. At first glance his story seemed reasonable enough. He said that he (Bryce) had in the middle of the afternoon received a telephone-message (telephones again!) from his secret-office confederate, Rose Klonec. The message warned him that De Lautrec was going for a treasonable meeting to a mysterious destination, and all the rest of it, and urged him to follow. Bryce said Rose Klonec knew he was only going to this—er—establishment of Chance; but Bryce cleverly explained it by saying she must have wished De Lautrec detained by Foreign Office men so that she could have the night with Ralph Douglas.

"Very well. Now, during our subsequent talk with De Lautrec, De Lautrec volunteered the information that all Saturday afternoon he, Rose Klonec, and her maid, had been out for a *picnic on the river*. Yet Bryce told us that she had telephoned him in the afternoon. It was not necessarily important. There were several explanations: (1) it was a lie on De Lautrec's part; (2) it was a casual error on Bryce's part; (3) she might have found a telephone even in company and on a picnic.

"Of these we might discard the 'casual error'

(2). A man like Bryce does not make such errors, especially when he has an important job on hand and needs to make preparations with a Foreign Office colleague for the chase. (1) seemed possible, for I shall tell you why I was far from satisfied with De Lautrec's behavior; and (3) quite probable.

"But I could not concentrate on this at the moment, because of that wild business of the puzzling circumstances of the murder, the cause of death, the complete false trail to Miss Toller, and such matters as we have now explained. It was only this morning that I could work coherently at it. I examined Annette Fauvel, Klonec's maid: with what result?

"On Saturday, so the maid stated, the three of them had left for their picnic at ten-thirty in the morning—they had driven directly to the river, never stopping, and all in the same car—they had hired a boat—and from the morning until the evening 'just before dark' Rose Klonec was never off the river. I made Annette repeat all that. The boatman was later questioned, and he confirmed her.

"Which eliminated both (1) and (3). It was not a lie on the part of De Lautrec, because he was telling the truth. She could have reached a telephone anywhere in Paris, except in the middle of the Seine. And the only alternative was that Bryce himself was lying.

"This threw a strange light on the situation. Rose Klonec—says Bryce—knew quite well that on Saturday night De Lautrec was going to gamble at the home of the Marquise de la Toursèche. Then how in hell's hinges was it that *Bryce* didn't know that too? By his own confession, he had been watching De Lautrec's movements for some time. We had heard from De Lautrec that he (De Lautrec) had been going there a long while. He had even fallen into a regular schedule: he would go about half-past ten in the evening, and he never left before dawn. It is so strange as to be almost impossible that a tireless follower like Bryce Douglas had no idea of this, and did not even know what the sinister house by the Hill of Acorns really was.

"In describing his pursuit of De Lautrec, Bryce gave us a thrilling situation, full of ghostly suspense. He and his picked-man Mercier waited outside the house for 'over three mortal hours,' until De Lautrec—due perhaps to an unusually early closing of the bank—?"

He glanced at Madame, who nodded. "Yes, he had broken it," she explained.

"—De Lautrec left. Bryce was very emphatic. It provided De Lautrec with an alibi. It also provided, you notice, an alibi for Bryce.

"But he was waiting there, wasn't he, in the company of a fellow-agent? No, he was not. By his own statement he was watching the front-gate, and his companion was watching the back-gate, in a fairly extensive wall. He himself acknowledged that both promised not to leave their posts in case the quarry slipped out. Now, if we have suspicious minds, we can think this: that Bryce Douglas knew such a fervent gambler as De Lautrec would not leave that house for many hours. Barring sudden death or an act of God, Bryce could be as sure of it as we are of most things in this world. It was not quite as tight-laced an alibi as Bryce might have devised; but it was a very good one, for (as you shall see) he was not devising an alibi for murder.

"Now, since I was certain Bryce was lying, it was well to ask the question: Why was it that I did not originally suspect him? Well, first, the lack of motive. Second, the fact that on one occasion he and the man in the brown raincoat had been seen —or *almost* seen—together.

"I could testify to this myself. On Wednesday night of last week, you recall, I had seen a tallish man in a brown raincoat climbing the wall round the Villa Marbre. (By the way, Bryce seems to have inclinations in this direction, for in his fanciful tale of his sinister watch before this house, he told us how at one time he had intended to climb the wall.) On Friday night I saw a man, apparently another man, certainly a shorter man, walk up openly to the gate of the Villa Marbre, and go in. I followed while he went into the grounds— both of us creeping: Lord!—and I saw him go round to the kitchen window at the rear, where a light was burning. Mark that: where a light was burning.

"He approached the window and peered through the shutters. The light inside went out. He jumped back. I approached him, and he told me how he had seen inside a figure in a brown raincoat and black hat, juggling with champagne-bottles.

"Reflecting on this, I thought for the first time of certain unusual things I had found in the kitchen of the Villa Marbre. I groan to acknowledge that I did not at first see anything significant in them—I was merely detaining you with a few

303

remarks, and a little improving talk about electric clocks, while my men took Miss Toller's hand-print from the car outside. I refer to the facts that (1) in the rear wall of the kitchen, *directly over the light-switch,* there was driven into the wall nearly to its head a white drawing-pin or thumb-tack; and (2) stretching along the back of the electric refrigerator, towards the window, there was a length of heavy black thread, evidently broken off, with a loop at the end of it.

"The electric-switch is the ordinary French or English type, with a projection which is pressed up or down. When the projection is down, the light is on. The window, though closely shuttered, was not quite closed. Now, if a loop in a piece of strong black thread were placed round the downward projection of the light-switch; and then run up over a firm thumb-tack driven into the wall to act as a pulley: and then run three feet or so to the window; then the end of it could easily be passed out through a slit in the shutter. You pull—the switch comes up. The light goes out. You yank—to break it off. But you yank too hard, and break your thread too close to the window...

"Yes, it is too bad.

"At this point, in the words of the improving Scottish poem, I said to myself, 'Auld bald Benco-lin, clay-cauld Bencolin, dour bald Bencolin, your wits have gone. They are unhinged. That little son-of-a-seacook, Bryce Douglas, *meant* you to see that whole performance. He arranged it for you, you jackanapes, to deceive you. When he paid his first visit to the villa on Wednesday night, in a certain disguise, he knew you had spied him climbing the wall and wondered if you had recognized him, for he knew that your eyes are sharp even if your wits are not. So he must test it. And he must make himself doubly sure by a little comedy. He would *create* the man-in-the-brown-raincoat before the man appeared for any sinister purpose.

" 'On Friday night, then,'—I am still speaking to myself, an unedifying process—'his first appearance at the villa you did not see. He probably climbed the rear wall, while you were watching at the front (the same trick he later played on Mercier here). He did what business he had to do in the villa, which was altering an original intention and putting in *one* prepared bottle of champagne in place of the six undoctored ones that had been there before. He arranged his drawing-pin and his string. He left the light on. He returned over the wall. He was then ready to come boldly to the front gate and let me follow him for an episode which should convince me.'

"I have now finished talking to myself.

"But," continued Bencolin, "had I realized it, Bryce let drop some very suggestive remarks when he was describing the brown-coated man in the kitchen, changing bottles (which was what he himself had been doing ten minutes before). Why does he come clear out there to meet Rose Klonec in a locked villa belonging to Ralph? And why— says he—won't he wait? Why does he go away when he sees the brown-coated man? *Because*, he says, *he is fairly sure the man inside is Ralph, preparing for a party.* He is already sowing suspicion on a grand scale, you see."

Ralph raised his head from staring at the green-baize table. His face looked heavy and bewildered.

"I've had too much in this case," he groaned. "Do you mean Bryce, Bryce of all people, arranged all this to throw suspicion on me? I can't believe it. I won't believe it."

Bencolin looked at him and nodded.

"But not suspicion of murder," Bencolin said gently; "that is the thing I wish to emphasize. And we may as well continue with that part of it.

"If, as then seemed to me certain, Bryce Douglas was the enigmatic figure in the case, how would the appearance of the man in the brown raincoat fit him?

"First of all, there is height. Whereupon we come to one of the sweeping, suggestive deductions of Jean-Baptiste Robinson, which I thought illuminating even when he missed the point. Jean-Baptiste says the figure is a woman. He declares that the woman wears footgear like a surgical boot, with a very high heel, which will add inches to height: in which the woman slips and almost lands at full length on the floor. Now, you will embarrass a woman with many articles of clothing—particularly men's trousers—but there is one thing with which you will never embarrass her, and that is high heels. There she is at home. Quite the reverse, it is a man who will be troubled above all things by high heels; he will carry himself in strange ways; he will be very apt to pitch at full length on a polished floor. Also, when Miss Toller saw him walking under the trees in the moonlight, it is not surprising that nothing in Bryce's carriage and gait struck her as familiar. Yes, our murderer was clearly from the first a man of a little under middle height.

"For the rest, do not be impressed by the moustache. It is a real moustache, and Bryce does not wear a false one in ordinary life, or his social behavior must at times be a little strained. There are men at half a dozen theatres on the boulevards who with actor's clay can model a moustache out of sight and have no difficulty in deceiving people in the front stalls. Bryce's wig need only be of the clumsiest—for blind Hortense's sight alone—a little more actor's clay and coloring will produce the 'pinkish spot' of a face she describes, and there is sufficient family resemblance already to make it quite reasonable. In fact, it is difficult to see how our brown-coated man could have been anybody but Bryce.

"The myriad of small and, to Bryce, pleasant details need not detain us: the letters, bleached out, with Ralph's signature at the bottom, and re-typed; the choice of Hortense because she could be made blind and because she had never met Ralph. As for the letters, Mabusse read them with one touch of the ultra-violet ray. There was one devilish complication, however, in the fact that Hortense took the letter to Stanfield, an old lover of Rose Klonec, and it nearly upset the whole plan; but in general—"

Ralph struck the table.

"But what the blazes was he going to DO?" he demanded. "If he didn't intend to kill her, what was he after? And the motive? And also something that I brought up myself today—"

"Let us get it in order," said Bencolin soothingly. "When Bryce brings his plan towards fulfillment, let us examine in conjunction with it the strange behavior of M. Louis De Lautrec.

"I have indicated that I was far from satisfied with De Lautrec's behavior from the first. But it seemed wrong in a curious way. He was not worried, personally worried, about the murder: it did not seem to concern him at all. Yet at that first interview he was very worried about something. It was a remarkable fact that, whichever way our conversation turned, it always came back to the subject of jewellery.

"I was prodding him about the three pieces of jewellery which—I then had reason to think—he blackmailed out of Rose Klonec on Saturday night. (And that part of the story is quite true: he really did get the emerald pendant, the diamond ring, and the ear-rings from her in the way he said he did.) He finally admitted this, though something else always appeared to be weighing on his mind. At every opportunity he would flash out with, 'So you think I stole her jewellery, eh?' Well, he tells me this, and I believe him; but still the man is not satisfied. He tries to explain his uneasiness by saying that the story, if told on the boulevards, would ruin him—which is precisely what it would not do. Rose Klonec was a widely known terror who had gained the dislike of most people. Anyone who could have outwitted her so neatly as De Lautrec had done over those three pieces of jewellery, and could have turned the tables in just that way, need expect only admiring approval.

"Now, De Lautrec was obviously very much impressed by the theory in *L'Intelligence* that a woman had committed the murder at the Villa Marbre. That is the way Jean-Baptiste Robinson affects some people, and the theory had many points of plausibility. Whereupon De Lautrec told me something so surprising as to make my head spin. I asked him how he knew Rose Klonec intended to go to the Villa Marbre on Saturday night—how, in addition any 'phantom Ralph Douglas' could have persuaded her to go—and he replied that she was persuaded by a *woman's* voice on the telephone, making an appointment for Ralph Douglas. He says he overheard this conversation.

"There were improbabilities in this account on the face of it: what woman? But immediately after this De Lautrec went elaborately out of his way in order to throw suspicion on Annette Fauvel, as possibly being the man in the brown raincoat and black hat. I naturally asked him what her motive might have been, and he merely shrugged his shoulders and looked wise.

"If this—I mean the voice of a woman making an appointment—seemed difficult to believe last night, I knew it was reeling falsehood this morning, when I became certain of Bryce Douglas's guilt. I knew Bryce had acted alone in the business. And this point supplied the answer to one final vexed question: how was the man in the brown raincoat able to persuade crafty Rose Klonec to come to the Villa Marbre, when Ralph Douglas never appeared himself in the business? *Because he was Ralph Douglas's brother.* Not only that, but he was associated with Rose in their mutual business; he could easily convey a private message to her with utter convincingness.

"Well, De Lautrec had sworn it was a woman: De Lautrec lied, and knew he lied. Did he know

309

or guess who really had communicated with her? In either case, why did he try to throw suspicion on Annette? Why should Annette be the man in the brown raincoat? Of course, there were Rose Klonec's jewels...

"Full stop. I questioned De Lautrec about the rest of that great jewel-collection, in which three pieces made a small show indeed. But now, instead of being passionately interested in them as he had been before, De Lautrec was passionately indifferent. He told me they were in a wall-safe in her apartments. The lawyer would come tomorrow to get them. At present the safe could not be opened, because nobody knew the combination. And so on, shrugging his shoulders. To me it seemed very unlikely that this man, who paid the rent of the place and had taken it over from the manager of the building, would not know the combination of what was, strictly speaking, his own wall-safe.

"The weight of inference had now piled up too far. There was as yet no suggestion of a theft of jewels. But at the same time De Lautrec was trying to throw suspicion on Annette—for something. What? Suppose De Lautrec had himself raided that safe, and was trying to lay a false trail towards Annette when the theft should be discovered? It was the only thing which could reasonably explain all his behavior, and it was worth following up.

"And if De Lautrec did this, when did he do it? It was right here that the two stories, that of the robbery and that of the murder, crossed each other at a significant angle.

"From information I obtained this afternoon,

and you obtained tonight, we can reconstruct the story of the robbery. Rose Klonec (like a prudent woman) had got made for herself a complete set of excellent replicas of all her jewels. But her practicality lured her into one great mistake—the worst mistake, aside from going to the Villa Marbre on Saturday night, she ever made. On Saturday evening De Lautrec threw his bomb and demanded some jewels as the price of her going to the villa. Rose was insane with rage. And even then she compromised. Two of the three pieces of jewellery she handed over to him were genuine. One —the emerald pendant, the most valuable—was bogus. That was her error.

"De Lautrec, believing them all genuine, was satisfied. He had then no intention of robbing her. He came here to the home of Madame la Marquise. From the first he began to win heavily, without needing any securities. But, when once he went to the other room for a drink, an odd thing happens..."

Madame de la Toursèche threw back her head and cackled with mirth.

"Yes, yes, yes. I told the little ones what it was tonight. M. De Lautrec broke off all his winnings to go into earnest conversation with M. Ledoux the jeweller; and afterwards he decided to keep out of the game for a while."

"Exactly. Now, he did not show the pendant voluntarily to the jeweller, and he did not show either of the other two. Communication with M. Ledoux at Amsterdam this afternoon satisfied us on these points. The pendant fell out of his pocket while they were drinking together. De Lautrec merely said, 'Interesting little thing, isn't it?' M.

Ledoux replied, 'Yes, for an imitation, it is not at all bad.'

"You have seen at least a few specimens of De Lautrec's flaming temper. Though he said nothing, he went into one of his worst furies right then. He knew that Rose had hoaxed him for the last time. She was not going to lose a few pieces of that cherished collection: she was going to lose all of it: and he was going to get it. He saw a way by which this could be done with comparative safety to himself. That very night, obviously, was the night Rose would be away all night at the Villa Marbre; and, if she pleased Ralph Douglas, she would not long remain in De Lautrec's apartments where he could get at the jewels. It was also the maid's night out. If he could contrive for himself a good alibi here at Madame's, he could snap his fingers at Rose afterwards. She would certainly denounce him; but she could not prove anything in the face of an airtight alibi.

"De Lautrec has a type of intelligence which is cunning rather than ingenious, like Bryce's. His alibi, as you have guessed, rested on the psychology of gaming-tables—which gave him his inspiration, because he knew it well—and on the peculiar lighting arrangements in this room.

"When the play is fast and the game absorbing, your rabid gamester (as all who play here are) is dead to everything except the board. It will require a major explosion to make him look round. He will not get up, he will not move. Furthermore, he is absolutely oblivious to the passing of time. We have all had the experience of seeing a group of addicts rouse themselves with a puzzled stare when someone mentions the time. But there are, you observe, no clocks in this room. On the contrary, everything is complete darkness except here—directly over the table.

"You see then, how it worked. If De Lautrec announced that he would stand out of the game for a time, very well. All the others in that tiny group were gathered round the table; had there been more people, it would have been more dangerous. As it was, he could slip from the house, climb the gate, get away in his car, take the jewels from the safe, replace them sardonically with false ones, and return here. Provided he did not take too long about it, all his fellow-gamblers would be willing to swear he had never even left the room ...particularly, you see, since he would immediately join in the game afterwards. The two halves of the game would then interlock, the various hands of the game becoming so jumbled together in everybody's mind that nobody would afterwards *even be able to swear at what time he was away from the table*."

Madame bobbed her head.

"I noticed it," she announced. "But then noticing such things is my business, you understand. And yet, though I noticed the length of time he was out of the game, I assuredly thought he was in the room."

"And now, with neat artistic effect, De Lautrec's story joins that of the redoubtable Bryce Douglas. Or, rather, it misses that of Bryce by a hair—just as Bryce and De Lautrec missed each other before the gates of this house. Less than an hour would suffice for what De Lautrec had to do. A little more than an hour would suffice for Bryce's trip to the Villa Marbre, his activities there, and his return. (In Bryce's case, that surprises you? You say it takes close on half an hour to go to the villa in a car? It does—from the center of the city. But consult your map of Paris and its environs, and see just where we are now. The Hill of Acorns is on the outer edge of Longchamp, in a cross-country line quite close to the Forest of Marly, another fact I found interesting.)

"Bryce, pretending to watch outside the gates, must have left here about half-past twelve. You will recall that he and Mercier came in a taxi; his own car had already been parked and hidden at the foot of the hill since he wished to give the appearance of being stranded in the wilds. De Lautrec must have left only a short time after-wards—and they missed each other neatly. Bryce has no suspicion De Lautrec is not still safely in the house. De Lautrec has no suspicion that there are supposed to be watchers outside.

"De Lautrec, having less to do, returned first. Bryce must have returned some minutes after-wards—again a deft missing of times. To both Bryce and De Lautrec everything seemed serene. De Lautrec, inside the house again, continued his winning streak; he asked for and got a deposit-box from Madame here, in which he locked most of his winnings and also, unseen, the jewels he had stolen. The only things he took away with him were a small part of his winnings, and the three original pieces of jewellery. Why? Because, though he had shown only one of them to M. Le-doux, he believed they were *all* false. It is surely apparent that, if he left most of his money win-nings behind in case he should be robbed in that lonely place, he would hardly have taken along three pieces of jewellery whose value must have totalled as much as he had won in the entire evening. But he was not going home. He was going direct to some night-haunt, and thence onward in such a way that he could provide for himself a three-day alibi.

"Imagine his shock when, as he leaves this house in a glow of satisfaction, he is set on by Foreign Office men—who say they have been watching the house all night! Heretofore he has been in only one quandary. Unfortunately, M. Ledoux the jeweller has already seen the emerald pendant. For all he knows, someone may have caught a glimpse of the other articles as well. Even though the pendant is an imitation, there are likely to be awkward questions when the news of the robbery comes out. Therefore the things must not be returned to Rose Klonec's apartments; he must keep them with him, and explain them away. For, remember, he could do that easily. That evening he had left 81 Boulevard des Invalides some time before Rose left it. He could not have robbed her before then, since she took some trinkets out of the safe to take to the villa Marbre. If his alibi at the gaming-house held, his whole alibi was perfect.

"But now the Foreign Office men intervened. And, after De Lautrec's shock of horror, he heard one of them (Bryce Douglas) speak up strongly and give him an absolute alibi. Here is Bryce swearing De Lautrec never left the house all evening: *Bryce merely preparing his own alibi.* De Lautrec must have been staggered, but he was grateful. It was only when he heard of the murder —when all the facts were in the evening's papers

—that I think De Lautrec suddenly smiled. He realized whose voice had made the appointment with Rose Klonec for the Villa Marbre; he may even have seen Bryce and Rose together. He realized, in short, why Bryce was giving him such a complete alibi.

"Was De Lautrec agreeable to this? Heartily, my friends, heartily. He must cover up Bryce all he could, for in doing so he was covering up himself. Thus the ends of the tale cross, the destinies converge; and De Lautrec concocts that clumsy fiction about a 'woman's voice' both to shift suspicion from his unconscious ally and to throw it in the direction of Annette Fauvel.

"To conclude this merry little account of cross-purposes and the perverseness of all human things, you shall hear what sly Mr. Bryce Douglas intended to do during his appearance as the man in the brown coat. What exactly was his plot? It was so to discredit his brother in the eyes of the world, and especially Magda Toller's, that everyone who met him would afterwards feel a qualm of disgust. Not fear or the vengeance of the law, you understand; not tall crimes and romantic evils; nothing but disgust."

He paused, and looked at Ralph.

"Will you understand me, Mr. Douglas," he went on, "if I say that that is how *he* saw you, and that he wished to make Miss Toller see it as well?"

Again there was a silence.

"Now take your mind back to a celebrated incident a year or more ago. I heard of it, unfortunately, only today; but it appears to have been widely published at the time and to have been read by all Paris. There was a dispute or quarrel at a night-club, during which you fought with Rose Klonec over her desire to handle a knife-thrower's weapons. She slashed at you, either accidentally or deliberately; and you told her that if she ever tried that again you would take a knife and spoil her face... No, I know the story was not true. But Paris believed it. And Bryce, impersonating you before Paris at the villa on Saturday night, intended in a modified form to—"

Ralph brought both his fists down on the table.

"You don't mean," he interrupted, "that the swine intended to take a knife and mark her face with it, so that it should seem I did it during a drunken brawl?"

"Not with a knife," said Bencolin. "With a razor. It was easier."

Ralph and Curtis looked at each other. Only Madame remained nodding and winking, with a gargoyle-grin of understanding.

"I know," Madame said simply.

"Yes. And he intended to do it in such a manner that Rose Klonec herself should never know you had not done it. That was the heart and essence of the scheme. She was to make such a scandal that—

"But you have heard the preparations of the first part of his scheme, how she was induced to the Villa Marbre. Now, somebody must see Ralph, somebody must identify him, somebody must be able to swear afterwards to his presence: hence Hortense. But Rose herself, of course, could not come face to face with the impostor. She must be drugged—if possible, both drugged *and* drunk—before Bryce the impersonator could enter the

317

villa. Hence the large assortment of good champagne to entice her; but, after the rejection of several plans, only the one bottle of skillfully and weirdly doctored Roederer. From the balcony he could watch, and make certain when she had taken it.

"When the scandal burst afterwards, there would be two interpretations of it.

"1. Rose Klonec's interpretation to take before the courts in suing him, as she would be quick to do. Rose would say, 'He always cherished a grudge. He enticed me there. He put a drug into something. When I was asleep, he made these scars on my face, which ruin me forever.' Rose would honestly believe that, because to her eyes it was the truth. But the popular belief would be different. The head-wagging world would say, 'Well, she is bound to tell us something like that, to make herself out as ladylike as she can. She didn't drink, eh? She didn't riot, eh? She didn't quarrel, eh?' And their interpretation would be:

"2. Rose and Ralph Douglas had picked up their affair again secretly. They made a rendez-vous at the Villa Marbre. There they had an intimate supper. The lady was not drugged, as she says: she was only roaring drunk, as the man was. There was a quarrel, at the end of which Ralph Douglas fulfilled his old threat—"

Bencolin paused.

"It is hardly necessary to elaborate, but this latter interpretation is the one Bryce wished everyone to take. He was prepared to show evidence of it. When she was asleep, he was going to take upstairs the prepared supper-table. When, the next morning, Mme. Klonec was found by her maid recovering from a stupor—the cuts not causing enough blood to endanger life, but merely to spoil beauty—there could be only one deduction. Round the room should be found scattered those conventional relics of a spree with which the films and novelettes have made us so familiar, and which would be instantly recognized by every sober housewife from here to the Butte. The empty bottles. The torn clothes. The ashtrays full of cigarette-stubs. The disarranged furniture ... do you not see our virtuous newspaper-readers looking at each other in a meaning way, and hear them saying, 'Oho!'

"That was why it was such a perfect plan. Its very falseness made it ring true. Here is Rose swearing before a court that she was drugged and attacked like a schoolgirl; and the contrary evidences jeering up at her from the other side. It was real life aped with brilliance. Whatever happens, the only one who suffers is Ralph."

Curtis interposed. "But, look here! If Bryce had acted as liaison officer—that is, if he had carried a message to her in Ralph's name—wouldn't he be drawn into it publicly too?"

"No. Do you see? She would not dare. This time Bryce's role would be completely calm, icy, and indifferent. 'My good woman,' he would say, 'you will not mention my name in this in any way whatever. I acted foolishly in conveying a message to you; but remember your circumstances now. You are no longer a poule-de-luxe. What employment have you? Only what you have had in the past, employment on good pay from Masset of the secret-office, and you can have it again. But you know my position; you know it must not be learned why you and I have been associating; you know my influence with Masset; you know that if you mention my name in any way, you will never earn a franc again.' If you can think of any more absolutely effective way of stopping the lady's mouth, I should be interested to hear it.

"Well, the whole plan broke down...you gentlemen have learned why. It was not only that Bryce's excessive ingenuity defeated itself and brewed liquid chloroform in a champagne bottle. But—waiting in the dark until she should drink the drug, waiting outside the villa—Bryce saw something which must have brought tears into his eyes. If you think that is an exaggeration, M. Douglas, you should have seen his face tonight when he learned that I knew.

"For he saw, coming into the grounds of the villa, Miss Magda Toller—the one person in all the world he wished to convince of Ralph's guilt.

"That is beautiful, eh? The auld, bald Bencolin removes a metaphorical hat. I salute the crooked Providence that walks a crooked mile. But there was worse. Bryce crept up the balcony stairs after Magda to see what was going on, when he could stand the suspense no longer. He had heard one woman stop talking, and he had heard another hysterical woman making threats as to how she would like to cut an artery and—" Bencolin stopped, brushing his hands together. "When he went up into the dressing-room to find out the reason for their silence, he found a good reason. He found one girl lying across a dressing-table, stupefied with the fumes of chloroform. He found a dead woman on the floor, killed by his alchemist's bottle. In two strokes his plan was defeated."

Bencolin leaned back in his chair. His face looked sallow and withered, and he shaded his eyes with his hand.

"There has been stated as a maxim of Bonaparte: 'Have two plans. Leave something to chance.' Bryce Douglas did not have two plans. But he made one on the spur of the moment—and again he drew it straight out of sensational fiction. He executed it in that blank fifteen to twenty minutes (an enormous time, my friends!) which one girl did not remember.

"She had cried out that she would like to kill Rose Klonec by making her bleed to death. He would now try to convince her that she had done actually so. Now, mark the important part: the point was not to have her arrested or even suspected of murder. Far from it! He would even take care that she left no fingerprints on that dressing-table—for, you recall, we found none and Miss Toller says nothing of wiping them off there. But he would convince her that she had committed a crime; he, the Foreign Office detective, would then solve it brilliantly. He would communicate with her in private, showing himself in a cool and heroic role, and he would explain how he would shield her. It was a part to his taste. It would turn all her sympathy towards him. And it was an alternate plan even more ingenious than the first—for, after all, he could *still* pretend that Ralph had picked up the old love-affair with Klonec at the Villa Marbre.

"You know what he did. It is the only case within my knowledge in which the murderer kills the same person twice. He cut the artery in the arm of a dead woman. There was some blood, because the woman was lying downwards over the bath with her arm hanging down. Obviously, he had to use the stiletto because that was the only weapon Miss Toller had seen. Then he left Miss Toller in the bathroom to recover from the chloroform, with the stiletto in her hand. He crept down the balcony stairs, and waited for her to come down. He even let her see him, because time was pressing and he wished to scare her away.

"But his reflections while waiting amounted to this: in this new situation, he had to have a scapegoat. He did not want Miss Toller arrested, and (heaven knows) he did not want himself arrested. The only possible scapegoat seemed to be the original one—Ralph. I will do Bryce Douglas the justice to say that he is no paragon of evil: he is only a bewildered, sensitive, and spiteful man whose ingenuity had in that case gone awry. On the other hand, he could not now plaster the rooms with indications of an amorous orgy: empty bottles, torn clothes, half-eaten supper, and so forth. Magda Toller had seen those rooms, and would know afterwards that there was something wrong with it, for Rose Klonec would not do much rioting after she was dead. Also, it was not certain how far he had deceived the girl—that is, how far she would believe in her own guilt. She might grow too puzzled; she might suspect; she might tell.

"He could, however, do this. He could go stamping in the back door of the house, in the role of Ralph arriving for an assignation. He could take the supper-tray, and bang upstairs with it. But, you see, the whole crux of his difficulties was just this: he dared not incriminate Ralph too far as the actual murderer. If he did so, as I have indicated, his scapegoat would be too successful as a scapegoat—and Magda Toller would have told what she thought to be the truth.

"Bryce was in a devilish dilemma, and for the first time, he lost his head. It is difficult to blame him, since in the coolness of the next few minutes he realized that his inspiration had not been quite so Napoleonic as he thought. That was the reason why he played that idiotic trick with the razor. It was the only thing he could think of to do.

"It has been constantly asked in this case why anyone should have sharpened a razor on rough whetstone. What has not been asked is why anyone should have sharpened the razor directly under the ears and eyes of Hortense; why, in a lighted kitchen, with the door to Hortense's bedroom ajar, the man stood in the middle of the floor sawing away with that razor, and making a noise for some time which would be certain to rouse her curiosity. Surely it is plain that he *meant* to draw her attention to it. His purpose was to show Ralph coming to the villa in a black frame of mind, intending to carry out his past threat if she showed any nonsense in their new assignation.

"The impersonator, imitating Ralph, goes upstairs with the supper-table. Hence the pliers— we were *meant* to find the pliers. We were meant to infer that Ralph banged on the locked door, getting no reply; that then, in a temper, he opened the door with the pliers. He sees the woman in bed, apparently asleep and indifferent, and he is still more angry. He pushes the serving-table across the room. He opens a bottle of champagne, pours out two glasses, and calls to the woman to get up and have a drink. (As a matter of fact, one of these glasses was the glass from which she had drunk the chloroform, carefully rinsed and wiped.) Then he approaches the bed and yells to her. She does not stir. He touches her, and finds that she is dead.

"This was the story Bryce meant us to read in the room—a philandering brother, with the devil in him, who would readily have cut her face open, but who did not do it nevertheless, because Rose Klonec had been murdered before he arrived. He meant to show us Ralph waiting there for a long time beside the body, swallowing drinks and smoking...hence all the cigarettes that Bryce lighted and put in a ring to smoulder away on the ashtray. What he forgot to do was crush them out and throw them into the ashtray in the ordinary way. The whole scene was as false as the weapons; the half-smoked cigarettes could tell us that. But one thing Bryce does not forget to do: he does not forget, when he slips out of that room within five minutes of having entered it, to take away that damning half-bottle of champagne from which no rinsing will quite remove the smell of chloroform, and to bury it in the grounds before he goes. He has created a double illusion of re-markable ingenuity and nastiness. He has made a murderess out of the girl he wants, and a cheap Apache out of the brother he dislikes. He is in a position to control the lives of both."

There was a long silence. Bencolin sat back and stared meditatively at the table.

"There's only one thing," said Ralph, who was

324

looking rather white, "that I've thought of time and again. I mentioned it to Dick today. If he went to all this trouble in every other respect, why didn't he at least try to make sure I had no alibi? That's the most important thing he should have gone after, and with it his scheme would have been complete, and yet—"

"He did," said Bencolin.

"He did?"

"Am I correctly informed that on Saturday afternoon you told him you were expecting your solicitor from London early on Sunday morning?"

"Yes, that's right. I mentioned it to Dick Curtis here when he first arrived—"

"And Bryce made you promise him solemnly that you would not go out on Saturday night; that you would be in your rooms by nine o'clock, so that you would have a clear head to talk business the next morning; and that if for any reason you could not do this, you were to go to his house early in the evening, and tell him so?"

"Yes! I'd promised to come and see him that night, but I decided to take Magda out to dinner instead, and I forgot it. Still, as I told Dick, I did mean to turn in very early." He brooded. "But what about Mrs. Toller? Is *she* concerned in this in any way?"

"Unfortunately, no. Hercule Renard, I am afraid, when he saw a tall woman hurrying away from the Villa Marbre, merely saw Miss Toller when he was lying flat on the ground—as I assumed Bryce to be very tall when I saw him on a wall in the moonlight. But one thing at least I can put to Mrs. Toller's elegant discredit. She was so eager to have you caught and accused of Rose

Klonec's murder that she almost persuaded Stanfield to charge you with having taken that pistol from his office. When she saw the case against you collapsing, she could not resist brightening it up a bit. I shall always wonder (though in this I am my usual suspicious self) whether she did not have a strong suspicion as to what Bryce was up to.

"You see, then, our position with regard to Bryce. We must break Bryce's alibi by breaking De Lautrec's. If—as I was almost certain—De Lautrec knew quite well who the murderer was, he could prove (1) that Bryce's tale of waiting all evening outside the gates of this house was a myth, (2) that it was Bryce who had made the appointment with Rose Klonec for the Villa Marbre —two points which, while no conclusive evidence of murder, would put Bryce in a bad corner, because they were the two points on which he had so consistently and frantically told lies. But to get De Lautrec to admit this was to make him confess his own robbery, which might prove difficult. The only way we could do it was to catch him barehanded with the jewels in his possession. Then, if he were promised immunity, he would tell the truth. And the only way to do that"—Bencolin began to grin—"was to get him to lead us straight to the jewels. The trouble was, you see, that I had no notion of where he had hidden them; even the theft itself was as yet undiscovered, because a triumphant lawyer had found the wall-safe full of paste replicas which he had not yet valued—*I* had them valued. The real jewels might be hidden anywhere in Paris. De Lautrec himself must show us where they were.

"He thought he was in a winning streak at cards. It was certain that he was going to plunge as he had never plunged before. Well, he should be given the opportunity. Through my friend the Comte de Maupasson (I remained hidden and unknown) there were introduced into this house two of the most persistent 'plunging' gamblers in Paris—Mrs. Richardson and M. Jourdain. There was also introduced a young millionaire of sporting taste, and another young man who was told to use his own judgment. You cannot accuse me of asking anybody to aid me. They did not know why they were here; I merely showed them a green-baize table and, in the words of the improving proverb, let nature take its course. If De Lautrec's luck could last against that combination, he almost deserved to get away with what he had done. I did not believe it could; anyway it was an experiment worth trying. For, once luck turned against him, his temper would get the better of his caution, and he would go after those jewels in desperation. That they were actually in the same house I did not know, but it made matters easy when he began to lose. The paper he signed was merely an outline of what he believed and knew Bryce Douglas to have done, in return for his own immunity. Of course, he had no idea that I had no intention of prosecuting him anyway—"

"Why not?"

"Because we could not have indicted him without bringing Bryce Douglas into it," said Bencolin. "And there is a reason, as I told you, why Bryce will go free. Bryce knows too much."

"Knows too much?"

"You forget his position. Have you ever heard of

Voirbo, the great chopping murderer of the late eighteen sixties? Voirbo, in addition to having committed an unpleasant crime, was a government-informer. He had poked a finger into many delicate pies. I warned you of this state of affairs at the beginning of the case; it sometimes happens here. In Voirbo's case, the affair was so sensational, and so clearly brought home to him by the great Macé, that it could not be shelved. But I will not say that the man's suicide in prison was ever particularly investigated afterwards. Bryce Douglas stands in a much more delicate position. I deal in facts, like a detective; but here I must talk in clouds, like a diplomat. He will leave France, of course. What they say to him or about him in England I cannot tell. If there is ever any trouble about it, or he makes one bad move here afterwards, we have always De Lautrec's statement. That is all I wanted. Let him go to heaven or to the devil: though I see him as not good enough for the one, or bad enough for the other."

"He's my brother," Ralph said bitterly, "so that's that; and I have no more to do with it. But this whole case has been a refreshing lesson. You thought Magda had committed a crime, and you were going to let her get away with it. Then De Lautrec commits grand larceny, and he gets away with it. Then Bryce commits murder, and HE gets away with it. You ought to write a book about police methods, and call it 'Crime Isn't Serious.' "

"It was very nearly serious for you."

Ralph drew a deep breath, and began to grin.

"Yes. Sorry. I've got that out of the affair, anyway. And you"—he looked at Curtis—"you get the girl."

"No hard feelings?"

"Hard feelings!" said Ralph. "I—no. She's not the gal I could manage or want to manage. Look here, I'll be frank. I want to be free. There was only one woman I was ever fond of, and you should have known it by the way I talked at her bedside."

"You mean—?"

"Yes, I mean Rose Klonec," said Ralph, getting to his feet. "And that's why I hate Bryce like hell."

He was silent, and it was a little while before he shrugged his shoulders.

"There's just one thing, though. Do you realize, old boy, that at one turn of the cards tonight you won over nine thousand good English pounds on the queen?"

"No," Curtis said frankly, "I don't realize it. I have an idea it's not real money—sorry, Madame, no offense! I mean I think it will disappear the moment I cross the Channel."

Ralph was grinning again, the eternal grin that would carry him through many more adventures than this, and yet never support him enough for a real adventure.

"Well, by gad," he exclaimed, "*I* couldn't have gone to *Trente-et-le-va* if my life depended on it. I shouldn't have had the nerve. I'll always wonder what would have happened if you two lunatics, you and De Lautrec, had carried out the business of having another shot at it. You would have staked your nine thousand pounds, and he would have staked Lord knows what. You could have whistled the old-time gamblers out of their graves, and patted them on the head for children; for if you'd won the turn of that card you would have won well over half a million pounds." He whistled. "I say, what *would* have happened?"

"Why don't you look and see?" cackled Madame, and laughed. "There are the cards, just as he shuffled and cut them for the deal," said she, pointing. "There by your elbow. *I* looked."

Ralph gingerly drew the pack out of its little box, and slowly began to run through it. Presently he laughed. Curtis laughed. Only Bencolin, getting out his intolerable pipe and leaning back affably in his chair, for one short moment looked serious.